The Scent of Home

Alan T. McKean

Black Rose Writing

www.blackrosewriting.com

ISBN: 978-1-61296-202-3

PUBLISHED BY BLACK ROSE WRITING

www.blackrosewriting.com

Printed in the United States of America

The Scent of Home is printed in Perpetua

Dedicated to the late much missed Professor Hamish Keir
and in memory of the brave men killed in Pickets Charge
Battle of Gettysburg ,day 3 July 1863.

.

The Scent of Home

PART 1

PROLOGUE

What do you do when you think your worst nightmare is past and you wake to find that each day's dream is more toxic with imagination than the last, and that your worst nightmare has followed you halfway across the world with the intent of killing or maiming you and taking the woman you love?

Caleb Bryant, my nemesis, had escaped death so often he could write a book on the subject. He was responsible for death and misery everywhere he went, including the gentle British Ambassador Sir Charles Gray in Foochow, China. He had, however, one major Achilles heel. He was in love with Lucy Oxford, my now-fiancée, and would use any means to get her. That feeling was not reciprocated on Lucy's part.

Bryant had yet to triumph in his evil plot, but he had come close enough to give us all a good scare. And as long as I can continue stopping him, hell will freeze over before he gets Lucy.

In case my journal recalling the events that have happened to me and the three important people in my life—and how we were flung together by various circumstances—is damaged or lost, I will provide a brief recap of events.

What I put down is factual. I can have no influence over whether or not you believe it. I only hope that you will give my account a hearing.

I am a time traveler who was sent back by a powerful but friendly organization—Vanguard—from the start of the 21st Century to the year 1867. My purpose was to secure the safety of Miss Lucy Oxford, the lovely red-haired, green-eyed heiress of a large estate in Aberdeenshire, Scotland. That charge included Lucy's companion, Caroline Harper—to whom we all owe our lives, thanks to her quick thinking on the danger-fraught journey back from China. Caroline is now the fiancée of Myles Connaught, the sailing master of the tea clipper Night Arrow, which won the 1867 tea race, even with us on board.

Additionally, I was to deliver, via the French Chargez d'affaires, a warning about a Prussian attack on France in a couple years time. Fortunately, we were also able to foil a plot by time-traveling Nazis who schemed to ship opium to American and British troops in 1944. Their nefarious plan nearly worked, but there again, I have found history does not always record everything just as it happened.

Most importantly, I rescued a young Chinese girl, now my adopted daughter Mi-Ling, from a life of exploitation and degradation in a child brothel in Foochow. To this young lady, I owe my life. Lucy and I are engaged and determined to make as good a home for Mi-Ling as possible—wherever "home" may be.

Vanguard's headquarters are located in a house near Huntly, Aberdeenshire, Scotland. By a strange coincidence, I am writing this journal about one-hundred-fifty years before the organization was created. You would have to ask Einstein about the physics of that.

We were assisted by two other time travelers, Angus McTurk, a British Army Regimental Sergeant Major and combat instructor, and Meryl Scott, who saved my life in China (time travel is not for the fainthearted), but nearly lost her own in the process. These two are now back in the 21st Century. I wish they were here. Meryl is a lovely girl with blonde hair, blue eyes and the courage of a lioness.

There is one other person to whom I owe much, Anton Devranov, a Russian exiled for a murder he committed in retribution for the brutal rapes and murders of his wife and daughter. He had recently been pardoned by the czar and was coming to our wedding. Anton saved my life in my first days in Foochow, when Bryant tried to forcibly remove Lucy from the British Ambassador's ball—and I objected.

Further, Bryant attempted to kill Sir Charles Gray. I managed to kill his paid assassin and stop Bryant the first time. Sadly, I could not foil the second attempt and Sir Charles was murdered. His assassin ultimately paid the penalty for his crime even though he thought he had escaped justice.

Caleb Bryant, like a lethal bad penny, has just turned up and he doesn't plan a social call. He intends murder—mine.

Now I will resume my account of the events as they took place.

CHAPTER 1

Near Huntly, Aberdeenshire, 1867

The threatening, but cryptic note, which Bryant had sent via two innocent local tradesmen was in my hand and I passed it to Lucy and Caroline. It said in bold, capital letters: "ACCOUNT OVERDUE, COMING FOR PAYMENT. SEE YOU AT THE WEDDING. BRYANT."

"Caroline, you were right," I said. "Bryant is not dead and I apologize for my 'head in the sand' attitude that dismissed the possibility of him having survived."

Caroline replied, "It looks as if we are back to square one, but you were not to know. I could have been wrong. I'm going to telegraph Myles. I think he has right to know about this situation. It's dangerous—for all of us."

Caroline was never one for rushing into things, thus when she chose a course of action it was nearly always right.

I said to Lucy, "Bryant doesn't know how many people are here, so he is going to be watching the place. I'll tell Jock Shepherd, the ghillie in charge of all the hunting on the estate, and get him and his helpers to keep a sharp lookout for unknown individuals wandering about toward the house, especially if they have field glasses. Meanwhile, it might be a good idea to stay away from windows. Bryant had access to a telescopic rifle when Sir Charles was murdered. He may have obtained another one."

Sandy and Duncan, the two men who had brought our food and the note, were in the kitchen keeping warm and eating. They stood up when we came in.

"Sit down, lads," I said. "If you see the man that gave you the note, will you pass this to him? He has a bill to pay." I gave them my note.

Inside I had written, Your account outstanding. Payment to be rendered. I had signed it, pp Sir Charles Gray.

Caroline gave Sandy and Duncan a telegram form for Myles detailing the sudden and unexpected threat. She also handed them ten shillings and told them to keep the change. "Don't mention this to anyone," she warned. "Not even to yourselves in case you talk in your sleep," she added mysteriously.

The guys went off quite happily, with much profuse thanking. Even with the cost of the telegram, what was left over amounted to probably a week's wages.

We felt we had to include Mi-Ling in what we decided about the future. She had had sufficient experience with Bryant to understand the threat and to realize that her life was in danger. He had wanted Branson, the turncoat agent, to kill Mi-Ling aboard The Night Arrow on the journey from China to London during the 1867 Tea Clipper Race. There was no reason why he would not try again.

What we had to figure out was, did Bryant just want Lucy, or did he want revenge?

Caroline remarked, "Drew, if he wants to hurt you, the quickest way is to do something to Mi-Ling—for example, kidnapping her to get you to meet him. Then he could kill you both. The safest one of us here is Lucy. Of course, he could always try to kidnap her, too."

"My next step," I said, "is definitely to tell Jock Shepherd what happened and to convince him that the danger is now real. I'll ask him to engage the other estate workers and get them to watch for Bryant or any strangers appearing."

Lucy, not surprisingly, was agitated. "Are we just going to sit here like rats in a trap?" she asked. "And wait for him to show up one night? We don't know how many hired hands he has. We need to tell the police."

Caroline sighed, "Luce, what are we going to tell the police? We have only Drew's statement that Bryant was the instigator in Sir Charles' death. The only other crime was the attempted kidnapping of Melissa Gray in Foochow, and all the witnesses are a three-month's sail away.

Bryant phrased his letter to make it look like a bill was overdue. Plenty of tradesmen and debt collectors have used such language."

Since we had included her in the discussion, Mi-Ling had been listening to all this. Her face was serious, but there was a light in that girl's eyes that no bad news could extinguish. She turned to us. "Papa, Amma, Carol-lady—when we come here, do you forget the dangers? Father God did not allow that bad man to harm us then. Does He now say, 'I not mean to get Mi-Ling to home. I change My mind and now let bad thing happen to her.' Father God not like that. When we were on big ship, I looking over the side watching the big fish in the water. I breathed beautiful scent like the soul of a rose and scent of jasmine, you call it, I think. Then another scent. Not flowers or perfume. But it fill me up inside so much that Mi-Ling have to stop breathing and say, 'Father God, what is that lovely scent Mi-Ling can smell?' He says, 'Mi-Ling, My child, that is the Scent of Home. Be brave.

"Mi-Ling will ask Father God to make us all brave." She wandered over to the window and sat down in a chair. I felt an inkling of fear. Mi-Ling did not seem to have her usual bounce. It seemed as if not enough air was getting to the fire burning in her heart. Could she have caught some sort of disease on the journey? She had probably come into contact with illnesses since leaving China, for which her body had developed no immunities. But the nuance of change was so slight that I failed to mention it to either Lucy or Caroline. With Bryant's menace, they had enough anxieties already.

I was hoping it would snow during the night. The benefit of snow would have been the revealing of footprints where no footprints should have been.

Lucy and Carolyn slept with guns under their pillows and we moved Mi-Ling into their room. It was no different than it had been aboard the Night Arrow on the way home.

I slept with the Webley under my pillow and a rifle behind a set of curtains. The fire in the rooms at night helped in both cases, disclosing every nook and cranny. We had new locks fitted to the back door, for we thought that would be the vulnerable entry point. There was a limit to what we could do in such a big house to protect it from breach.

How do you fortify a castle with no garrison?

We made it safely and peacefully to December 20, although I occasionally fell into worry about the change I perceived in Mi-Ling and had contemplated several times asking Lucy and Caroline if they had noticed it. Her spunk had faded and the eager anticipation with which she had met every day since her rescue in Foochow seemed dulled. Snow had just fallen, but there was no wind blowing to cause it to drift. A carriage with two figures in it headed toward the house. The first warning I received was Caroline's voice, "Drew, we have company."

The arrivals were a man and a woman with an enormous amount of luggage. The man got out of the coach and I breathed a sigh of relief. He did not have a limp as Bryant would have had. He approached the door and hammered the knocker. Warily, I opened the door and was happily confronted by Anton. "This is a fine welcome, brother!" he joked. "You look like a calf that cannot find the place where he is supposed to suckle." The infectious laugh followed.

"Come in, Anton!" I exclaimed, embracing him. "Come in—and your traveling companion as well. Don't make her sit outside in the cold!"

Anton's companion shook herself, to brush aside the cold and snow, and when she did, the scent of coconut drifted to me from her hair. My heart missed a beat. Only one girl I knew used the scent of coconut; my former girlfriend, Meryl. But it couldn't be her...could it?

They both entered the house and the driver began to unload their luggage, leaving it in the hall.

"It's not as cold as it looks." Anton said cheerfully. "You have face like a funeral and this is supposed to be a wedding." He looked round and I remembered to officially introduce him to Lucy. He had seen her at from a distance at the Ambassador's Ball in China, but they had not met. He kissed the back of Lucy's hand. "You have speechless beauty. Words fail. Only the heart can absorb."

Lucy smiled and said, "And I am glad to meet you, as well, Mr. Devranov."

"Please, call me Anton. If you call me Mr. Devranov, it seems like a bill collector asking for payment."

While this merry interchange was going on, the rest of us—Caroline, Mi-Ling and I—stood around wondering what to say. We felt like extras in a play. Anton's traveling companion emitted a gentle cough.

He started, suddenly remembering her. "May I introduce Miss Svetlana Simeonova," Anton boomed. A hand was extended, but her face was hidden under a broad-brimmed hat.

"I am delighted to meet you," I said, trying to remember to breathe when I smelled again that faint scent of coconut.

"All this way," the mysterious lady said. "I feel we have been traveling for years and not even a SavaJava in sight." Then, as I gasped, she removed her hat.

I had never expected to see Meryl again. Now, amazingly, here she stood in front of me. I managed to keep my eyes from popping out of my head, but I could not stop my heart from singing.

"May I call you Svetlana?" I asked

"Of course," she replied. "Unless you know me by another name?"

I looked into Meryl's eyes and saw my heart reflected back to me. I remembered, then, that Meryl knew this house probably even better than I did—only from some 150 years into the future.

Women are quicker on the uptake than men when it comes to another woman. Lucy was regarding "Svetlana" with suspicion and Caroline's welcome was somewhat frosty.

"Are you going to keep us standing about in this barn of a hallway?" Anton demanded. "Where is the fire? Old Russian saying, 'The bear cannot reach the fish in the river while the ice is frozen over.'"

"Very good," I said, realizing after the words left my mouth that they were only half-hearted. My whole heart was engaged in the miracle of Meryl standing before me.

"I knew you would like it!" Anton exclaimed happily. "It is amazing how much you can miss old Russian sayings."

We went into the warm sitting room and had tea and cake. The tea was not bad, but not as good as it had been in China.

"Okay," I said to them. "Do you want the bad news? Or the bad news?"

Then I told Anton, "I had better explain to your companion. She has been thrust into this."

Meryl looked at me impassively. Then, when she thought no one was looking except me, she wrinkled her nose and a smile flashed across her face. Nobody had seen her—except Mi-Ling. I knew I needed to talk to Meryl alone, but how?

Anton said, "It takes bad news to help you appreciate the good— like vodka in a hot room. When you go to the bottle, it has all evaporated. Then you wake up realizing you had only been dreaming. Still, life was getting tedious. I brought my hunting rifle for sport. Do you have swine to shoot at like we do?"

"Only Bryant," Caroline responded grimly.

"Bryant is alive and he is in the area," I explained. "He has threatened us and now we are stuck here. Some of the estate workers know his intent, but we have no evidence to present to the police."

"Hmm." said Anton. "It could be worser as the peasant said when he was chased by the bear. I am not sure how, but it could be worser. Old Russian saying. It loses a little in the translation." He then brightened up. "Just think, if you knew Russian—you could read old Russian sayings in the original language."

Since the conversation portended morbidity, Caroline crossed the room to Mi-Ling. "It will be time for lunch soon," she said. "Nothing like naughts and crosses to work up an appetite. Come on Mi-Ling, let's play a few games."

Mi-Ling followed Caroline obediently, but she lacked excitement at the prospect of playing one of her favorite games. She looked at me as she left the room in Caroline's wake. She had a look on her face that was either puzzlement or hurt. Or, perhaps, she really was feeling unwell— a scary thought.

"Maybe you can fill me in, Lucy, about the much troubles here?" Anton asked. "There is nothing so uplifting as the society of beautiful women. Meanwhile, Drew can show Svetlana around your wonderful property."

Meryl and I walked slowly away from the house, keeping a respectable distance between us. I turned to face her when we were out of sight of the house. "Do you know how awful it was shoving you into that time machine in China not knowing whether you would live or die from that sword wound? Are you okay? I mean, are you fully recovered? If it is any comfort, Bryant now walks with a severe limp, since that time you came to my aid. I would have killed him, but he ran away and all my knife got hold of was the back of his cowardly leg fleeing. I don't know if Angus McTurk filled you in on the details, but what a journey we had! I owe my life to Mi-Ling. She shot Lancaster, Bryant's sailing master, when he was trying to kill me." I chuntled on like an excited school boy.

She smiled at me and turned her head slightly to one side. "Shhh, darling, everything is fine and so am I."

"I'm supposed to marry Lucy and start a life in America. We have this place up for sale." Added silence, apart from the cooing of doves. "Meryl, when I threw that time switch at the start of all this, I knew I loved you. So often, all I could hear was your voice telling me you would always love me. Do you? No, don't answer in case the answer is no." But I couldn't stop myself. "Are you and Anton lovers?" Heavens, I thought. Our conversation was about as calm as a melting iceberg.

"Anton has tried to seduce me without success, Drew. So put your mind at rest. Yes, darling, I still love you. Now it's my turn to ask. Have you and Lucy been intimate yet—made love? Had sex? However you want me to phrase it."

I blushed slightly and answered, "No, only by promise for after the marriage. We have hugged and kissed, yes. But that's all."

Believing me, she nodded and we continued walking, stamping against the cold and snow.

We went into a small cottage on the estate and began to look around inside. "Listen carefully," she said. "You've found the time terminal here, I take it?"

I nodded.

"Since your first trip, the time car has been fine-tuned. It can now arrive or depart within minutes and operate in a small time frame."

I hummed and hawed. "Let me understand…are you saying that you could leave here at say—Tuesday, December 25 at three o'clock, travel somewhere, and then return at 3:10 p.m.—while the ten minutes that passed here could be weeks where ever you travel to? Whew!"

Meryl nodded. "There is one more thing, Drew. You're needed for another mission."

"You're kidding! I only just got through this one. Not to mention the fact that we both almost got killed."

"Par for the course, honey bunny. You're in the club now. I have a file for you."

I looked at her, still somewhat shocked. "Why am I getting the sense of déjà vu?"

She smiled and crinkled her nose. "It might be awkward to meet like this again. So far, we've been out seven minutes. It's like this. Some 'visitors' to America in 1863, are trying to persuade General Lee to accept British help before Gettysburg. If Lee does, it could swing the tide and divide America. An America of two separate countries would not be able to stand or to withstand over time. Plus, Americans themselves should decide their country's future without anyone's interference. Read the file. Then we can arrange another meeting. We had better get back for now, darling, before anyone starts to miss us or ask questions."

When we got back we were cold. Lucy and Anton were flushed from sitting near the fire.

I went to my room and hid the file, then came back down in time to hear a laughing Anton and part of a conversation

"And so all they could do was put the vodka back in the lamp and then say 'sorry for the mistake." He laughed encouragingly and Lucy laughed with him.

It was the uncharacteristic behavior of Mi-Ling to Meryl that alarmed me. She was almost rude to Meryl and Mi-Ling was never rude to anyone. Then I remembered that Mi-Ling had seen the smile that passed between Meryl and me. Did she think that the future that she had eagerly anticipated was evaporating in the heat and fire of Meryl's presence? Or was my guilty conscience playing tricks on me?

CHAPTER 2

That night after a game of bridge, I decided to retire early. The file was burning a hole in my imagination.

"Never mind," said Anton. "In a few day's time, no more going to bed alone. I am glad the walls of this house are thick." He grinned, then sighed. "That is the trouble with a good imagination. Old Russian Saying, 'When the bull slips his halter, he is not just looking for clover.'"

Laughing, I grabbed a book from a shelf and threw it at him. "Go oil your rifle!"

Anton picked up the book. "I hope not a prophetic choice, brother, *Fyodor Dostoyevsky, House of the Dead.*" The laughter stopped.

I could imagine that Caroline would be glad to get back to sea with Myles. As bad as going round the Cape of Good Hope or Cape Horn would be in the future, nobody like Bryant would be trying to shoot her or Myles.

I kissed Lucy goodnight and she whispered in my ear, "Soon love, soon."

The trouble was now that I had seen Meryl again, I was thinking more about clover than I was of what Lucy could offer love wise on our wedding night.

When I got to my room, I had to carefully heat the pages of the file in front of the fire. This revealed the writing, an old but effective way of disguising a message. The curtains in the house were thick, which was good. It would be difficult for anyone outside to see any shadows if I decided to get up and move about while reading.

We had to go back to June 30, 1863, Gettysburg, Pennsylvania, where the biggest battle in the American War Between the States was about to commence. There was a group of people (the briefing was non-specific) that wanted to persuade General Robert E. Lee, commander of the Confederate Army of Northern Virginia, to accept British help against the Union forces. The plot was that British Forces were to use the British Navy to break the Union Blockade, land, and draw away Union forces which would have been sent to reinforce Union General George Meade at Gettysburg.

If victory was achieved, Lee could advance to Washington and present peace terms to Abraham Lincoln, effectively splitting the United States into two separate countries. Whether Lee would be happy with a victory dependent on British guns remained to be seen.

A strong Confederacy would provide abundant supplies of raw cotton for the many spinning mills in Britain at the time. The cost of that cotton would have to be a lot less than was presently charged and the planters' standard of living would take a tumble. An independent Confederacy would also have a major effect on World History, especially in the World Wars of 1917-18, and 1942-45. Not only that, but the new countries themselves, not having resolved their differences, might later enter into another conflict. God forbid.

The key thing was that General Lee had to give his permission for the use of British forces or else it was a non-starter. Lee, history maintained, was a man of integrity who practiced a strong Christian faith. What could they be plotting to do to get someone with that strength of character to change his mind?

This time I would have to wear a uniform and be aware—aware of what happened historically at Gettysburg. I had been given the rank of major.

If I fell into the hands of the Union Army, my diplomatic status might be conveniently forgotten and I could be hanged as a spy. Suddenly, dealing with Bryant seemed a lot easier. As it turned out, it was to be a lot more heartbreaking.

Meryl was to pose as my wife. We had all the paperwork. Lieutenant McTurk was to be my aide de camp. I was glad to see that Angus was getting at least some of the recognition he deserved through his commission.

The question we must answer: who was planning this and how

could I get to see General Lee? Being an observer from Britain was something, but overstepping the mark could have dire consequences. If those trying to persuade Lee to ask for British help were Germans or Prussians, it might be possible to pick them out. But what if they were Americans set on changing history for their own agenda?

I wrote a note to Meryl saying that we should try leaving at 2 a.m. the following morning, even though that was close to the wedding. If the time machine worked right and didn't let us down, we would seem to have only been gone for ten minutes and should be back before we were missed. Unless Anton were to come through and try to seduce Meryl again as we were leaving, we should get peace. It was a daring, nerve-wracking plan, but I hoped Meryl would agree to going at that time.

I had to remember my 1867 military drill and there were helpful notes in the file to refresh my memory. I fell asleep shouldering arms and awoke to one of the rare bright, brisk days of sunny winter, as if the sun were in training to become summer at a later, as yet unspecified date.

The people in the house had breakfast at various times. Caroline was up first and Mi-Ling was with her. Mi-Ling ran up to me with a big broad smile and took my hand. "Good morning, Papa! Soon you and Amma be married and, as it say at end of story, 'We all live ever after happy.'"

I hugged my daughter and kissed the top of her head. I was thankful that she seemed bright and chipper—only, was it my imagination or did she have the makings of dark circles under her eyes?

Meryl came into the room, yawning slightly, and at the sight of her, Mi-Ling's face clouded over and she turned sullen and silent.

"Good morning, Svetlana. I trust you slept well?" No sooner was that enquiry made than Lucy came into the room and went over to where breakfast was laid out waiting. She did not seem hungry even though the scrambled eggs were fresh.

"Did you sleep well, darling?" I asked Lucy. She nodded half-heartedly and then brightening said, "Not as well as I hope to do in a few day's time. I'm just thankful that there were no visits from Mr. Bryant."

A thought that surely was echoed by us all.

I tried to sound pensive to cover up my growing apathy about Lucy and the wedding. "Bryant said he would see us at the wedding. That would be the time when any attempt to create trouble would have maximum effect and maximum publicity."

Anton arrived finally, which made me wonder when they ate breakfast in Russia. He managed rolls and marmalade, and tea with lemon in it.

"Why does morning always come so soon?" he asked grumpily. "The light here forces its way into your eyes and then they open. In my dream I was lying next to the most beautiful girl I ever saw." Then he looked at Meryl. "Present company accepted. Old Russian saying, 'Who eats crusts when there is fresh bread on the table?'"

Connie came to play and we let Mi-Ling and Connie go down to the kitchen. They had become fast friends with Mrs. Fraser, the cook, a formidable lady who could probably have made Angus McTurk anxious. Mrs. Fraser was as gentle and soft with the girls as a newborn spring lamb.

Caroline was reading and watching the road every now and again. Whether she was sentry or waiting for a reply from Myles was hard to tell. She had a bonnie engagement ring on her finger but she missed her beau. She asked finally, "What's the point in being told you have been gifted a thousand pounds if it is still in the bank? I wish Myles were here."

There was a clear space where everyone present was lost in their own thoughts and no one was looking. I passed the letter to Meryl about tonight quickly and she slipped it into the folds of her gown.

So the day dragged by, with even Mr. Thorburn, the minister, coming to go through the final wedding arrangements. He managed to keep a straight face when Anton asked why he wore his collar back to front. He replied that he had a lot on his mind and a stiff collar helped support his head, which was filled with weighty thoughts.

Anton replied with interest, "You must have book of old Russian sayings."

So for the rest of the day, we just kept watch as things began to arrive for the wedding. Lucy and I went to Huntly to get her dress fitted for the final time, even though I had to stay outside the shop. You haven't lived till you have stood for an hour in a street in 1867, especially with the night soil still evident—not to mention the mud.

Afternoon naps proved a good surcease, as we did not know when or where we would get to rest again and we needed to be fresh. So I rested in the afternoon and so did Svetlana, in her room. Sadly, sleep evaded me. I knew now that I loved Meryl. Yet, I was scheduled to marry Lucy in a few days. I liked Lucy and held a great respect for her. I didn't want to hurt her. I had promised her mother that I would look after her and not break her heart. How would it all end? And depending on the outcome, what about Mi-Ling? How I loved my brave little girl! And how it worried me that, even when she had played with Connie earlier in the day, she had exhibited a lethargic side that I had never seen before. Yet, during my nap, I should toss all these worries out into the afternoon gloom to chase themselves around and leave me alone. Tired people got careless and that could be fatal.

Evening finally arrived. Anton and I played games of billiards. Sometimes he won and sometimes I lost!

I did not know where the time tunnel would empty us out on the other side, but hoped it was not a long hike to Gettysburg. As it turned out, I need not have worried. Oh, the wonders of modern technology! I wondered when they would develop a pocket version of the time tunnel. Our papers had been signed by Alexander Stephen, Vice President of the Confederate States of America, (CSA). They were countersigned by John Breckenridge, Secretary for War. I thought, what a lousy portfolio to get—dealing with war and fighting. I am all about love and peace, not violence. Still, someone had to do it and I had apparently been elected.

There were also papers from our own government requesting we be allowed to observe and requesting that every help and assistance be given us. I wondered if there were any more observers from other countries, but this we would only know once we got there. General Lee was not to be harmed and was to be protected at all costs.

****

Meryl and I met met at 2 a.m. downstairs. It was our first chance to really be alone. She was carrying a case in one hand and her shoes in the other hand. "The heels click on the stairs," she explained apologetically.

"Don't explain or apologize for anything," I whispered. "Just hold me." After a long, long hug, I asked her, "Do you know how much I have missed just holding you? I remember our last night together. And when I was in danger—when I thought that I would never see you again—what broke my heart was just that thought. That I would never see you again. Yet, darling, it was the opposite possibility that kept me going—the thought that someday, by some miracle, I might see you again, hold you again."

"Drew, darling. Our paths have taken separate directions. Please, let's just concentrate on completing this mission. We've been given it for a reason. Then let's see how things turn out. Darling, Mi-Ling needs you. She seems to resent me, and I don't blame her. She's a bright little girl. She feels that I'm a threat because I might separate the two people she loves the most in the world and expects to live together with her in happiness." She looked deeply into my eyes and two blonde curls bounced down over her blue eyes.

I sighed and agreed reluctantly. "You're right. We must concentrate on the task at hand."

I pressed the button to summon the time car and it came— complete with Angus McTurk.

He looked at us both and smiled, then handed me my firearm. It was an Adams Beaumont revolver and he gave me a quick crash course on how to load and fire, though the percussion caps were a bit fiddly. "It's got a mighty kickback so take that into account. If you hit someone with a shot from this, you'll not need to fire a second time."

We loaded in the luggage and set time car in motion, dialing in June 30, 1867. A separate dial operated the destination. I wondered what happened if you changed the time and forgot to change the destination.

Complete with a feeling of déjà vu, and a plea of God help us, we settled into the time car that would—if we did our jobs well—maintain history as it was written 21st century books. Then, with our flair for the dramatic, we looked at one another and said, "All for one and one for all."

Dramatic it might have been—only we knew in our hearts we meant it.

Part 2
Gettysburg, June 30th 1863

Gettysburg 1889

"In great deeds something abides. On great fields something stays. Forms change and pass, bodies disappear, but spirits linger, to consecrate ground for the vision—place of souls, and reverent men and women from afar, and generations that know us not, and that we know not of, heart drawn to see where and by whom great things were suffered and done for them, shall come to this deathless field, to ponder and dream, and lo the shadow of a mighty presence shall wrap them in its bosom and the power of the vision pass into their souls."

General Joshua Lawrence Chamberlain.
Former Colonel of the 20th Maine Infantry at Gettysburg in 1863.

CHAPTER 3

We arrived in the distinguished setting of an old barn that also served as a stable behind the Brafferton Inn, where we hoped to stay. We got our luggage and hired a small buckboard. Then we went for a trot round the town, trying to look as if we were actually going somewhere. The plan was to then go to the front of the Brafferton Inn, claim our pre-booked rooms, and chill out. There did not seem to be an air of panic. It should be two o'clock on the afternoon of June 30th.

General Lee would not arrive, according to historical accounts, until about 2.30 p.m. on July 1st. We did not want to attract attention to ourselves, so when we spoke, we put on our best American accents. Strangely enough, the most successful at that was Angus McTurk. Angus had played poker one day in a saloon in Abilene in 1887. (I never did understand the reason he was there.) Angus, when someone asked to see his hand, put down a royal flush in diamonds. His opponent also put down a royal flush in diamonds. It was Angus who had walked out of the saloon in one piece.

The sun was headed downward and the town seemed to bustle with life in all its variety. Some folk, wagons loaded up with all their worldly goods, were leaving town, hoping not to run into a Confederate Cavalry vedette—for this was Union Territory and the presence of the Confederate Army of Northern Virginia near the town was an unknown quantity.

We got back to the Brafferton and claimed our rooms. We had previously decided that we needed to try to find where Lee's headquarters would be—getting the lay of the land so to speak—while there was still comparative freedom of movement. It never dawned on the town's people, that because of the events of the next three days especially, their town would become one of the most famous places in the United States.

When Angus met us in the hall of the Brafferton, he wore a black-frocked coat, white shirt, a black bootlace tie of some sort, wide-brimmed hat, and black trousers and boots. He looked like Wyatt Earp, except for not having a Buntline special revolver. When we asked about the hat he said, "Aye. I won it from Wyatt Earp in a poker game. He wanted to put up his shirt, but as it was a warm day and much perspiration was in evidence, I said I would settle for the hat. Well, I am going for a wee mosey. I'll catch up with you later. Don't do anything I wouldn't do. See you for dinner."

He left and we knew that Angus would learn quite a bit. He had his own methods of finding things out.

Meryl and I walked, arm in arm, on down the street. In spite of the danger and uncertainty of our mission, I couldn't help the flood of joy in my heart just from being with her again. I tried to talk myself into a guilt trip for feeling such joy, but it fell flat. I was too happy for self-incrimination and self-castigation. Meryl said, once we got out of the earshot of anyone, "The Confederates should be here tomorrow and they will bump into General Buford's Cavalry and the shooting will start." She seemed lost and alone in her thoughts and I did not intrude. I had no right to intrude. I was supposed to belong to Lucy. We were mere days away from our wedding, for heaven's sake!

We walked a bit further. Meryl picked up a flower that had fallen from a Magnolia tree and inhaled its fragrance. Somehow, it was hard to tell where the beauty of the too-soon fallen flower ended and Meryl's beauty began.

"It would go well in your hair," I remarked, and the sun seemed cold in the reflection of her responsive smile.

We came to the Thomson House, the place in which General Lee would have his headquarters. "See, note and inwardly digest," she said indicating the house with her head. "I could settle here, Drew," she mused dreamily. And then as if reminded why we came, she clicked into professional mode and said, "I hope we can handle this. I feel as if I am being balanced on a knife blade and don't know where to fall. You've got your pass?"

I nodded. "In my boots. Where's yours?"

Tapping her bosom, she smiled at me and replied, "In that safe place, which all of us girls have."

It was the first time I had ever felt jealous of a piece of paper.

What we didn't know at the time was that things would be resolved in a way neither of us expected, by a hand that seemed the most unlikely.

In the Brafferton Inn, we met up again with Angus, who was talking to a couple of people and broke off his conversation when he saw us. "Major Faulkner, Mrs. Faulkner, it is good to see you again," he said, tipping his hat to Meryl, who smiled demurely in response.

We invited, "Please, join us at our table."

"Nothing would give me more pleasure," he responded gallantly.

The food was good, Angus and my steaks done to perfection. Meryl ordered crab cakes. For dessert, there was a fruit salad. It did not seem as if there was a war on, but I suppose the owner did not want to panic his customers. Everything appeared to be business as usual. In passing conversation with the owner, he remarked, "I heard that Jeb Stuart got captured by federal cavalry but managed to get away. General Lee will need his eyes for the battle."

We continued the conversation, saying that we hoped the Federal Cavalry could protect us, and asking, "Will this war ever be over?"

One conversation at another table drifted over. "They say Lee has 90,000 men with him and many of them have no boots and ain't been fed for weeks, an' they're meaner than a nest full of hornets."

With this kind of conversation going on, the locals were giving General Lee an easy time of it.

We noticed that Angus had a small earpiece and wondered what it was for. When the conversation at the other tables got louder, he conveyed that it was a Kairon detector. Kairon enabled us to time travel. Could it do the same for anyone else? Without a whole lot of explanation, we guessed that what he was picking up were signals or pulses. The closer he got to a source of Kairon, the more frequent the pulses became. By some stroke of luck, it was possible that the people for whom we were looking were at another table.

After checking out the people in the dining room, Angus said he was going past the Farnsworth House Inn and the Dobbin Tavern, both places where you could pick up useful scuttlebutt, and where he could run his check for Kairon. "If the people we're after are from the future, they, too, will know where Lee has his headquarters and will be prepared."

He looked at Meryl and me and added. "We have to be up early tomorrow. The action will start just after dawn. Let's hope we live long enough to do what we came here for. If we don't, then the time we came from may be ruled by different people than it was when we left it."

When Angus left, Meryl and I looked at each other like two moonstruck teenagers. "Now what do we do?" I asked.

"Well, we could go to bed and get some sleep," she suggested. "Keeping in mind the mission we're on, we don't know when we're next going to get to bed."

We went up to the room we shared, since our identification listed us as husband and wife. Meryl looked around thoughtfully and offered, "I'm going to the dressing room. You can get undressed in here."

A maid brought two jugs of hot water when she saw us heading to our rooms. We both washed up, then slipped into bed.

"You lay that side and I lay this side and we should be able to sleep," Meryl directed. When we moved, the springs on the bed creaked and we lay there for ten minutes, deeply aware of each other. Our scents mingled to create a passionate cocktail that made each of us aware of our need and desire for each other.

Had a stranger been passing our room door, they would have heard cries and groans and gasps of breath and pleasure. If that same person had passed by our room again, coming back from the errand and looked inside, they would have seen two sleeping figures wrapped in each others arms and lost in love.

CHAPTER 4

July 1st, 1863

We awoke the following morning. My arm was around Meryl and I snuggled up against her. She woke up and kissed me. "Darling, we have to get dressed, and, yes, I love you."

"Maybe there is more warm water outside our doors," I ventured. When I checked, the warm water was there and we were able to get a wash. I did Meryl's back for her and we dressed and went down for breakfast. We could hear the sound of distant gunfire. Angus was at one of the tables and we joined him.

"About time you two showed up," he observed. "I won't ask any questions. Let's just focus on today. There's still a box at the stable we need. Mrs. Faulkner, wait here. Drew and I will go look."

We left Meryl tucking into breakfast. She had an amazingly practical streak, making the most of the food presented to her. None of us could count on meals being regular.

Angus and I walked slowly back to the barn behind the inn. Angus went over to the darkest corner of the barn. "Should be just about here," he surmised. As he put his hand down to get the box, he jumped back and pulled his revolver. "Just come out real slowly," he directed, seemingly speaking to the hay.

The hay moved and a black figure wearing torn, ragged clothing arose and stood up.

"Who are you?" Angus demanded.

"My name is Sebastian," the figure mumbled with shaking voice. He looked around. "Where am I anyways?"

"You're in Gettysburg, Pennsylvania."

Sebastian's eyes opened wide, "Law! Thank the Good Lord! He's done kept me safe and got me to the north."

Angus looked at him and motioned him to sit down. "Are you a former slave?" he asked quietly.

"Yes, sir, I is. Former."

"You've been in northern territory for a while—except you've landed in the middle of a battle. The Confederates have invaded and fighting is about to start here. The Union soldiers will be driven off," Angus continued, "before they win the victory."

"So what is I gonna do?" Sebastian asked, clearly frightened and shaken from Angus' news.

Something came back to me—words from the Old Testament spoken by Cain when God asked him where Able was, the brother whom Cain had murdered. Cain had retorted, "Am I my brother's keeper?" Feeling like Cain at the moment, I thought, Just leave him. Get the stuff you came in here to get and ignore him. Yet, I knew if Sebastian tried to leave the town with Confederate Cavalry buzzing around, he would get caught and sent back to his former master, or perhaps killed. The infantry of Heth's Division might deal with him out of hand.

We would be taking a big risk in providing aid to a former slave and I felt that Meryl was entitled to have a say in this. Yet, I knew what her answer would be—affirmative. Still, how could we help him?

The barn was empty and Sebastian stepped out into the open. His wrists showed bruising from abuse and his ankles, just visible where his long legs showed beneath frayed britches, bore the scars of chains.

The box we had come to look for contained clothing, some of which we gave Sebastian to wear. He washed in a horse trough, and fortunately, no one else came to the barn while he was washing and dressing in borrowed clothes.

I had taken some bread rolls with me from the inn, and these I gave to him. They didn't touch the sides of his mouth as he wolfed them down.

"We'll get you more food," Angus promised, "but you must listen to me. Do you understand?"

Sebastian nodded and looked attentive. "Yes, sir."

"You must pretend to be a slave again. I don't like even using that evil word, 'slave.' So let's just say that you must pretend to be our servant."

Sebastian shook his head stubbornly. "Naw, sir. Ain't gonna be a slave no more. No matters how you say it or spell it, it ain't gonna happen."

"Think, man," Angus directed, with urgency in his voice. "If you don't pretend to be our slave, they will kill you. We are talking about three days before they go. Three days isn't a long time to pretend being a servant if it saves your life."

The man looked puzzled, asking, "How you know they gonna lose?"

"There are many Union divisions on their way here," Angus explained, "but it will take until tomorrow before all the soldiers get here. When the Confederates take over, you must act as if you are our slave, loaned to us by a Confederate friend for our journey here and to attend to our needs. Just for three days, you must support us." Angus paused, then added, "There is a third member of our party. A lady. She's this man's wife."

"I understand," Sebastian said, buttoning up the shirt I had given him. Before he slipped it on, I saw the scars across his back from beatings and realized that the deeper scars were inside, their damage hidden from our eyes.

I took up where Angus had left off. "Go back into the hay and stay still. Try to go as far back as you can into the darkness. I will try to bring you more food."

We went back to the inn. Meryl had gone up to the room. We explained what had happened and what we hoped to accomplish.

"Has he agreed to this?" Meryl asked.

"Yes, we thought it was the best thing," we said in unison.

She walked up and down the room. "I'm going over to the barn to see if I can talk to him and put his mind at rest. He must be terrified, and he has no reason to trust either of you—two more white people who might have lied to him."

Meryl recounted the next chain of events later. She had gone down to the barn and called Sebastian's name. It took some time before he responded and she had just started to reassure him. Meryl had her back to the hay as they talked, and it was only a slight movement in the hay that had drawn Sebastian's attention. He, alone, had spotted the copperhead snake slithering out from the hay and coiling up behind Meryl in a striking position.

Sebastian acted instinctively, thrusting Meryl out of danger and dealing a death blow to the serpent. In the momentary panic, Meryl fell backwards, hitting her head on the edge of a stable door and losing consciousness. While Sebastian was attempting to help Meryl, a Confederate captain and two troopers strolled into the barn.

Meanwhile, up in the hotel room, I urged Angus to return to the barn. "Something must be wrong," I explained to him, going by my gut instinct. "Meryl's been gone too long."

Thankfully, Angus and I had changed into uniform before we headed back down to the barn. We entered through a small door at the back and found Sebastian with a rope round his neck and the Confederate officer hitting him.

"Assaulting a white woman, you filthy piece of trash! We know what we do with the likes of you!" They started to pull the rope up and it tightened around Sebastian's neck. He saw us and the wild white-eyed fear in his pleading eyes hit me in the gut.

"Stop!" I ordered. "That's my servant and the woman is my wife."

"Who in tarnation are you?" the officer asked.

"Major Andrew Faulkner of her Britannic Majesty's 92 Gordon Highlanders. This is my ADC, Lt. Angus McTurk. I would thank you to release my servant. I have a pass signed by Vice President Alexander Stephens and Secretary of War John Breckenridge." I held out the paper.

"British be damned! You ain't nothing but a Yankee spy and we deal with spies only one way."

"Look at my pass, for God's sake," I said.

He swore and pulled the hammer back on his pistol.

Then a voice cut in—a soft voice with a unique air of command and a Virginian accent, "Captain, you will do me the courtesy of lowering your pistol and releasing your prisoners. All your prisoners."

The Captain and the two troopers sprang to attention. Robert E. Lee—Commanding General of the Army of Northern Virginia walked in with his ADC, four troopers, and two officers—one of whom looked like General Longstreet.

I handed my pass to Major Taylor, whom I knew to be Lees' ADC.

In the meantime, Meryl regained consciousness and confirmed Sebastian's story. Had there been any remaining doubt, the dead body of the snake served as a silent witness.

Lee raised his hat to Meryl. "Mrs. Faulkner, I trust you are recovered from your accident and have suffered no injury." He turned to me and offered his hand. I stood to attention and saluted him.

"That is quite unnecessary, Major. You do not wear this uniform."

I looked at him and said respectfully and truthfully, "I was not saluting the uniform, sir. I was saluting the man wearing it."

Major Taylor had read the passes and said to Lee, "The passes are in order, General."

Lee responded, "These four people enjoy my protection for as long as we remain here, Captain."

Then to us. "Now if you will excuse me, there is a battle to fight. My headquarters will be at the McPherson house and I should be glad to see you at a time when we are not otherwise engaged. He bowed to Meryl. "I suggest that you return to a place of safety, Ma'am."

He honored us with another look and a slight nod of his head. "Good day, gentlemen. I saluted again. This time it was returned.

The captain, whose name was Vincent, and who had so nearly had brought our trip to a premature end, mounted his horse after Lee left and said bitterly, "Granny's eyes can't be everywhere. Watch your back."

"I hope you have a nice day, too, Captain." I would have said more, but felt the pull of Angus' hand on my sleeve. Then, too, there was a distinct feeling of déjà vu that served as a reminder of Bryant—and also of Lucy, whom I was scheduled to marry but had suddenly realized, since being with Meryl again, did not love. I knew that as soon as possible, I must talk to Meryl about the future. And what of Mi-Ling's future in 1867?

Sebastian said under his breath, "Law! Thank you, Lord Jesus for safety," to which I quickly and unashamedly echoed with a hearty, Amen —then wondered why I had. Church talk and Amens were not part of my usual repertoire.

Angus watched the captain's back as he left the barn. Turning to me he said, "You know, the Kairon locator was going ten to the dozen in my ear when that laddie was close by. Interesting, eh? Despite General Lee's protection, we had better keep our heads down and try and hang onto our equipment."

Meryl and I got back to our room, which was still intact. We found there were some Confederate officers billeted in the hotel, which might mean it would remain a place of safety.

"Now we wait," Meryl said, as we wandered aimlessly about our room.

"I can't marry Lucy," I blurted out. "And I have to tell her as quickly as possible. This is 1867, or will be. The one protection a woman has in these days is Breach of Promise. It means that when I tell her, Lucy can take everything leave me with nothing."

"What about Mi-Ling?" Meryl asked.

I continued walking up and down the room. "I have to tell Lucy about us. That I don't love her. I thought I did—but I was sadly mistaken. You're the one I have loved all along. But to tell Lucy now— three days before the wedding? How cruel is that! As to Mi-Ling, I wish I knew. Thinking about her and her disappointment rips my heart right out of my chest."

"You could go through with the wedding as if nothing had happened."

"That I could not do, darling. The trouble is that the heart does not ask if it's okay to love. It just goes ahead and does it."

Meryl patted the bed beside her. "Come on, my hero. I need a cuddle—and could do with a coffee." The coffee had to wait. I pointed out to Meryl that it was an inopportune time to go for coffee. "What about the cuddle?" she purred.

We could hear the sound of shelling, gunfire and explosions. This, we had to remind ourselves, was not a film set. These were not technically safe explosions. They were the real thing.

"Dear God," I said. "Get us out of this." Then I wondered why I was talking to God—praying to Him—when I still wasn't quite sure that He existed. But with explosions rocking the building and causing the windows to groan, I very much hoped that He was real, and that He cared about what happened to us.

You might be surprised at me admitting fear, Reader. But if you're reading this account, you are probably in some cozy warm place, with no feeling or fear of being shot at by someone who can't see you. When the cannon ball they have just loaded into their cannon falls short, you are the unfortunate obstacle between it and its final resting place. Hour after hour, knowing that all round there was fighting. Praying for darkness so there could be some kind of a break, a respite. Hunger and especially thirst because there was a lot of sunshine going about, it was hot.

Angus came to our room door and knocked. "Are you two decent?"

"Just a minute," we said, followed shortly by a, "come in."

He came through the door looking thoughtful. "Thon Captain Vincent had a strong Kairon signal. I wish I could have got near some of his chums. If my suspicions are right, General Lee is going to be seeing more of him, whether he wants to or not. The other thing is, it's not safe for Sebastian to stay in the barn. If he's caught on his own, he may be killed. All we can do is bring him up here—if you folks don't mind."

I greatly minded. I wanted to be alone with Meryl. But not at the risk of Sebastian's life.

"Are the Union forces aware that there is a possible invasion force ready to attack?" I asked. "If they do attack and we get caught by the Union outside of these uniforms, we'll be treated as spies. You, too, Meryl. If we stop those who are trying to persuade Lee to get British help, then we have to be out of here before the Union forces reoccupy the town."

Meryl looked thoughtful. "I keep raking my mind, but what I

remember reading is that Lee and the other Confederate officers would have been in favor of Britain coming in on the Confederate side."

Angus explained, "I believe they didn't think through the implications—like freeing the slaves. The government of the time would have demanded that. They would have wanted favorable prices for buying cotton to feed the many cotton mills. There would have been a demand for cheap British imports to be allowed in, and there would always be the threat that British forces could be withdrawn if the South didn't agree."

I added, "Then the North would re-impose the blockade. And there was always the possibility of a Union invasion of Canada. If Lee accepts this, does he realize that, diplomatically, it could be the case of casting off Washington, and then having—if not rule—at least extreme influence from London again? The whole reason why 1776 took place would be negated."

"I guess there is no such thing as a free meal," Meryl mused. "1863 Britain had the most powerful Navy on earth, and they would want a lot in return."

I said, "General Lee is a soldier—a brilliant general of great genius —but he is not a diplomat. He is under pressure just now. When you are under pressure you don't always see the long-term results of the decisions you make."

At this point, Sebastian came to the door. Meryl went to answer. "We were just talking about you, Sebastian. "It's not safe for you to remain in the barn. Please join us here. It will be the safest place for you."

He looked surprised and asked, "Y'all don't mind no black folk a'hangin' 'round yous? Why you should do this for me? I ain't even your real slave."

I remembered Sir Charles Gray, the British Ambassador in Foochow, and what his attitude had been to the Chinese, whom many others despised. He treated them with kindness as fellow humans, and with the love of Christ. I kind of wondered what he would have done with Sebastian, yet in my heart I knew the answer. Then it dawned on me that in 1863, Sir Charles was still alive.

"Can you sleep in our changing room?" I suggested. "That way we all get some privacy."

Sebastian looked uncomfortable with the idea. "Sure enough, I can do that. But I ain't likin' the idea of comin' between husband and wife. You folks need to be private."

"Do you have a wife? Do you have children?" Meryl wanted to know.

The big man's eyes began to brim with tears. "My childrens died from disease. Bad water. Cholera, as they says. My wife was taken away and sold somewheres. Can't nobody tells me where."

Angus looked at him and said slowly, "You must hate Confederates with every fiber of your being."

The tear-filled eyes of the black man looked at him in surprise. "Naw, sir. I don't hate. The Lord done said we was to love our enemies and keep on a'prayin' fer them who uses you the wrong way. I reckon if the Lord done say that, it must be important to Him. It's easy to say you believe somethin' till you're put to the test. Hate ain't no way to live. If'n I hate, what be the difference between me and them? Why should I bring my heart down to their level?"

His simple, humble words filled the room with a louder silence than the noise of battle raging outside.

"The Confederates ain't all bad," Sebastian added. "They's some kind, fine God a'fearin' folks among them. Jesus said, 'If you forgive men their trespasses'—that be the things they done do wrong to you, so your heavenly Father will forgive you your trespasses. But if'n you don't, then God won't forgive you. In the end, I reckon it ain't goin' to matter none what man says, but it do matter what God says."

As I listened to Sebastian, I realized that all my preconceived ideas of what it meant to be a "man" and "manly" had just been shot to pieces —with no weightier a weapon than words.

"Still, you must miss your wife," Merle said.

Sebastian looked at her and smiled. "Law, yes! My only possibility of seeing Bessie Mae again is by prayer. The Good Lord know where she is and He kin have us meet again but I have to keep a'praying for it—and you can't pray and hate at the same time."

Then he asked hesitantly, "Miz Faulkner, would you mind if I went to have a rest in that room you said I could borrow? I'm plenty tired and it will be nice not to see soldiers and snakes, though the Lord has been real good to me. And another thing about it, when I'm free, I'm not goin' near another ditch. I've done hid from cavalry in ditches more times than I care to say. They ain't never caught me, praise the Lord! Funny thing was just before you found me, I hid from a cavalry patrol and I'm right sure the officer saw me He looked right into my eyes, yet he didn't say nuthin' I even remember his name cause one of his troopers used it – Lootenant Luke Carter."

****

That evening, because some Confederate officers were dining there, we got a meal as well—all of us including Angus, though this time we sat at separate tables. We had to take Sebastian's meal up to him in our room since black people were not permitted in the dining area. This was a time to listen more than talk. There was a band outside, for the fighting seemed to be over for the day. Yet it would be a long night for the injured on the battlefield. The one extreme problem was that was hard to get clean water. Any water, in fact.

Three officers who were dining at the inn looked at us. One raised his hat and came over to our table. "Excuse me for interrupting, sir, but I don't recognize your uniform."

I stood up and offered my hand. "Major Andrew Falconer of her Britannic Majesty's 92nd Gordon Highlanders. Here is my pass signed by Vice President Stephens and Secretary of War Breckenridge. This is my wife, Meryl, and my ADC, Lt. Angus McTurk."

The Officer looked at Meryl, who dried her lips with a napkin and focused her baby-blue eyes on him and said, "Colonel, if I'm not mistaken. I'm delighted to meet you."

He smiled. "Colonel Beauregard Lovejoy 14th Tennessee Infantry.

At your service, ma'am."

"Honored to meet you, Colonel Lovejoy." She extended her hand, which Colonel Lovejoy kissed.

I asked McTurk later, "How come you kept a straight face when he introduced himself as Lovejoy?"

"Simple, laddie. He is probably a better shot than I am. Sometimes it takes wisdom to survive time travel."

Colonel Lovejoy introduced his fellow officers. "This fellow is Major Frederick Fellows." Fellows bowed.

"This is Captain William Gordon and Lootenant Harry Ambrose." They both acknowledged my nod.

Captain Gordon spoke with the trace of a Scottish accent and with a shade of suspicion in his eyes. "Where was it that the Gordon Highlanders mustered again?"

I smiled and replied, "Why, in Aberdeen."

"Of course," he agreed. "How could I forget? But I've been over here a long time now. Still, I've been to Aberdeen. It has a lovely city center—all that pink-colored sandstone."

"With all due respect, Captain, you have been away a long time. The center of Aberdeen is built of beautiful gray granite, the color of which is not unlike your uniform." Whew, I thought, I'm glad he fired a test question that I could answer.

Looking into his eyes, I saw the shade of suspicion lifting.

"Your commander-in-chief, General Lee, is greatly respected in the British Army," I said. "His victories are studied. One hopes that Gettysburg may be among them."

I saw Angus' eyes flash me a warning. I was supposed to be neutral and should avoid even tacit support of one side against the other. Even in 1863, walls had ears, and we were not out of this situation yet.

The main topic of conversation seemed to be if General Ewell should attack Cemetery Hill tomorrow. We knew Cemetery Hill was where General Meade had his headquarters and, consequently, was where the telegraph office was located, but we could say nothing.

What we could not guess was that how many people knew about

the British invasion fleet off the coast. Nor could we know how Lee's supporters felt about it. Would what could be seen as an invasion take greater precedence as a unifying factor than state's rights? I had this picture of the Blue and the Gray uniting to suddenly fight the Scarlet.

I was lost in that daydream when I became aware that Colonel Lovejoy was addressing me. "Will your countrymen come and assist us, Major?"

I rubbed my hand over my forehead. "Well, Colonel, I don't want to speak ill of my native land."

He nodded his head. "Why, so I should be disposed to imagine."

"The trouble is, Colonel, that once the fighting is over and we soldiers go back to barracks, then the politicians take over. My country has the biggest navy in the world. I didn't say the best—but certainly the biggest. Many times round about 1776, the navy of the young United States defeated Britain.

"You know in life, Colonel, you don't get something for nothing. Britain would be looking for you to free the slaves as the first price for her help. Then I suspect my country would seek cheap cotton to feed the massive cotton mills in Britain, and at least in southern ports, they would be looking for very favorable terms for your imports. They would also, in the back of their minds, fear a Yankee invasion of Canada. You may manage to throw off Washington only to exchange it for London."

Colonel Lovejoy scratched his chin and responded, "I'm sure that our people have seen all this. At least, I hope they have. As far as I recall, there have been no direct negotiations between Richmond and London."

"Colonel, with all due respect, General Lee is a soldier and an excellent commander. His victories are legend. But he's also a commander under pressure who sees the opportunity for a sudden influx of friendly troops which will assure him of victory. But he might be unaware of the size of the bill laying on the table awaiting payment. And in respect of bills, gentlemen, may we buy you gentlemen your dinner?"

The Colonel looked at me and replied, "Why, sir, that's very kind of you, and the lady too." His eyes strayed to Meryl who turned her head to one side and threw in the fluttering of lashes over her baby blue eyes, a killer combination that reduced male resistance to zero.

He continued, "There is no way that we could refuse a gift from such a fair hand. I will pass on what you say at the first opportunity to General Lee. Thank you for this most thought-provoking conversation. But we must turn our attention to more mundane consideration—like the removal of as many Yankees as possible tomorrow."

When we got back to the room, we found that Sebastian had spirited himself into the space of a small room down the hall. "If y'all need me, just call," he said with quiet dignity before retiring.

We went to bed with a sense of make and break about tomorrow. We also felt that we had found one needle in the haystack when there were supposed to be two. We worked on the principal that most organizations worked in twos, even the bad guys. Where was the other needle in one whale of a big haystack?

CHAPTER 5

July 2nd 1863

I remember being at the funeral of a good friend and having one of the mourners remark to me in passing, "Turned out fine again. Nice day for a funeral."

Remembering that made me wonder if you got a nice day for a battle. There was firing and a hive of activity outside. Orders and counter orders. The rumbling of artillery and ammunition caissons going helter skelter and the sound of music—Dixie and Hurrah for the Bonnie Blue Flag.

Folk were singing and through the window, somehow, came the smell of a myriad of cook fires. How many of these boys going off would come back? How many of the boys in blue on the other side? Some of the mothers and newly-made widows would get a condolence telegram, but there would be many dying in the corner of the battlefield with nobody to miss them and with only God to notice. War might be necessary sometimes, but there was nothing romantic about it. I realized that in two-hundred years, little had changed except the enemy.

We knew from history that on day two, apart from skirmishing, fighting did not take place until the afternoon. General Lee would be planning where on the Union Line he would attack and General Meade would be trying to second guess him. This would be a good time to look for a window of opportunity to see him.

Later, the fighting in the wheat field, the peach orchard and Devil's Den would take place, as well as the attack on Little Round Top.

At Little Round Top, the defense put up by the men of the 20th Maine and their commander, Colonel Joshua Chamberlain, and his officers, would culminate in a famous, dangerous, desperate, downhill bayonet charge that would later make their memorial the most visited in the Gettysburg battlefield.

All this was still to come. When we live through something, we don't realize that it is history taking place. It's a weird feeling when you are on the spot as history takes place. Not only do you see and hear, but you even smell the events. You hear the philosophical voices of the men. You smell the powder smoke, the fear, goober peas and biscuits cooking. You smell the fresh coffee that someone found. You hear the jittery horses and smell the moist leather. You become aware of the scent of familiar things that make for eternity and are inherent in every generation.

We had no need to look for General Lee. He found us, or at least Captain Gordon, whom we had met the night before, found us. "Good morning, sir." He saluted and I returned the salute. "General Lee's complements, and would you wait on him at his headquarters at 10:30? He asked for the three of you to come. He didn't feel it was proper to leave a lady on her own in the midst of a battle," he explained impassively.

"Please convey to General Lee that we will be delighted to wait on him at that time and we hope he is well," I replied.

Captain Gordon acknowledged the answer and sent his horse galloping away to deliver our message. Angus and I walked on down the street and to the edge of the town. Feeling that her presence might be distracting, Meryl had stayed in the hotel—so we would need to get her for the meeting with Lee.

McTurk and I passed a group of guys around a coffee pot on the outskirts of town towards the Union Line. "Hey, Fellahs," they mocked. "I wouldn't be gettin' any closer to the Union lines, with them bright red uniforms. They ain't no way they can miss you!" They laughed boisterously.

McTurk asked calmly, "You mean like the fellah in the green uniform a'comin' round that rock?" McTurk pushed the guy with the coffee pot to the ground just as one of Bredan's sharpshooters fired, the shot landing between McTurk and the soldier. Five or six rifles replied and the green-uniformed soldier, in the words of one of the men in gray, "aw shucks, he done skidaddled." The coffee pot had landed the right way up, and when the Union soldier 'skidaddled' out of range, the Alabamians—for that is where they hailed from—invited us to join them and thanked McTurk for the warning.

"You British sure talk funny," one of them said.

McTurk replied, "Yep. It's all the tea we drink. Your coffee's good, though."

"It's Union coffee, but the soldier who had it, well, he didn't need it no more, so he donated it to the Confederate States of America Army Welfare fund. Mighty nice of him."

His friends agreed with much nodding of heads. "We're all a'fixin'to go to a place called Little Round Top," one of them explained. "Ain't nobody there. All we got to do is march up the hill and set up camp. Nice safe place let the rest get on with the battle. Yep, so the Major says—safe an' real quiet."

We got up to leave and Angus said, "If we were you, we wouldn't be countin' too much on that there place bein' quiet. Keep your heads down, fellahs."

We thought it would be a good time to pick up Meryl and Sebastian and head for General Lee's headquarters in the McPherson House. How long we would have to wait we did not know, but seeing General Lee was the whole purpose of us having traveled here to this time. The four of us set off.

The one-story house in which Lee's headquarters was situated was built in 1789, crafted with stone of various shades. There was a wooden balcony to the rear and worn wooden steps up to the front to the door, with a rail around the porch. It was a lovely building. All it would have taken to transform it into a home would have been a rocking chair on the front porch with a cat curled up asleep on the seat.

Sadly, its peaceful existence had been shattered by war and by the trappings of battle. Instead of a cat on the porch, a soldier stood on the balcony with a rifle in his arms. The rifle had a telescopic sight and his locus gave him the best view around.

There were two soldiers flanking the front door of the house and two standing at the back, each armed with a pistol and sporting a broad-brimmed hat, which was necessary to keep the rising sun at bay. They were dressed, one in gray, and the other in that particular homespun Confederate combination called butternut. The fact that their uniforms did not match in no way belayed their excellent quality as soldiers.

I noticed the corral behind the house was unoccupied, and it looked as if General Lee might have been out examining the disposition of at least part of his forces. I wondered what a general did before a battle. I suspected that he dug deeply into his store of optimism in the hopes that he could spread it amongst his men. I also knew that when he awoke, the first Person, Lee would have gone to that day would not have been an orderly or officer but God.

At the front of the house, Major Taylor was engaged in speaking to a lieutenant, to whom he handed a pack of what looked like dispatches. He patted the man on the shoulder. The lieutenant stepped back and saluted and Major Taylor returned the salute.

Angus still wore the earpiece of the Kairon detector. As the lieutenant went past, Angus gave me a surreptitious nod. We went over to Major Taylor. He treated Meryl to a bow and a "Ma'am," then gave all of us a hearty, "Good morning. General Lee's not here just now, but he will be back presently. Would you care to wait inside?" Then looking at Meryl pointedly, he added, "It will keep the lady out of the sun." Turning his attention to Sebastian he informed us, "Your slave can wait inside the door." With that, he conducted us inside.

Meryl sat down and Sebastian stood. Angus and I paced up and down. We heard the noises of an army rousing—clanking, creaking and the sound of hammer striking anvil. Singing drifted in, sounding optimistic, inspired by the hopes of victory and memories of home. We heard the sound of boots on the wooden steps and General Lee entered the room. Major Taylor went to him to remind him who we were, and the look of recollection played across his face. He came over and shook hands.

"I thank you for taking the trouble to come and meet with me.

Colonel Lovejoy passed on some of the things you said. I was interested to hear more." He hung his hat on the peg behind the door. "I would offer you coffee, but we are short of drinking containers."

I replied, "Please, sir, don't concern yourself with such matters. We have had sufficient breakfast and the hotel manager was able to produce some coffee, so our thirst has been assuaged."

He smiled the smile of a wise teacher who was pleased with the contents of his pupil's essay, and pointing to the neighboring room said, "There will be less occasion for disturbance if we go in here. Major Taylor, please see that I am not disturbed for the next thirty minutes."

We started to follow him, including Meryl. General Lee turned to her. "Mrs. Faulkner, there is no need for you to trouble yourself over such matters. Major Taylor will take good care of you while your husband and I converse."

Meryl smiled and responded pleasantly, "General Lee, five months ago I was nearly killed in a sword fight in China. I have been shot at and nearly killed several times and have killed men in self-defense and when the service of my country demanded it. I have been asked to be here and I must see it through unless my presence causes you offence."

Lee bowed and said, "Forgive me, Mrs. Faulkner. Sometimes the unexpected is not confined to the battlefield. Please come in and be seated. You are entirely welcome."

We retired to the inner room.

"To your knowledge, Major, are the British going to come in on our side?" General Lee asked me.

I replied, "Sir, the removal of slavery would be a prerequisite. Also the provision of cheap cotton to feed the cotton mills that pepper the land."

Lee nodded. "I see."

"Sir, may I speak freely—laying aside the fact that I am a Scot and part of the British Isles?" I asked.

Lee gave an affirmative nod to my question.

"Sir, British intervention may help give a victory just now, but there is a real danger that you would, as the Confederate States of America, be exchanging rule from Washington for rule from London. You fought in 1776 to be free. The war you fight now is part of the growing pains of a great nation. It is for Americans to settle the shape of that nation, as some have begun to do already by the laying down of their lives on both sides."

General Lee looked at me, and after taking a mouthful of water said, "Major, I am gratified by your forthrightness. But this is a war that those on the outside looking in may not fully understand."

My stomach felt tight with fear, knowing that so much might depend on my next words. How had I ended up in this situation? "Sir, I beg to state that it is precisely for that reason that those on the outside should not be asked or allowed to participate in it."

General Lee slowly nodded his head and replied, "Major, I will consider what you have said."

It was at that point that there was a commotion outside the door. We heard Major Walker's voice, "General Lee has asked not to be disturbed." Then, with a puzzled tone of voice, "General Lee! I'm sorry. I didn't know you were there."

Lee's voice came from behind the door, "Captain Vincent and I do not wish to be disturbed. Is that understood, Walker?"

"Yes, General, of course," came the reply.

I saw Angus slide his pistol under a cloth on a chair directly behind him and unbutton his holster and kick it below a chair. At that point, Vincent and the lieutenant we saw talking to Major Walker earlier entered the room—along with General Lee and a trooper.

When the door opened and Meryl saw General Lee, she got up with a start from her seat, knocking over a container of ink on General Lee's desk, some of which spilled onto General Lee's sleeve. "Oh," she said, putting her hand to her mouth. "I'm dreadfully sorry."

We were all surprised, but Meryl had recovered the fastest. What she had done, although we did not realize it at the time, was to mark the real Lee for identification purposes. Now, I realized why she was in this organization—her fast thinking.

The false Lee walked over to the desk behind which General Lee sat. "You will vacate that chair, whoever you are."

General Lee looked at him. The false Lee repeated the order. Captain Vincent pulled out a pistol and pointed it at General Lee. "We have no time for this. You—whoever you are—get off the chair now!" He pulled the hammer back on his pistol.

General Lee looked at him calmly. If you shoot me, Mr. Vincent, what explanation will you give for the presence of two General Lees?"

Vincent sneered. "Granny, we are going to send you on a little trip. You see, you must order the British into the fight. With that, America will become divided and weak so that she will fail to fight in the future when the world will be at war and need her strength. We can tell all of you this because you are all going to enjoy our hospitality."

I said, "I see, but we are citizens of her Majesty Queen Victoria and the British Empire. You kidnap us and you will be hunted down. My country's empire covers…"

Vincent snarled, "Shut up, English scum. The day of your miserable empire is past! We will build a new order. We are part of PATCH, People Allied To Change History. Though, I doubt you have the intelligence to comprehend something so lofty and profound."

Moving around the desk next to the other Lee, the false Lee continued, "Soon the world will hear of us because we intend to patch up the mistakes of the past. We travel into the past to build a new future, a future of power and strength."

General Lee looked at him with a shake of his head, "Travel to the past? You are deranged, sir. I'm afraid the sun has got to you. The future, like the outcome of this war, rests in the hands of Almighty God."

Vincent sneered. "Almighty God? With the power we have, we don't need God."

The false Lee called out, "Walker, get in here now."

Walker entered, leaving the door about a quarter of the way open behind him. "Yes, General?" He fell silent because he was covered by a pistol.

"Now," Vincent said, "time for your little holiday." He took a silver-covered box very similar to the one that operated our time machine out of his pocket. He pressed it two or three times and warned, "It better work, Reynolds, or you're in trouble." At that point, an archway opened and everyone's attention was diverted to it.

While everyone's attention was focused on the glowing archway in the middle of the room, I saw the door edge open. Sebastian slipped inside, clutching a pistol. He was almost invisible against the wall, but Angus saw him, too. Sebastian moved silently. He pistol whipped the trooper. Angus dived for the gun under the cushion and pointed it at the lieutenant. Sebastian covered both Lees and Vincent.

Vincent smiled at him. "Very good, boy. Now you can be a real hero. Kill him"—he pointed to Lee—"the source of all your troubles, the general of the army that has enslaved your people. Just think what a hero you will be! He's your enemy. Shoot him."

Sebastian looked at him. "The Lord say, 'Vengeance is mine. I will repay.' General Lee wears a gray uniform, but he's a brother in Christ. You just said yerself you don't need God. That makes you God's enemy, and bein' God's enemy makes you my enemy."

Major Walker, who had been silent, suddenly asked, "Yes, but who is the enemy? Which one is the real General Lee?"

"I am. And when we summon British help, we can win this war. Victory will be ours," the false Lee promised.

Sebastian looked at them both. "I know which one is the real Lee. The man who speaks God right proud. But if'n y'all won't believe me, and need more witness than this dark man's skin, there be someone who can tell."

A light of recognition flooded Meryl's face. "Yes!" she exclaimed. "The horse. A horse will recognize its own master."

Walker and Angus took the two Lees out to the back, one by one, and when they had finished, came back inside. Major Walker pointed to the real Lee. "Traveler recognized him right away and came from the other side of the corral." He indicated the other Lee. "With him, Traveler never moved. Nor did this man, whoever he is, know Traveler's name."

Meryl pointed to General Lee. "Plus, when the other Lee came in, I purposely spilled ink over the real General Lee's sleeve so we could identify him."

Lee looked at his sleeve and smiled at Meryl. "Mrs. Faulkner, you truly are an exception, and exceptional as well. Major, you are blessed to have such a wife."

"Thank you, sir," I replied, trying not to think about Bellefield and the painful bridge that must be crossed when we returned. What was going to happen to Lucy? And what about Mi-Ling? I suddenly realized that I missed my soon-to-be-adopted daughter dreadfully. An empty ache echoed through my heart and only Mi-Ling's bright smile and quiet joy could make the hurting stop. Steady, I told myself. Focus. You're not through with this mission yet.

Angus stepped forward and addressed the false General Lee. "You go back where you came from." He pointed to the trooper. "You, too." Obediently, they went through the time portal, which now looked a bit more wobbly. Then Angus spoke to the lieutenant. "Turn out your pockets before you go."

A collection of bits and pieces came out and were put on the table. These Angus studied before he ordered, "The spare control for the portal."

"There is none," came the denial.

Angus pulled back the hammer of his pistol and shook his head ruefully. "Nasty gun, this. Got a habit of going off accidentally. Duced inconvenient some times."

The second control was flung down on the table and the lieutenant went through the portal. Vincent started to follow.

"Not you," McTurk said.

"But what are you going to do with me?"

McTurk threw the switch and the portal closed. He crushed the switch of both controls.

Vincent yelped. "But I'm stranded here!"

McTurk looked at him and said, "In my army, for threatening to murder the commanding officer in war time you would have been court-martialed and shot."

General Lee looked at Vincent and said to Major Walker. "Major Walker, be so good as to prepare Mr. Vincent's discharge papers. The Army of Northern Virginia has no further need of his services and we're giving him a dishonorable discharge."

Then to Vincent, "Get your things and get out of my sight and remove that uniform for, sir, you are not fit to wear it."

Vincent drew in several breaths. "I will tell what happened here today," he threatened. "What I saw. It will be all over the papers in Richmond as soon as I get back."

Sebastian shook his head. "Mmm, Mr. Vincent, ain't no one in the world is gonna believe you."

"Yes," I agreed. "Who is going to believe you? Two General Lees, and going back in time? Why that's rank foolishness."

"But you can't do this to me!"

Major Walker had left the room and returned with a piece of paper for General Lee to sign. Lee signed it and handed it to Vincent. "Now, get out of my sight."

I watched one of the would-be tyrants of the new order leave.

"Sic semper tyrannis," Meryl said.

The next time that phrase would be heard would be from the lips of John Wilkes Booth when he murdered President Abraham Lincoln, words so false as to be stellar.

General Lee heaved a big sigh. "I shall be so glad when all this is finished." He extended his hand to Sebastian. "Thank you. I am in your debt."

As I watched black and white shake hands in 1863, I knew I was watching something I would remember until my dying day. They looked into each other's eyes and suddenly I realized that only God could have engineered this. It was the strangest thing, but I felt as if God had taken up residence in my heart. Suddenly, I knew that God could do the impossible.

Sebastian let go of General Lee's hand and said, "General Lee, you are not in my debt. We both be in Jesus' debt."

Lee nodded that sage-like nod that seemed to set him apart from the others around him. "Yes. We are all in the hands of the Lord and He will work out this day, one way or the other. You are free, Mr. Sebastian. I will give you a paper that states that fact. Nobody will harm you. Thank you again."

Sebastian smiled and said, "General Lee, we didn't do nothin' today. Ain't it wonderful that no matter how much we think we know about the Lord, they's always room to learn more? And ain't it even more wonderful that He be a God of surprises?"

"Sir," I said to Lee. "We've taken up enough of your time. If we may be allowed to continue to observe?"

"Of course," Lee assured us. "And thank you for your prompt action." He looked at McTurk. "If you ever seek a change of uniform, there is a command waiting you here."

McTurk replied, "I will give the matter my earnest consideration."

"As to the events that took place here …?"

We said we could not think of anything that happened that was out of the ordinary. There need be no fears on that. We shook hands and parted. McTurk and I saluted and Lee returned the salute.

We decided to head back for the hotel. We went to our room and just stood there for a while looking at one another. We guessed that Lee would not be asking for outside help and wondered how a different commander would have coped with the situation. McTurk said thoughtfully, "I fear we may still have a problem. If you were Vincent, what would you do?"

Meryl answered promptly. "Maybe seek revenge? He has information that would interest the Yankees. He's not from the North or the South. He doesn't care who wins. All he wants is power."

McTurk nodded. "True. And he would want to get back at us. We're not looking at someone with a rational mind. Think about Bryant and how far he has taken his desire for revenge—halfway round the world."

"I would rather not think about Bryant and his desire for revenge, Angus, if you don't mind." I considered briefly, where would Vincent go? Then I informed the others, "Remember in the stable when he had plans to kill you, Sebastian?"

"I ain't likely to forget that even if 'n I was paid to. Naw, sir! I love the Lord but I have to be kinda glad that He didn't call for me at that particular time."

McTurk asked suddenly, "Didn't he have two laddies with him? Two troopers?"

We all nodded.

"And," McTurk finished, "wasn't it just one that went through the time tunnel?"

Again we affirmed.

"So," Meryl put in, "we have two. A tyrant and the trainee tyrant. What can they do? General Lee discharged Vincent."

Sebastian said, "Even though General Lee has give an order, how important will that be in the face of everything else that's going on? This be a big battlefield. How soon folks gonna get to know 'bout an order like that? And if it's a settin' on Major Walker's desk like a lazy chicken hen, when's he gonna to get to it? He's busier than a bee round honey."

"Sebastian," McTurk asked. "You're a quick thinker and a straight thinker. How would you like to join us be part of the team? We have no secrets from you. You've heard everything."

"Shore 'nuff, y'all really do travel through time? You ain't like Vincent and his men?"

"We are trying to stop them," Meryl explained. "We know the damage they can do."

"This here be 1863. What time y'all come from?"

"Round about 2013," McTurk answered.

"Whew!" Sebastian blew out his cheeks. "That's a right far piece of years. That must mean y'all know the past as well as the future."

"Before you ask, yes, the South surrenders in two years' time and America grows to be a powerful nation. One nation under God, indivisible, with liberty and justice for all. But it was a hard road," I told Sebastian.

"Does General Lee survive the war?" Sebastian asked.

"Yes," I said. "And even today he is honored as the great general that he was."

Sebastian thought and took a deep breath. "I shore am glad to hear that."

"You'll get a salary," Meryl said encouragingly.

Sebastian looked at her. "How dangerous is that?"

Meryl laughed. "It's not dangerous, Sebastian. It means you'll get paid."

"Paid? Law, that just takes a bit of getting' used to. Y'all really want me? Even though I'm …"

"Don't say it, Sebastian," McTurk interrupted. "Where we come from, your skin color makes no difference. All are equal in the Lord's sight. Black people can gain the highest offices of state now. They own their own houses and businesses. They have won their battle for equality and respect for the most part. But, unfortunately, there will always be angry, bitter people who must tear down others to build up themselves."

"Well," Sebastian said with a philosophical shake of his large, strong shoulders. "Don't seem to be a lot happening here. I speak French if that be any help." His dark face broke into a lively smile and he shook his head. "Law! The Lord sure do move in mysterious ways. Bessie May used to say to me, 'Sebastian, if'n you fell in a river you'd come out a'clutchin' a couple of big ole fish.'"

We laughed.

The laughter died quickly as I realized, "The answer is staring us in the face! Where would these two try to get to? If they go to the Union side and give them information, it will only help a Union victory. Lee won't listen to them if they keep going on about the British. The British force is awaiting a word from Lee that won't come."

There was a silence then McTurk hit his fist in his hand. "How stupid! Of course, the telegraph office. They could still attempt to cause a British force to land. Send a telegram purporting to come from Lee, and all hell is let loose."

Meryl added, "Lee would never have given a code word for such a major offensive, even if there was one, to a captain. Vincent was only a captain."

"He don't need what General Lee know," Sebastian said thoughtfully. "What if there be someone mad as him among the British? Someone there must know the message General Lee would send, even if'n it's, 'cut the cherry pie, mamma, 'ahm comin' home.' If someone there know what to say and Vincent contacts them, they can put the whole thing into action."

"Yeah," said Meryl. "This is only day two of the battle. There's still another day."

"Another day?" Sebastian said. "How long do this fight go on for? If'n they go on into the 4th of July, don't reckon it's gonna to be much of a holiday."

"How do we get to the telegraph office?" I asked.

"Take a taxi," Meryl quipped.

"What be a taxi?" Sebastian asked.

McTurk patted him on the back. "Come on, laddie, you'll learn. Now, excuse me for a moment. I need to make a brief check outside."

"Did I say somethin' wrong?" Sebastain asked, puzzled.

"Not a thing. But Taxis haven't been invented yet," Meryl explained, treating him to a broad smile.

Sebastian shook his head. "Not invented yet? Law, but this time travel sure do mess with your mind. You mean that we could go see anyone that has ever lived, talk to them?"

Meryl thought for a moment. "Well, really—yes—anyone who has ever lived."

Sebastian looked at her. "Anyone? Even the Lord Jesus?"

There was a silence in the room

Meryl said hesitatingly, "The answer is, yes. As long as He was real and really had lived."

Sebastian looked at her."That shore is one trip I'd like to make!"

McTurk hurried back into the room. "We need to get to the telegraph office if it's still functioning. If it isn't there, there might be a telegraph train near it. That will be the easiest one for Vincent to get to. The one at Mead's HQ on Cemetery Ridge could be well guarded. It will have a direct line to the War Department in Washington. There isn't one to the White House. President Lincoln goes to the War Department each day to read and reply to the telegrams his commanders send. There are telegraph links at Army Division and Corps level. Whether they all work is another story. The PATCH people could have someone at the HQ."

Meryl asked, "Why not just cut the wire?"

I objected. "Wouldn't that interfere with the course of the battle if folk can't communicate?"

"You can't make an omelet without breaking eggs," Meryl retorted.

"Listen," McTurk put in. "We know historically how this battle ended, but suppose because we cut the wires it turns out the other way?"

"A southern victory?" I asked. "At that point, the British would almost certainly come in and we would have achieved the PATCH people's purpose for them."

Sebastian had been listening to all this. "I hate to interrupt you folks' deep thinking, but shouldn't we outta do something? All Vincent's got is his own self to talk to, an' you can answer your own self a lot quicker than you can answer three other people all talking at once. Him on his way to the telegraph an' still wearing Gray—it don't take a whole heap of horse sense to know where he gonna go. If'n he pokes his head up at Mede's house, someone gonna be obliging and shoot it off fer him."

"So we just go to the telegraph office and look?" I asked.

"Shore 'nuff," Sebastian said. "Faint heart never got to the cookin' pot first."

Leaving Meryl and Sebastian behind, Angus and I headed to the telegraph office, which by some miracle, was still standing and functioning. The young trooper happened to be outside. McTurk grabbed him and yanked him around to the side of the house, whipping out his pistol. "Listen, sonny, where are you from?"

"Bandera, Texas."

"Lots of Russian immigrants there?" McTurk quizzed.

"No," the boy answered, puzzled by the question. "Polish. They came to make cypress shingles from the trees along the Medina River."

With a quick nod of his head to indicate that the trooper had passed the test, Angus said, "Listen, Laddie. Vincent has been discharged from the army by General Lee. If I were you, I'd get back to my regiment double quick. You know where it is. If anyone stops you, we'll cover for you with General Lee. Get your rifle and cartridge case and a water bottle and get going and keep your head down. What's your name?"

"Trooper James McTurk. My ancestors came from Scotland."

"How did they get from Scotland to Texas?"

The kid grinned broadly. "You can read about it when my book comes out." He ran off.

The telegraph office was empty apart from the operator. Vincent had his back to us. We assumed he was writing out his message to pass along to the clerk. The clerk was operating his camelback Morse key.

McTurk crept up behind Vincent and put a gun in his ribs. "Nice and easy does it, laddie. Keep your mouth shut. My Adams can go off accidentally. It's got a mind of its own."

I had about ten seconds to think up an excuse for removing an officer from sending a telegram. I went round the counter putting on my best southern accent and hoping that the telegraph operator didn't know his uniforms. "Major Thaddeus Moxton, Confederate Judge Advocates Office. I must ask you for any texts of telegrams this man has sent."

The nervous clerk replied, "He…he was just writing his message out for me to send. I didn't know! Please! I've got a wife and children."

"Thank you for your cooperation," I said reassuringly. "You're doing a good job and yours is the communication of the future. When this war is over, this country will need men like you."

He pushed his wire framed glasses up onto his nose. "You think so?"

I patted him on the shoulder and said, "I know so." Then to Angus. "Right, Lieutenant. Forward march with the prisoner." As we left, I thought, Now we have him—what are we going to do with him?

I wonder if you've ever been in a sticky situation and suddenly rescue has come out of the blue and you've exclaimed, Hey the cavalry has arrived!, and given a cheer. Well, that's what happened. Right out of the blue, the cavalry arrived, except it was not only out of the blue, but that the guys on the horses wore blue uniforms and they were going hell bent for leather up the street while we stood wondering what to do. The boys in blue were heading for us and on the pennon flag there was the number two. They saw Vincent's gray uniform which gave the game away that he was Confederate. They saw our uniforms and the pity was that none of them had a book describing uniforms of the Confederate Army during the War Between the States. According to the cavalry, we were three Reb officers and they came down on us shooting and hollering.

Vincent was hit. He didn't stand a chance and couldn't defend himself because we had taken his revolver. They were also shooting at us. Real Yankee bullets knocking holes out the woodwork and whining off to heaven alone knew where. We couldn't fire back—we were supposed to stay neutral. Well, where do you go? When you can't go up, the other way is down. Below the telegraph office, there was a gap between the floor of the balcony and the dirt. It was into that gap that both McTurk and I rolled as shots thudded into the floor of the balcony outside the telegraph office. We rolled into the dark—well at least some of it was illumined. But it was mostly dark, dank and stinky.

We heard shouting. "Them Reb officers have rolled under the building. Let's get 'em."

No sooner had the cavalry come to get us, than coming from the other end of the street came a blood curdling yell. "Yankee Cavalry, boys! Let's get 'em—UYEEHAA!"

We had been saved by the cavalry from the cavalry. It could only happen to us. God bless Jeb Stuart's boys!

We gave it time and McTurk said "I think it's safe to move now." Then we heard the warning hiss.

"Lie still," McTurk ordered. "Don't move."

My mind went back to China and the one-hundred-pacer hog-nosed viper that had decided to join me in the cave. Had it not been for McTurk's quick reaction, you wouldn't be reading this now. Right, calm,

I told myself. It hasn't rattled, so it is not a rattlesnake. There are no water moccasins in Pennsylvania. That means if it's venomous, it has to be a copperhead. The chances are it wants out into the sun to warm up and find food. I heard this thumping in my ears and thought that half the town must hear it in spite of the frequent firing of arms. Then I realized the thumping was my heart. My bladder wanted to empty. Freezing me, I felt motion as the unknown serpent crawled over the back of my leg and worked its way across my shoulder. Lord, I breathed silently. I would really appreciate your help about now. I'm trusting You—which was true. There was no where else I could go for help.

With agonizingly slowness, the snake headed for the light and the pond in back of the telegraph office. I seemed to have found the only copperhead in Pennsylvania that needed a walker to help it get outside.

"Steady, laddie," McTurk said encouragingly. "He's more afraid of you than you are of him."

That was a lie.

"Steady…still, still," McTurk directed.

The terror of having a poisonous snake go past about three inches away from one's face is not the way I would recommend spending a warm sunny afternoon in July. Then the snake was gone. I tell you, I got out from under that building faster than thought could form the idea in my mind.

McTurk and I rolled out and into the legs of some six horses.

"Major, I trust you have not been inconvenienced by that visit from the Yankee Cavalry."

I looked over to see two dead Union cavalry lying on the street. Then I looked up. The figure on horseback was blacked out by the sun but the voice was unmistakable. General Lee.

"No, sir," I said. "We are both fine, but I can't say the same for Captain Vincent. It was regrettable sir. It looks like his time ran out. Still, he died in the face of the enemy, defending the lives of the two British observers. I hope he will be remembered that way."

"I thank you for your generosity of spirit to my officer. I will have Major Walker note accordingly. If you will excuse us, I think my presence is required elsewhere."

After General Lee and his entourage left, McTurk said to me, "Aye, Laddie. That was nicely done."

"That Yankee Cavalry did us a favor. We'd better get back to the hotel or Meryl will be having kittens," I replied.

"It's not for me, laddie, to interfere in someone else's life, but you must decide which of the bonnie lassies you want when you get back to 1867. And that means that one of them is going to get hurt. Anything you have been through until now—and that includes snakes, sharks, pirates and Yankee Cavalry—is going to seem easy in comparison. It's a choice that only you can make because you are going to have to live with the consequences. And I hope, laddie, that you will take into consideration that bonnie wee lass who saved your life on Night Arrow, your adopted daughter, Mi-Ling."

I assured McTurk, "I never forget Mi-Ling for more than brief moments at a time. Like when a copperhead snake is crawling over me. Actually, I keep worrying about her. She just didn't seem quite right when we left. Like she was taking on a sickness. It scares me."

I sighed deeply and added, "You're right, Angus. And now that we've accomplished what we came here to do, it makes my decision even closer. On another point, and not trying to keep from racing back to Lucy and being rushed into making the necessary decision, but I would like to be there at Pickett's Charge tomorrow. I have read about it so often. It would be rewarding to see what took place."

"Okay," McTurk said. "Then we get back and get you and young Meryl sorted out, or not, as need be."

"On the ship, in the tea race, it was so clear. Everything seemed to fall into place," I groaned.

McTurk stopped. "Think of breathing," he advised.

"A very useful practice," I agreed.

Ignoring my deep philosophy, he continued, "What's the one thing you can't do without when you are breathing?"

"Oxygen."

"Right. The one thing you can't do without. Nitrogen is necessary, but nitrogen on its own will kill you. It takes oxygen to keep you alive. Which one of these girls is your oxygen? The one you can't live without?" He looked at me like a teacher trying to explain some intractable theorem to a dull pupil. Then he added, "There's a third possibility. If you're going to get called on to do time traveling, then you may not have met the right girl yet."

"Now you have got me really confused," I responded. "And no matter what happens, I want the best for Mi-Ling. But at the moment, let's go see Meryl."

We entered the Brafferton, which had suffered a few cracked window panes from the distant explosions of war. We knocked on the room door and went in.

Meryl lay across the bed groaning. Sebastian lay on the floor.

"What the ...." I ran to Meryl. "What happened? Are you hurt?"

Somewhat dazed, she asked, "Is Sebastian okay? If it hadn't been for him, the three of them would have raped me."

"What three? Who were they? What happened here?" I demanded.

Meryl took my hand. "Three Yankee cavalrymen. Sebastian came out and surprised them. They came in through the window. I was caught unaware. They took one of the cases as Sebastain beat them off. Is he okay?"

Sebastian had been severely beaten, but fortunately appeared to have sustained no lasting injuries. I checked the luggage. The missing case had housed the Uzi SMG.

"Where did they go? How long ago?" I panted.

"Minutes ago," Meryl said. "They wanted a change of clothes. "Ohhh...ugg..."

McTurk looked at me. "We've got to get that case before they open it. They will probably head for the stable to look for horses. I think they may be deserters."

Sebastian told us to "git goin', and promised to take care of Meryl, who was trying to be brave and stop groaning for our sakes.

We went out the window and let ourselves down onto the street. We ran to the stable at as quick a slow pace as we could mange, reminding ourselves that we must appear to be observers, not participants.

"Remember, they may see you before you see them," McTurk directed. "Your eyes have to adjust. Let me go in first to the left. You count to four, then follow round."

He went in and I counted four and followed, hiding in the hay until my eyes adjusted.

One was trying to hit the metal case with a hammer. The other two were talking. "Let's go back and have some fun with that sweetie in the hotel room. Yes, sir. I could set her tingling and I would…"

The third one said "We need to go back and get us some clothes. I can't get this blasted thing open."

"Oh, I could open her up. Yes, sir!" The first one said.

"Will you shut up! We need to be thinking about our hides. If Confederates come in on us, we're going to be in a firefight."

We decided it was time to make a move. McTurk went out first with his revolver and I followed. "Okay, get your hands up. You're our prisoners," I directed.

They turned and looked at us. "First, you better tell us what uniforms those are that you're wearing."

"Confederate Judge Advocates office," I said.

"That tells us that you aren't proper soldiers," the one who had tried to open the lock objected.

"Don't waste time worrying about the color of our uniforms," McTurk advised. "Now, we are going outside and you will become prisoners unless you make a sudden move."

Then we heard a click behind us.

"They won't be going anywhere with you fellows. Drop your guns."

You stupid idiot, I berated myself, you thought there were only three—but there are four. One must have been at the other stable door keeping watch.

The one who had been trying to open the box said in a mock southern accent, "Well, hush mah mouth. I do declare, Beauregard, we done got us two Reb officers. High rankin' by the looks of them reb uniforms." The others joined in with their moronic laughter.

The comedian carried on, "Why look at them purty red uniforms. You can tell they've seen a lot of combat. Bang! Oh, my! I just gotta run away and hide from all them nasty guns or I just might get mah uniform dirty." The others hooted with laughter.

The guy who was behind us said, "Hey, Sam, that's a good take off. Next thing you'll be buying a plantation and gettin' yourself some blacks to work it."

We have to pretend to be more afraid than we are, I decided. "We are prisoners of war and demand to be treated as such," I said.

"I'm going to take you to General Hancock and he can talk to you."

"Yeah," the others agreed. "There might be a promotion in it."

"Hey, let's go back to the hotel first and celebrate with that sweet little blonde thing. We can take turns. She had that black man in her room."

We started to head out and this time the fourth soldier was behind us. "Right, Joe?" one of the men in the front threw back at Joe.

No response.

"Joe, stop joshing around..."

The other three turned around to where Joe had been and we were in front of them.

Sebastian shot out and grabbed the comedian. McTurk and I took care of the other two. Well—McTurk took care of them and I assisted. They were out.

Sebastian had the other guy by the throat. He spoke between his teeth. "I ain't mad 'bout you hittin' me. What riles me real bad is a man as would hit a woman. You be nothin' but stinkin' trash."

"Sebastian, no!" I warned. "He's not even worth killing. If you kill him like this you'll never forgive yourself."

"I shore would like to try," Sebastian responded. He looked at the guy who was shaking like a leaf. "If'n it hadn't been for them other two, I would have killed you. We're gonna hand you over to the Confederates." He hit the guy where Meryl had been hit and spat, "The measure you give out is the measure you git back." The guy's nose started to bleed.

"Oh," said McTurk. "What a shame to get that pretty blue uniform all red—MOVE!"

Horses ran into the stable. If they belonged to the Union Cavalry, we were in hot water right up to our necks. The look on the prisoners' faces turned to despair as they recognized the new arrivals as Confederate Cavalry.

One glance told me it was Luke Carter. I said to McTurk, "You do the talking. I used to know this guy in the future that used to be the past."

Lieutenant Carter looked at us. Then recognition came into his face. You're part of the British Delegation. Funny, I was just talking to Colonel Freemantle of the…what was it he said?"

"The Coldstream Guards," McTurk offered.

"You know him then?" Luke asked.

"We know of him," McTurk corrected. "Inter-regiment rivalry."

Luke nodded. "Yeah, we have that, too. It's all good sport as you English would say. Well, we will take charge of your prisoners."

"Oh, the big guy there—he does a real pretty southern accent and likes hitting women," McTurk added. "And if it had not been for Sebastian, here, they would have got the drop on us."

"You would help a Gray Uniform?" Luke asked Sebastian.

"Lieutenant, hitting a woman while your friends watch is wrong no matter what the color of uniform or of your skin."

Luke nodded. "Yup. You're sure right there. Well, thanks. In time I hope I meet up with you folks again."

"Sure thing," McTurk and I ventured.

When they had left with the prisoners, we retrieved the dented case and went back to the room where Meryl was sleeping. After making sure she was okay, we split and went separate ways. It was about six o'clock and fighting continued.

I managed to get some bread, meat, and light beer for Meryl to drink. There had been the promise of coffee, but so far it was only a promise. When Meryl awoke, I gave her the food and related the events.

"If it hadn't been for Sebastian, we would have been caught. There was a fourth one that we hadn't seen. Sebastian saw him. We owe him a lot."

"Are we going back now?" Meryl asked.

"I asked Angus about staying to see Pickett's Charge tomorrow."

"Sorry, Honey Bunny, but I'm so sore that I'm not going to be much good to you in bed tonight," Meryl smiled apologetically.

"Don't be silly! What matters most to me is you and your health. I love you! You come first. You must rest," I assured her. "As for me, I'm for an early night. I guess I'm still recovering from that snake crawling over me. Then, when we get back to Bellefield, I have to sort things out with Lucy and Mi-Ling."

She sighed. "I know I do love you, Drew. It would be easier for both of us if I didn't. When I thought these guys were going to kill me, it was not seeing you again that stuck in my mind." She sighed again and added, "Boy, I could sure go for a SavaJava coffee."

There was a knock at the door and we invited, "come in," in unison, even though I had my hand on my pistol.

Sebastian put his head round the door. "Are you okay, Miz Meryl? I've been worried near 'bout sick over you."

Meryl smiled at him. "Thank you, Sebastian. That's sweet of you. Please don't worry. And thanks for all you did." She held out her hand and Sebastian took it while she gripped her thanks.

"My thanks, too," I added. "It's great to have you on the team. I never even saw you in the barn."

Sebastian proclaimed solemnly, "Having black skin can be real useful sometimes." We laughed and he left to return to his own room.

I got into bed with Meryl and took her in my arms and fell asleep. My dreams were a mélange of copperheads, Yankee Cavalry and freshly brewed coffee. The sound of shooting fell off into the distance.

CHAPTER 6

July 3rd —Gettysburg, Day 3

I guess Meryl and I had hardly moved all night. We must have been more exhausted than we realized. With the task accomplished, as far as we knew, the pressure was off a bit.

There was breakfast in the hotel and Meryl and I met Angus downstairs. "Let's try and stay out of trouble," he said. "And when the boys come back from Pickett's Charge, we can cheer them and then leave—get you folks back to Scotland."

"What about Sebastian?" Meryl asked.

"I can take him back and process him into our organization. He is a fast thinker and good planner, just what we need. He was mad with that Union soldier for hitting you."

We took breakfast back to Sebastian. Meryl smiled and thanked him for his advocacy of the day before, and I swear—he blushed.

I told Sebastian and Meryl, "When Angus and I get back, we should move quickly and get going. The Union will be more prevalent once General Lee is forced to retire. With our Confederate documents, we'll be in danger."

Meryl said, "If my memory serves me correctly, the Confederate Cannonade starts at one o'clock. You and Angus better get going if you want to be there." She paused and asked, "Sebastian, will you stay with me? Please?"

"If you don't mind," he said to me.

"No. Thank you for doing that," I responded.

"You be most welcome. This time I aim to keep a gun handy just in case they be folks from either side what would rather loot than fight."

"Darling," Meryl said to me, "keep your head down. I don't want to lose you. I love you."

It was the first time Meryl had said anything like that in front of others. It suddenly made her very vulnerable. I smiled at her. "Pray that I will be kept safe. I love you, too." She nodded and smiled. "Besides," I added, "you still owe me a SavaJava."

"Now that's not usin' your brain," Sebastian objected. "If anyone gonna' to keep you safe, it be the Lord. "

"Don't be puzzled, my friend," Meryl told Sebastian, taking his arm. "I'll explain everything."

Unexpectedly, the big man's eyes welled up with tears. "Friend," he said, repeating the word with wonder. "Ain't nobody wid white skin ever called me that before."

****

We got near to Cemetery Ridge at about one o'clock, just as there was the sound of a cannon going off like a signal for the firing to begin. If you think you have heard loud noises, they are nothing compared to this. Two miles of Confederate Cannon, almost axle to axle, went off with about three seconds between each roar. The thump on the ground made your teeth rattle. The whine and scream of shells and shot as they headed towards the Union Line were deafening.

Up on Cemetery Ridge grew the famous—or infamous—clump of trees that General Lee had selected as the rallying point for the men who were soon to emerge from Spangler's Woods and the fields behind. Some would enter into immortality there. As Pickett's Charge was gathering, we could see little of them, for all attention was focused on the artillery. Colonel Alexander's cannon had to silence the Union artillery before the infantry could advance. Shot after shot, shell after shell. There was an explosion behind the Union Line as first one, then two ammunition caissons, blew up to a loud cheer from the Confederate Lines. The shells were not hitting the wall at Cemetery Ridge, but going over. Tightly packed behind that wall lay waiting Union riflemen. Angus and I knew they were there, a sea of blue waiting to flood the wall, pouring massive rifle fire into the oncoming ranks. The Confederates did not know this. These ranks were still in Spangler's Wood with dreams of glory, the last push—the one act that would turn the battle.

Whump, bang—ear drums hammered. They had been fighting for three years and their ears had become accustomed to the noise pollution of battle. Not so with Angus and me. I was getting a headache, yet I could not move. I was riveted to the spot.

Then Union shells began to land, sometimes throwing up great clods of dirt and grass, blowing bushes. Then the first one landed near men. The men were tossed into the air like rag dolls and blood splattered across the ground.

The men began to form up, ready for the march into history. Northern shells landed and exploded. There was no place of safety. Yet, I challenged my cowardly spirit. If these brave sons of Virginia and North Carolina could face this unflinchingly, then I could not and would not seek sanctuary. The words of General Armistead rang in my mind, "The cowards and the mother's boys have long since gone home." Cowardice, they say, is infectious. But so is courage.

Angus came up beside me. "No, laddie. I've seen that look in your eyes in the eyes of many men. You can't go with them or die with them. This is happening now so it need not happen again."

The Union shells were still landing, but with less intensity although no less noise. The Union gunners knew the infantry was coming.

As the blue battle flag of Virginia reached out to embrace the wind, I saw the motto sic simper tyrannis, and what looked like King David over the dead giant Goliath. Thus it is with all tyrants. I knew in my heart that the real tyrant here was not wearing either a Blue or a Gray uniform. The real tyrant was death, who was waiting to reap his sickening and wasteful harvest from among this human wheat.

I could see the North Carolina battle flag further down the line, with the rows of equally brave men under it. Under both was the unifying flag of the Confederacy that had brought these men together.

Angus did not have to point out General Pickett, seeking to

encourage his men. "Up, men, and to your posts." Crash. Bang. Pickett's big black horse moved slightly to one side. "Do not forget today that you are from old Virginia." The look in his eyes said that he was sorry for his rank. He wanted to go with them—"My boys."

The Union guns were practically silent and that was taken as a sign that the Union artillery had been silenced. Bands started up and the lines of Gray-spattered human wheat moved forward.

Angus tapped my shoulder and pointed to a lone figure under a tree with his head in his hands. "General Longstreet," he said.

The big man looked up, then stood up and watched as the men started to move forward. I wanted to shout a warning, but who would listen? This could no more be stopped than one could stop the wind. They were going off to be the seed planted during an event that would help bring a fractured country back together again. One nation under God.

The only tunes I recognized were Dixie and The Bonnie Blue Flag, as the guys in the band played their hearts out.

The shouted orders became a confused symphony. The lines of wheat were being punched through and others stepped in from behind to fill the gap. The words of William Shakespeare, which he had put into the mouth of the English King Henry V at the Battle of Agincourt, came to my mind. I had had to learn them at school. In 1415, a small English Army defeated a huge French force at Agincourt. It was St. Crispin's Feast Day and Henry said to his men:

> *And Crispin Crispian shall ne'er go by*
> *From this day to the ending of the world*
> *That we in it shall be remembered;*
> *We few, we happy few, we band of brothers;*
> *For he today that sheds his blood with me*
> *Shall be my brother be he ne'er so vile*
> *This day shall gentle his condition:*
> *And gentlemen in England now a-bed*
> *Shall think themselves accurs'd they were not here*

And hold their manhoods cheap whiles any speaks
That fought with us upon St Crispin's Day

(William Shakespeare Henry V Act IV scene three)

The lines of wheat were no longer straight. Smoke wreathed the battle field as if God Himself was seeking to hide the carnage from those watching. I saw arms and legs and heads fly into the air, yet I could not look away as canister shot tore into them and grapeshot did its grim work.

Before my time traveling started, I had been to Gettysburg, the peaceful pilgrim-filled park, and had walked this very ground. I remembered that as I had walked towards the Union lines with the cannon muzzles lined up, I thought, how did these boys do it? Now I was seeing the same ground again and seeing how they did it—their courage answered my curiosity.

Then suddenly, by the wall on Cemetery Ridge, there was a sea of blue as varied as the colours on a moving ocean and the rows of waving wheat wavered more but kept going

forward, ever forward. The Confederates fell in twos and threes, sixes and sevens, and through the field glasses Angus had given me, I could see General Armistead with his black hat on the point of his sword to reassure his men—his few his precious few—his band of brothers. The Confederates got to the wall and started to turn captured cannons on the enemy, then the sword and hat were gone, and a sea of blue surged around the survivors.

I looked behind and saw General Longstreet watching. He dropped his head in his hands—for he had foreseen what others had not: that no 15,000 men ever born could have taken that hill. Now he had the ungratifying and hateful realization that he had been right. Like with the mythical daughter of King Priam of Troy, Cassandra, who was condemned to tell the truth but have nobody believe her—the satisfaction of having been right turned to ashes when he saw the realization.

Cannon on the hill were still blasting. Men feet away from the muzzles were blown to bits. And then the Confederates began to turn and come back. It was more than flesh and blood could stand. They had gone into history.

In my own country of Scotland, there had been a battle just over the border with England. It was called Flodden. In 1513, a Scots and English army had met. It had been a disaster for the Scots. The English had lost 1,500 soldiers, but the Scots had lost 12,000, including King James IV, and all his officers and nobles. There was a poem written to remember that event. It told of how it would be the wives and children who would weep and mourn. The last line goes,

For the flowers o' the forest are all wede away.

Translated it means, for the flowers of the forest are all blown away. Just exactly what had happened here.

The men of Pickett's Charge had been blown away. Yet as bruised and battered as the survivors were, they met with General Lee, not with the cheering with which they had gone out to battle with, but with the resolution that the Army of Northern Virginia would fight with their commander another day.

"Come on," I said to Angus, "let's go. I feel like an intruder with no right to be here. This is private." We headed back for the hotel.

A figure stopped us, "Colonel Freemantle, her majesty's Coldstream guards." We did not salute, even though he outranked us. He did not have on a uniform.

"That was a sight of courage," he said. "I hope someone writes about it."

I looked at him. "Sir, why don't you? Now, if you would excuse us..."

I had seen and lived through a sight I would never forget. I was in no mood for small talk. Neither was Angus. If I could have been in one place, in one time, at that time, it would have been in Gettysburg Park.

Meryl and Sebastian had everything together and were ready to leave. We needed to go. That reminded me of Mi-Ling and of Lucy and of decisions I did not want to make—but must. I was the only one who could make them. I did not realize at the time that there would be somewhat of a delay before I could put any decision into action.

We carefully walked over to the stable and Sebastian asked, "I don't mean to be awkward or nothin' but once we get into that machine, where are we goin'?"

Meryl explained, "Drew and I are going to Scotland in 1867, and you and Angus are going to modern times some one-hundred-and-fifty years later."

Sebastian kind of worked all this out in his mind. "That sure sounds like one looong distance. When I wasn't free, the master used to take me with him in the buggy. I would do the driving, he would direct. Excepting, he didn't know left from right or north from south. 'Sebastian,' seys he, 'if you know that I am wrong, you gotta tell me. I must ask you to do that no matter what. Got that?"

"Sure thing, Mr. Burnham. I gotta tell you if you is goin' the wrong way, but, master, with all due respect—you gotta listen to what I seys.' Shore nuff', he did."

"Why did you leave if you got on so well?" McTurk asked.

"Because the son was not like the father."

We did not ask more questions.

Angus summoned the time car and we got in. We said goodbye to Gettysburg. It had been a gut-wrenching time for the team. After warning Sebastian, we set the dial, pressed the switch and moved off on another journey through time, a journey that should follow The Scent of Time and take us home.

PART 3

LOST IN VIRGINIA

CHAPTER 7

The time car came to a shuddering halt as if it had arrived at a junction in the road and encountered a set of red lights. Then there was nothing —even though the light inside remained on. We looked at one another with that feeling you get when you can't decide whether something is wrong, or just not quite right.

"Well, let's hope we're home," I said, attempting to sound positive. "Lucy might have some stew and dumplings for us." I didn't want to think about what else awaited me when I told her about Meryl.

Angus and I picked up a gun and knife and slid the door open. We expected to see the basement at Bellefield—except to my knowledge— there were no birds singing in the basement at Bellefield. We looked out into a forest. A great deal of forest. Tall trees, conifers of some kind, reached up into the sky. I knew very little about whatever "ology" was connected to the study of trees, but I did know that these kind of trees were not found in Scotland. Also, frost and snow should cover the ground in December and the ground was clear.

"Where are we, Angus?" I asked.

"Laddie, I might be more concerned about when, if I were you."

"It seems to be peaceful," I said hopefully. "At least we haven't landed in the middle of a war."

"AYEEEEKA WHOO!"

The next thing we knew, three Native Americans, seriously intent on hurting us, came rushing forward. They carried a knife and a tomahawk each, and additionally, had a rifle slung over their backs. If you shoot someone, you may find that they have friends who take a serious dislike to you. Pictures of the caricatures of Native Americans that I had seen flashed through my mind. In these, they were holding up one hand and saying, "peace." But these guys had knives and my scalp began to crawl as I arrived at the same conclusion that Angus had already reached: our scalps should crawl no further.

We shot two of them and Angus parried the blow of a tomahawk, killing the third. "Man, these boys were fierce! Let's hope there are no more of them. That noise of shooting would waken anyone's curiosity who heard it," Angus remarked.

We looked at the fallen Indians. Two of them wore buckskin shirts and all of them wore leggings and moccasins. Their faces were marked with lines of various patterns. Their guns were flintlocks.

Angus studied the muskets, two of which were shorter than the third. "These two," he said, pointing to the shorter guns, "are trade rifles. They have a fox on a plate at the side. They were put out by the Hudson's Bay Company." He picked up the third, longer, rifle. "This beauty is a Pennsylvania Long Rifle. It must have come from some poor soul who probably lost his scalp as well."

By this time, Sebastian and Meryl had exited the time car cautiously. Meryl looked at the tree dead braves and asked, "Social call?"

Sebastian looked at them and said, "Man! Them's injuns!" He picked up the tomahawk and took one of the knives. "Well, they ain't gonna need these no more. Hey—I thought you folks said that Scotland was a friendly kind of place."

"It is and this is not," I replied.

"Say what! If this ain't Scotland, then where in the Lord's name are we?"

"It looks like...actually, I have no idea." I answered.

"Sebastian looked around. "Man, where did all them trees come from! How did we get here, anyways? Did somebody take a wrong turning? These guns look old. Have we gone back in time instead of forward—and what time is it now? Man, I'm confused!"

"Join the club," I invited.

He sighed. "I take it this weren't supposed to happen?"

"Right," said Angus. "Council of war. We look to be somewhere in Virginia and it looks like, perhaps, the 18th century."

"Och, aye," I said. "Or more appropriately, Fennimore Cooper's book, *The Last of the Mohicans*.

"No, that was about four hundred miles north," Angus corrected.

"There must have been a time when there wasn't a war going on," I said hopefully. "Perhaps we've hit that, at least. Look: can we see if we can get out of here? If the machine will work? Angus, I trust your judgment and you may be right about where and when we are. But it's at least fairly obvious that we've gone backwards instead of forwards, judging by these guys."

Angus remained quiet, so I added, "Do time machines have a manual? There must be procedures to go through when things go wrong."

Angus nodded. "You and Sebastian keep watch. Meryl and I will tinker about and see if we can get this thing going."

Sebastian knew how to load the rifles. He took the long rifle and I took what appeared to be the better of the two muskets. We had a knife each, counting my Bowie knife. We further armed ourselves by each taking a tomahawk. Sebastian ran his finger along the edge of the one he held. "Man that's sharp! You scared?"

"Yes, sir," I replied.

"That's a relief! I thought it was just my knees a'knocking together."

Then Angus reappeared and said, "Right, guys. We're stuck. It may also be that the polarity of the Kairon has been reversed, so the forward setting works by going back and vice versa."

Sebastian said, "So it looks like we better start getting used to wherever we are."

Meryl looked at him. "Sebastian, do you realize the significance of what Angus said?"

"Miz Meryl, when you've been a slave, you learn right quick to either adapt or die. Me? I've always favored staying alive."

There was no cavalry to come to the rescue and no film director to shout, "cut." We were stuck, and basically what Sebastian said was dead right. The cavalry can, however arrive in an unexpected form.

"Lord, if you can hear me, I sure am scared and we could sure use some help." No sooner had I finished praying, than the help began to walk towards us.

More Native Americans approached. Their appearance was different and they walked quietly toward us, showing no sign of aggression.

Sebastian said, "Put your guns up. I reckon these here guys mean peace."

There were four of them, and the one whom we judged to be the oldest spoke as he looked at the dead warriors.

"Shawnee. Our enemies. You have killed our enemies. We offer you our friendship."

"What may we call you?" McTurk asked.

"We are Powhatan, friend of the English."

McTurk extended his hand and the speaker, who seemed to be the leader, took it.

"Is there a settlement nearby?" McTurk asked.

"Yes. You wish we take you there?"

It was a great relief that nobody seemed to ask the obvious questions—those being, what are you doing here and how the name of goodness did you get here?

The tall Powhatan looked at the time car and walked around it, searching the ground. He said something to the speaker, whose name turned out to be Nita. Nita said, "We will return and hide your cabin."

We began walking. I noticed that Meryl fell back to where the tall Powhatan was walking. "Hello, I am Meryl," I heard her say. "What can we call you?"

He looked at her. "I am called Kitchi." As they walked, he kept turning and looking at her. Meryl noticed and asked, "Is something wrong?"

"No," Kitchi said. "It is like the time I was out hunting and I saw a white deer. I had never seen one before. I could not kill it." Kitchi stopped. "I do not mean to cause offence, but I have never before seen a woman with the sun in her hair. That, I am sorry to say if it offends the one who is your husband."

She smiled. "He is not easily offended."

They were about to continue walking when Kitchi suddenly threw out his arm. "Stop, onyare!" The snake shot across Meryl's path. It seemed as anxious to avoid her as she was to avoid it.

"Thank you, Kitchi!" she exclaimed.

"I am sorry. I hope I do not frighten you. If you are to survive here, there are many things about the forest you must learn."

"You speak very good English," she noted.

"I went to school in the mission. To be able to speak another tongue is good and necessary."

Lord, we could be stuck here forever, I thought. I will never see Mi-Ling again. She will think that I left her. That I went away because I didn't love her. What am I going to do?

I thought I might be the eternal optimist, but surely someone would come and look for us, wouldn't they? Sebastian and Meryl are going to adapt quickest and McTurk would be welcome in any militia or army, I realized, but what am I going to do?

We seemed to be walking for sometime. McTurk went up ahead with Nita. Meryl and Kitchi were still walking together. Sebastian and I walked together and the other two Powhatans in the party were at the rear, keeping an eye open for more Shawnee. I assumed they did not want to be caught out.

"You look as though you got to your food cupboard to find the mice had done gotten there first," Sebastian noted.

"We could be stuck here for good. You're already adapting," I accused.

"Slave school of survival. There's always somethin' to do."

"Angus will get a job as a fighter anywhere."

"Yup. Reckon so."

"Well, what the heck am I going to do in seventeen-something?"

"Well, what you do wherever you come from?"

I sighed and the pictures of Edinburgh swept back to me. How good it looked at this precise moment of memory. "I illustrated books with pictures and drew maps and things."

"Law! Well, reckon you could print or write somethin' and get someone to print it. How 'bout stories for childrens 'bout life in the future? Childrens would love 'em, but reckon nobody else would much believe 'em. But reckon that's what makes a good story—you done don't have to believe it. All you gotta want is for it to happen. An' you and Miss Meryl could make you a home. Reckon you be one blessed man."

We began to see signs of life—cabins, houses, shops, fences, domestic animals and even a horse or two. Then we came to an inn and discovered that we were in Alexandria, Virginia.

The inn had been constructed from logs, but it was the only one, and the owner seemed friendly enough. The hall was bigger inside than it looked from outside and there were tables around and one or two pewter tankards on the tables. The place looked clean.

Angus addressed the owner, "How are you this fine morning?"

"Very well, sir. You new to these parts?"

"Yes," Angus said. "We've been in Kentuckee and may want to move here." He handed the man two coins. At the sight of the money, the owner's eyes lit up.

Angus smiled and said, "Let me know when this is used up."

The owner returned Angus' smile. "Yes, sir! Only I wouldn't be lettin' on that you have this, if I was you. Just a piece of friendly advice."

Angus nodded. "Of course. I understand. Thanks for looking out after us."

"Also," the man pointed out, "your clothes make you stand out. They may have something to make you blend in more at the trading post. That's part of survival here, blending in. The Powhatan are friendly, but some of the others—Indian and non-Indian— are not friendly to the English. I would go about in pairs if I were you."

"Yes, we already found that out. Some Shawnee attacked us. We defended ourselves and got brought here by some Powhatan."

The owner directed us to our rooms. Meryl and I got the same room. It would be best if we continued to pretend to be married, yet in my heart, I wished we really were married. Perhaps I was just a jealous man, head-over-heels in love with her, but it seemed to me that Meryl and Kitchi had enjoyed their walk and conversation a bit too much. It was a short time later that Sebastian and Angus joined us.

"We need to make getting out of here our priority," Angus told us. "To get out of here, we need Kairon and we need to get it back to our machine."

"It might as well be on the moon," Meryl said." In fact, it might be on the moon."

"I don't suppose there would be any of the PATCH people here?" I conjectured.

"Why?" Meryl asked.

"Well, they might have a time car and that time car might have Kairon. Kairon we could use to put into ours and get out of here," I explained.

"What would they be doing here?" Meryl asked. "I could see the point of trying to persuade Lee and change history that way—but here, in Alexandria?'

I argued. "PATCH will be aware that their attempt at Gettysburg failed. They'll want to try again. The attempt they made to bring the British into the Civil War was engineered to weaken the America of the future. When they try again, that's the tack they will take. One event that will weaken or hamper America and keep it from being the nation it is."

I continued. "If this is 1750-something, America wasn't founded as a nation until 1776. Who was here, assuming PATCH is here, in the 1750s? Someone who's going to play a pivotal roll in 1776."

Meryl said, "Perhaps one of the Founding Fathers."

"It has to be," I agreed. "Who was indispensable?"

"Thomas Jefferson," Meryl suggested. "He drafted the Declaration of Independence."

Angus said, "I'm going to find out what year we're in. We need to know." He left the room.

Sebastian had been listening to our speculation. He shook his head. "You folks is thinking like English, not like Americans. To Americans, the one figure that unites them all is George Washington. My old master used to let me read his library books. The library was the one place his son never came to. All as he was interested in was whiskey and women —black or white. But, anyways, what I knows is that the one figure is George Washington."

Meryl and I exchanged glances. We knew Sebastian was right. Remove Washington and there was no figure to replace him. There would be other good Presidents, but only one Washington.

Angus came back and informed us, "It is 1755, about the 29th of June. Major General Braddock has just arrived to conduct an attack on the French-occupied fort, Fort Duquesne."

Sebastian put in with the air of a history lecturer, "Didn't he get whupped?"

Angus smiled. "Whupped and a half. Only about a third of the men made it back, Braddock wasn't one of them."

Meryl looked pale. "Wasn't George Washington with him at least for part of the time?"

I said, "Why do I think I am not going to like this next bit?"

Meryl continued, "Didn't George Washington get back okay, but with a few musket ball holes in his coat?"

"Before I go sticking my vulnerable neck into something like that," I asked, "how do we know any PATCH people are here to want to try and stop him at this point? Why not wait till Valley Forge or Cowpens and pick him off then?"

"PATCH is like cancer," Angus said. "They like to work in secret, a minor act here and there. George Washington is practically unknown, just another commander. The damage for the future United States would be incalculable. So we're going to enlist in the militia—at least I am."

We looked at him.

"Hang it all! You might be good, but in a battle like that you'll need someone to watch your back," I thundered. "That watcher seems to be me. No protest. You've saved my life several times over, so now it's pay back time."

"What are Sebastian and I going to do while you two go off?" Meryl asked bleakly.

"Sebastian will help you. I'll give you half of what gold we have left," Angus said.

"What you mean," Meryl said crossly, "is that Sebastian can protect me."

"Look," Angus said. "If I need back up, so do you. We're all in this together, remember."

"One thing 'bout me, Miz Meryl," Sebastian joked, "You won't lose me in no crowd."

She smiled and I thought how beautiful she was. There was the competent, good agent, efficient and able. Then there was the other half of her: the woman who needed to be loved and told she was loved and shown she was loved. I had done precious little loving. I had taken the gift of physical love she had offered, but had not told her how much I loved her and what she meant to me as the woman I wanted to share my life with. Kitchi, whom some in future generations might have ignorantly referred to as a "savage" had wooed Meryl more than I had, appreciating the sunlight caught and reflected in her hair. When had I ever said something like that to Meryl? Suddenly, I longed to talk to Lucy—to tell her as gently as possible that I did not love her and could not marry her. Even more, I must try to explain all this to Mi-Ling and ask her if she could give Meryl a chance to be her "Amma."

"Meryl, please take care," I said somewhat breathlessly.

"Me take care? It's you that could get scalped or killed or bitten by a snake. Then what am I going to do?"

After she said that, we both realized suddenly how deep our feelings were for each other. Yet, we had only just found them. They had been like gold hidden under the surface we had developed to protect ourselves from vulnerability.

"I will take care of him," Angus promised gruffly.

"Meryl, I love you," I said in front of the others and I felt that a dam had burst on the inside of my heart to allow the waters to start flowing again.

Angus said, "I'm going to see if we can get some kit and any clothes we need to blend in—plus a blanket each and some food and something to carry water."

"I'll come with you in case you gets lost," Sebastian said. "Plus I reckon I've had a bunch of practice toting stuff."

That left Meryl and I alone together. "Did you mean what you said?" she asked.

"I would marry you now," I told her. "But I don't think a marriage certificate dated 1755 would be taken seriously in 1867. That night I left for China and you told me you loved me, I knew you meant it. When I found out that they had sent you to Aberdeen, I felt so miserable. When I knew I was going back some one-hundred-and-fifty years away from you, it was even worse. The feeling of emptiness never left me and I used to smell your perfume. When I closed my eyes, I could imagine you were at least in the room—but how I longed to hear your voice. When I saw you in China and you nearly got killed by Bryant—to put you into the machine and leave you was horrendous. I wanted to climb in with you and forget the mission. I had to send you away, because in 1867, there would have been no medical treatment and you would have died."

She put her head on my shoulder. "What kept me going was the possibility of seeing you again somehow. They wanted you to marry Lucy, but I knew she wasn't right for you." She crinkled her nose and smiled at me.

When we kissed, it was like starting all over again. I just wanted to hold her and drink in every sight of her and feel every touch. It was as if I were again seeing her for the first time, this time through eyes of love. She had become part of me, the second beat of my heart, my breathing out or in and all that my eyes longed to see. Yet, I knew things were not totally settled between us. I wanted to see Mi-Ling again—to try to be the father to her that she needed. Somehow, even though I had never learned to fully believe in Him or count on Him, I knew God would help me with Mi-Ling. He loved her, too.

It is amazing how much peace you get when you know what you must do and with whom you must share your life. I remember the words of a song, "For you for the rest of my life, for you for the best of my life, for you alone only for you." Perhaps it was the impending danger that made me realize that if I were going to come back to Meryl from Fort Duquesne, I would need help not only from Angus—but from Jesus as well.

Meryl and I looked out through the window of our room. "You know," she said. "How many other couples get the chance not just to be together, but to be together at any time in history? When would you like to settle?"

"With you," I said, "but I am not sure when. Not back to that gray existence in Edinburgh. Perhaps we could go someplace where we could make a difference, a real difference.

The important thing for me is to be with the girl who has the sun in her hair."

"Here you," she said with mock severity, poking my ribs, "no pinching other people's chat-up lines. Think up your own." She gave me a broad smile. Her nose crinkled and a strand of hair fell across her face. The cornflower blue of her eyes shone like gems that had been taken from a royal crown. The afternoon sun fell across her face and took my breath away. I had never seen anything, anyone, so beautiful. If dancing with Lucy all those months ago had seemed like holding springtime in my arms, now with Meryl, I was holding summer, a new summer of promise that was just beginning. She was not only a woman, she was the only woman for me. I put my arms round her, drawing me to her, and enjoyed that moment when conversation seemed superfluous and when more was spoken heart to heart than any ear could hear.

We must have drifted off to sleep. When Angus and Sebastian returned, the only thing that was missing from all they had obtained was a plastic bag in which to put them. Plastic hadn't been invented yet. They had water canteens and a couple of canvas bags. Angus gave Meryl a pistol, a powder horn and some spare flints. "I know you can use a rifle, but a pistol might prove more handy."

"Can I go look for a skirt or dress that doesn't look Civil War?" Meryl asked. "I can hide this pistol in one of the pockets." Angus gave her some money and she and Sebastian left together.

"The PATCH people, if they are here," Angus said, "may be in the militia that is gathering. They could blend in."

I paced the floor, attempting to think. "If they get in the battle, they don't mind if they don't get away. To them, the cause is the thing."

"Yeah," Angus snorted. "Great cause—sending someone else to get themselves killed so that you can achieve your aim while your hide is nice and safe."

"Kin I git me Daniel Boone hat?" I joked.

"Kin do better than that, boy," Angus informed me. "The boy Daniel Boone is one of the wagon drivers even though he's only about nineteen."

"Even at nineteen he might be a feller worth looking out for. You'll need to use the Kairon detector. If they are here, one of them at least, must have a time car control."

"Yep," Angus agreed. "If some Shawnee hasn't got it nailed to his lodge pole."

CHAPTER 8

The troops were mustering at the Carlyle House in Alexandria, a large gray Palladian-style mansion built by the merchant Thomas Carlyle. General Braddock had made it his headquarters before heading for Wills Creek where the forces were starting to muster. There would be troops at the Carlyle House and we wanted to check as many as we could with the Kairon meter.

The difference this time would be that, because we had sent some of the PATCH people back through the time tunnel, they would now be aware that there was an organization that knew about them.

If Professor Reynolds, an ex-colleague of my brilliant Uncle Adrian, was one of the driving forces behind them, he would figure out that it had to be one or two of the time travel experts that were running our show, and not just faceless civil servants. Maybe he would think of Adrian, maybe not. Either way, he and his murderous plan had to be stopped.

It was a fair distance to Willis Creek, and how we were going to get there, I wasn't quite sure. We had to check here and at the muster point at Willis Creek. If we didn't find any PATCH people at either location, I wasn't sure what the next step would be. I did know that after Braddock's defeat, all hell would be let loose on the frontier, and if Washington was safe we would have to get away quickly.

I was going to support the troops of King George II, who ten years before had chopped up the Jacobite Army at Culloden, near Inverness, in Scotland. They had been obeying orders. Their commander, the Duke of Cumberland, had ordered the burning to death of wounded Jacobite officers who were sheltering in a barn after the battle. Cumberland ordered the barn to be set on fire. In England, the duke of Cumberland was known as "Sweet William." In Scotland, he was known as "Stinking

Billy." Now, I had no choice. I was fighting on their side.

Before we left, Angus and Sebastian gave Meryl and me the gift of time alone together. Meryl started to cry when they had gone. She was worried about them. She had found clothes that allowed her to blend in. Fortunately, one of the ministers' families had offered to have Sebastian and Meryl stay with them when Angus and I left, which was a relief for me. Sebastian said he would help in the garden, and since the minister was ill, Meryl offered to help his wife take care of him. It seemed like a winning situation for everyone—except me. I didn't want to leave Meryl behind. I didn't want to be away from her for even hours. Besides, call me jealous and suspicious, but Kitchi wasn't all that far away either. I didn't want him calling on Meryl after I left.

All too soon, Angus and I prepared to head down to the Carlyle House.

"Drew, promise me you'll come back!" Meryl cried. The panic in her voice was reassuring.

"I will come back," I promised. "You're my reason to come back. I can't live without you. Let's get married as quickly as we can, even if we have to stay here."

"If we get back," Meryl said, "I will try to make a good mother for Mi-Ling. You'll have to help me, Drew. I've never been a mother before."

I kissed her on her lovely nose, loving the way it crinkled when she thought of a joke. "As I have never been a father before. But we will manage, darling. Together."

As Angus and I walked away, Meryl called out after me. "Don't you dare get yourself killed, Drew, or I'll never forgive you! Please come back to me."

Angus patted me on the shoulder. "Thanks for coming with me, Laddie. My back feels a lot safer."

We got a small Union Jack and passed by the troops. There were not a lot of them, but we came to the last group and I saw the expression on Angus' face change to a frown. His gaze was in the direction of an blue-coated officer on an appaloosa. He must have been

Virginian, or in the regiment. That meant he could get close to Washington without arousing suspicion. So we kept him in sight while we cheered along with the crowd.

"God bless good King George," Angus cried, and for some of the way the cry was taken up as the party started to head to Fort Cumberland. The last wagon in the train was about to pass when we saw three Indians jump on the back and begin passing out things. The young driver saw it too, and pulled out his rifle to stop them. One Indian hit the driver and was about to whack him with a tomahawk when Angus hit him. I hit the other one. The third Indian looked at the two of us and legged it. The driver lay in the road. We checked him and found that he had bruising on his forehead, but no broken skin.

He shook his head. "What in the name of all that is wonderful was I doing?" he asked. Then he smiled at us. "Hey, thanks, fellers. Much obliged for your help." He held out his hand. "Name's Boone. Daniel Boone."

We introduced ourselves. "Where are you fellahs headin'?" he asked.

"We're heading for Willis Creek to muster for the expedition."

He smiled his broad smile. "Well, I reckon you could use a ride then, huh?"

We nodded and I found I was whispering in my heart, Thank you, Jesus. For only Jesus could have put us on a wagon with the soon-to-be-famous Daniel Boone. The situation we were in meant that breathing was of a greater priority than keeping fit through engaging in long hikes.

The British line was long as we headed for Fort Cumberland. It looked like a good place to hide if the French and the Shawnee, and who ever else happened to be in the vicinity, decided to come hollering out the woods at us.

Daniel's eyes constantly scanned the land. "Injuns eyes are everywhere," he explained. "So unless you've got eyes like a hawk, you can't see hide nor hair of 'em until they come out hollering at you."

"Yes," Angus agreed. "We met some Shawnee and they tried to kill us."

"You know, I'm right pleased they didn't succeed." Daniel laughed. "Don't reckon I'll ever get used to goin' through forests and trails and over mountains."

"Oh," Angus said with a sage-like look, "I reckon you'll kinda get the hang of it."

What many folk don't realize is that in Virginia, at night, there are a whole posse of critters that bite, sting, creep and crawl—and that are real anxious to make your acquaintance. That includes the high-pitched whine of mosquitoes. What I noticed was that the guys who smoked clay pipes seemed to be less troubled. Every time insects got bad, they would surround themselves with a blue haze and you could almost hear the bugs coughing. Angus and I joined suit. I didn't have to inhale and I hoped when this was over, I could stop. For food, dried meat seemed to be popular, but it was cold without a fire. We got issued bread.

Daniel taught us several things about being in the forest. Rattlesnakes, he said, liked heat. If you were careless at night, they were "mighty partial to cozying up with to you to get warm." I decided to sleep in the wagon. Not every snake was poisonous or dangerous, but how could you tell in the dark? Suppose there was a rattler with amnesia who forgot to rattle before it bit? Oh! I was letting my mind run away with me.

If they still have cowboy pictures by the time someone reads this, and you see them all cozy round a nice camp fire sound asleep—well it's not like that. No, nothing like it.

The following morning Angus said, "You were lucky you didn't get your throat cut or your scalp lifted. We need to stick together. They pick off folk away from the herd."

I knew he was right and was thankful to be alive and able to join the others for breakfast. We could see where the pathfinders had needed to widen the road to Fort Cumberland and would try to do the same to Fort Duquesne. However, the French and their Native American allies were not about to wait while the British and Virginians got themselves in a front seat before the fort. Traveling by wagon was agonizingly slow and everything seemed to creak and groan. The artillery was awkward. I mean, how in the name of goodness do you fire a cannon in the middle of a forest? I knew the cannon was going to be used to batter Fort Duquesne, but what a hard job shifting it was!

As Angus had already warned, you had to be careful not to fall behind. If you did, you could be caught and scalped. We saved one guy at the rear end of the column from that very fate. Then we shot two Shawnee who had caught someone who limped. Daniel hauled the lame man into the back of the wagon.

We had been going for several days when I asked Daniel out of curiosity what was in the kegs in the back of the wagon. He informed me it was gunpowder and musket balls. This was one of several wagons that had gunpowder interspersed in the convoy.

Well, there was one other problem that became apparent after a few days. Virginia was hot and humid at this time of year, and you got thirsty. There was no bottled water, merely good, fresh spring water—complete with dysentery. Dysentery began to wreck havoc on the travelers. When it comes to this bodily function in 1755, on a wagon train bound for Fort Cumberland, forget privacy and modesty. Nobody wanted to be caught in a quiet place either by a potluck scalping party or by curious timber rattlesnakes.

Do you notice on the films nobody ever seems to need a comfort stop? Well in 1755, a lot of people with or without dysentery needed a comfort stop. Next time you go to the supermarket to buy toilet paper, or toilet roll, and you grumble about the price—believe me when I say that if you don't have it—you miss it. Boy, do you miss it! What did they use instead? Well, leaves, of which there were plenty in the forest. Ignorantly snatching up the leaves of poisonous plants proved a bad idea. Corn-on-the-cob was included in the rations. You (or the animals if the corn was dry) ate the corn off the cob and kept the cob for that use that should have been private—but wasn't on a wagon train through the forest.

After a few days, the French could have smelled us before they saw us. Everybody was in the same miserable state. This was real life where everything went on in the raw. After a while that was just what you were

—raw in a certain part of your anatomy. I was glad for Meryl's sake that she had stayed behind—that had protected her behind, so to speak.

When the cannon got stuck in a rut, or a wheel came off the wagon, then it was a case of all hands to sort things out. General Braddock would ride up and down, anxious that nobody fell behind.

It was the lack of sleep that got to you: the noises, the insects, the feeling of something crawling over your legs, the intent listening for Indians. It made you feel like a mother with a newborn baby. The mother constantly awakens to see if the little one needs anything and the accumulated tiredness can wear down even the strongest and most good-willed parent. We suffered the same malady. You could not afford the luxury of being wrong about the Indians—or the wildlife, which was even more varied and plentiful. And, counting black bears—really big!

The other thing is that in going through this huge forest, even though a clearing had been ripped out, you lose track of time—not just hours and minutes—but days. That was very disorientating.

We had experienced hardship without glory and were overjoyed when we at last entered a clearing and saw a large camp and stockaded fort and guessed we had arrived at Fort Cumberland. The only trouble was that Angus and I knew what was coming next. At least, we knew it in our heads. Nothing could have prepared us for the actual horror of it.

Daniel said to us, "Looky here, I could sure use you fellers here if you don't mind being a wagon train guard and maybe missing out on some of the fighting."

We said we didn't mind missing out on the fighting and pointed out that if our boys didn't get their powder and ball, then that fighting was going to be a mite one-sided. I was scared, imagining Indians or French behind every tree. Soon enough, that fear would become a reality.

Still, there was a good spirit in the camp among the Redcoats and Virginians, in spite of weariness. There was even the thought that the French in Fort Duquesne would see us coming and abandon the fort. But Angus and I realized that French ambition was made of sterner stuff.

Many of the men were not used to military discipline and obeying orders.

The officers, including General Braddock, tried to get them in line so they could volley fire—that is all fire at the one time. It worked with the Redcoat regulars, but the Virginians had the sense to see that the way to fight an enemy who is hidden behind a tree is not to stand out in the open in a line. Braddock expected the same of his French adversaries. They would stand facing each other out in the open, exchanging volleys until one side had had enough.

The forming in line worked for a bit, but in the camp there was nobody shooting at you or waiting to scalp you. It was not difficult to obey commands when there was no great noise, nor a forest full of Indians howling like banshees.

Still thankful that she was staying with the minister, I wondered how Meryl was getting along. I hoped Sebastian was being treated well. I missed Meryl desperately and longed to be with her again.

I thought of and missed Mi-Ling desperately, too, and wondered if I would ever see her again. Anything could be going on at Bellefield. If our time machine hadn't broken down, we would have been back before we had even missed. But now, Lucy remained in grave danger from Bryant. I vowed to do my best to end that situation if we got back. Then, as I had so often, I wondered what had gone wrong. I had always assumed that Lucy would not fall in love with me. It had never occurred to me, after seeing her picture at Bellefield and meeting her, that it would be me who would not fall in love with her. She had everything else but my heart. When you hear of soldiers in combat zones saying how much they miss their family, believe me, missing is a mild word compared to the reality of the depression and emptiness.

Then came the day when we saw the young Major George Washington for the first time. He had been ill, but was making a major effort to keep up the spirits of his men. It's strange that when you see an historical figure in real life, they look human. George Washington looked like a young man trying to make his way in the world. If we had told him what lay ahead, he would not have believed us. It made me think that God knows things about our future that we don't know, and that if He told us before hand, we might not believe Him. Washington did not know his future—but he trusted God for that future.

General Braddock's forces had drilled, marched, lined up. They had volley fired and cheered. The only thing they had not done was to practice the type of fighting they would need to combat the coming Indian and French attack. It was not until after this that the British Army was to develop the use of skirmishers. These guys would particularly target enemy officers or non-commissioned officers (NCOs) and try to break down the chain of command in the opposing forces. If everyone was out in the open, it was much easier to see the officers and NCOs. The NCOs carried halberds, a type of long spear, as a badge of office.

The French, on the other hand, would stay in the trees, shoot, move to another spot, shoot again. The guys in the open only had puffs of smoke to tell them where the enemy was, while the French and Indians had lines of scarlet coats to aim at.

At the end of May, I think, we headed out at long last, bands playing and spread out in a long column, with maybe a musket shot of distance between units.

Angus said to me, "Right, laddie. Eyes peeled. You are most certainly under watch by the enemy. I'm trying to keep an eye on Major Washington. He has two people on his side trying to kill him. I haven't found the second, but I'm making the assumption it's an NCO. At Gettysburg, PATCH didn't try to kill General Lee, but only to temporarily replace him. Here, the idea is to get Washington out of the road and replaced. PATCH seems to like two-men teams, even through Vincent made it three.

"If these are trained operatives, they may not risk three here. If there is a mistake and the killer fails, the murderer may find that, in comparison to Indians, a host of furious Virginians is much worse. If they catch him they might even hand him over to the Indians."

We were doing something like three miles in a day and George Washington put forward the idea of splitting the force, using a fast group to race ahead. Braddock, Orme and the other commanders agreed, and orders were soon shouted as cavalry came to the fore. This would allow the slower section and the bulk of the wagons and artillery to move at a slower pace while the quicker moving troops could ford the Monongahela River before any Indians got there. If they wanted to hold up Braddock's forces, the ford was the place to do it. Colonel Dunbar drew the short straw. He would command the rearguard.

Angus, Daniel, and I were to be in the fast columns. As dangerous as moving gunpowder was, at least you were watched and guarded. Nobody wanted any accidents.

You stopped thinking after a while and tried to shut out of your mind what lay in the woods. You just concentrated on what you could see. It really was so far, so good. Angus and I knew what was coming. The others didn't. Lt. Colonel Gage, with an advanced guard, who Braddock sent to the fording place, was unimpeded. It made Angus and I think that, perhaps we had been mistaken about the horrific events we had read about in history books.

Sadly, instead of moving quickly to catch the French as unawares as we could, we stopped to dot every topographical 'I' and cross every topographical 'T'. We came to a wide and bushy clearing, or it might have been a ravine. Then the firing started, along with the whoops of Indians.

In true European fashion, Gage's column went into line and returned fire, but most of the shots were absorbed by trees. The French and Indians knew that once a volley was fired, it would be at least fifteen seconds before the musket could be reloaded and fired again. Fifteen seconds was more than enough time for the Indian to come round the side of the tree, behind which he was sheltering, and get the next shot off, then move to another place in the next fifteen seconds.

At first, the British seemed successful, even bringing up two cannon. But again, so much of the fire hit the trees. Our men started to crouch down and to look for trees to shelter behind.

The Virginians fought from behind the trees where they could get cover. Braddock got his men on their feet at sword point, calling them cowards and demanding that they stand straight. He tried to do the same thing to the Virginians. All that he accomplished was to turn his men into sitting ducks.

I heard one man say to Washington, "Major, we can't fight what we can't see."

Braddock was using his sword point to threaten his troops. The fire was returned less and less frequently. We tried to guard the wagon and Daniel said, "We need to get outta here real quick."

I turned from the wagon in time to see one soldier who had fallen, severely injured. An Indian appeared from the forest and scalped him. The soldier was still alive and he screamed piteously. I heard the knife go through his scalp. I will never forget that sickening sound to my dying day. The Indian picked up his bloody trophy. There was an axe in the back of the wagon and my thought was, over my dead body, you will get away with that! The Indian never saw me. I ran at him and swung the axe in rage and blood lust, whacking off his arm. The arm holding his bloody trophy fell to the ground and I swung again and the axe went into his body. He dropped like a stone.

Between the exchange of weapon fire, I managed to check on the soldier, but he was already dead. I got back to the wagon, and as I jumped back in, Angus said, "I would hate to meet you when you really got upset."

I think I could load and fire a musket in my sleep. We had to get back to the ford at the Monongahela River before the Indians and French did. Angus had been watching George Washington and the captain he knew to be from PATCH, but where was the other Patch operative?

Angus said in between loading and firing. "It may be that one or both of these guys has a control for their time car. The controls that the guys at Gettysburg had were like ours. These may be the same, and if we can get their Kairon unit, we can either use their time car or take the Kairon and put it into ours and get out of here. Remember, these guys came to kill George Washington. They're professional assassins."

Things were starting to fall apart, and we had to get back to the ford. There were individual fights and Washington and Gage were trying to fight rearguard actions. Then we heard Braddock had been hit and a rumor started that he had been shot by someone from our side. Served him right, I thought uncharitably. A lot of men had died because of his stubborn pride.

The retreat began to speed up, and two wagons were ahead of us. One wagon was fine, but the wheel came off another and the driver was thrown out to the ground.

"It's a woman," Angus said. "Daniel, slow down!" A couple of Indians came out the woods and headed for the woman. She had a pistol in her skirt, but it misfired. The Indian let out a whoop and tried to grab her. He had seen the mis-firing pistol in her hand, but had not seen the knife in her other hand. She slammed it into his ribs. The second Indian rushed her with his Tomahawk and was intercepted by Angus. The two started fighting. The woman picked herself up and grabbed the Indian. With Angus on one hand and the woman on the other, the Indian was doomed. Angus steered the woman back to the wagon. Washington was helping and encouraging his outnumbered forces. One of the Virginians looked around and saw that Washington's back was turned. The guy took out a knife and aimed at Washington, steadying himself to throw with deadly intent.

"Go on," Angus gritted, issuing a dare. "Move!" He picked up the Indian's discarded tomahawk and threw it at the Virginian, burying it deeply in his back. Angus rushed over and pretended to help as he searched the dying man's kit. Exploring the man's white rucksack, Angus found a silver object, which he pocketed

Two others joined Angus to help the wounded man. Daniel and I doubted that the wounded man would recover, no matter how much human intervention he received.

"Daniel," I begged, "slow down and let Angus catch up."

"He better get movin' fast," Daniel responded. "We're fallin' behind."

To my horror, Angus slipped and fell. Someone in a white uniform at the edge of the forest aimed at him. Panicked, I turned and attempted to grab a rifle, but the girl had found one first. She fired. The French soldier went spinning backwards. Angus caught up with us.

I hauled Angus into the wagon and told him, "This lady just saved your life."

"It has been a long time since I was called a lady, but I thank you," she said with a trace of a French accent. Her raven black hair fell across her face and she had, of all things, violet-colored eyes.

She addressed Angus, "Are you recovered? I am glad you still have your hair."

There was a look in Angus' face that I had not seen before. It was a mixture of respect, admiration, and dare I say it—love. Love at first sight. I could not help but smile and noted that the girl was not wearing a wedding ring.

"I'm fine, thanks to you. That was good shooting. But shouldn't you be on the other side in this battle? You sound as if you're French."

Her full lips pouted and she tossed her raven locks defiantly. "You do not know what it is like to be a Huguenot under the rule of Louis Quinze. You are treated like scum!"

"What is your name?" Angus asked, as they both fired off another musket.

"That's fine fellers," Daniel said. "Jest talk and shoot, talk and shoot —or at least—don't stop shooting."

"Abigail Carreau," the girl said with pride. "What are you called?"

Maintaining our endeavor to re-load and shoot, everyone in the wagon introduced themselves to Abigail. When Angus told her his name, she smiled. This was in the middle of a battle, and she appeared undaunted about what was going on around her. "But I shall call you instead, eh bien mon brave." And, from then on, that was how Abigail referred to Angus. "Mon Brave. I saw the look in Angus' eyes. He liked it and I didn't blame him.

It's amazing what can happen in the middle of a battle. And it's equally amazing that even the most seemingly impervious heart can melt if looked at with love and respect. Fortunately, Abigail was not married. She informed Angus of that right away.

We fought our way to the river ford, and again, our cavalry had secured it. But the folks who had been left behind with the slow moving part of the expedition had been badly chopped about by the Indians and were attempting to move the wounded, even the walking wounded. It was gut-wrenching, but Washington was wonderful. He seemed to be everywhere at the same time. Unfortunately, so was the Virginian captain.

This time, I had been exposed to a close-up of broken bodies, screams and sounds of battle. Not everyone died quickly or cleanly, and there is no such thing as a glorious death. I had never seen so much blood before. Then there was the additional horror: the sight of moving wounded—scalped, crawling, groaning, crying. Those who would never see their wives or children again, dying on the forest floor, their nails digging into the wet leaves. The atmosphere was thick with sorrow, agony, broken dreams and shattered futures.

Angus showed me the control that he had taken from the dead PATCH operative. Did the second one know his buddy was dead? He would have been as aware of the disaster that we were walking into as we had been. Could we just shoot someone in cold blood? If we did, where would be the difference between them and us? It would be much harder for him to kill Washington in Alexandria than it was here.

Just then, Angus overheard a conversation as the captain rode up to Washington.

"Follow me, sir. It's just over here in these trees sir …"

They headed in the woods together and McTurk ran in after them. They were entering the one area in the forest where there were no Indians, as far as I could see. I had to restrain Abigail to keep her from going in after Angus.

"He's a big boy. He can take care of himself."

"You are supposed to be his friend, yet you let him go without covering his back? It only takes one knife …" and she drew her hand across her throat.

I nodded. "Okay." She gave me her pistol. I already had my Bowie knife. I slung a musket over my shoulder.

"The musket will catch in the branches," she warned me. She was right.

When I got into the woods, I heard Washington say, "Guy, I don't see anything. I don't understand why you've brought me here."

Guy raised his pistol and pointed it at Washington. I expected the usual PATCH prattle of how superior they were.

Lord, we could sure use a couple of hostiles to turn up at this point. Thankfully, they did. A French infantry man in a buckskin jacket over his uniform appeared, along with two Indians. Bloody scalps hung on the Indians' belts.

Angus sprang from cover and hit Washington's horse. "Get out of here, sir," he ordered Washington urgently.

Guy was taken by surprise at Angus' sudden appearance. The Indian and Frenchman fired. Guy was forced to defend himself, and so was Angus. I ran in and got one of the Indians with my pistol, which left me with just my Bowie knife. The second Indian dived at me while the Frenchman shot Guy's horse. Horse and rider crashed to the ground. The Indian fighting me was strong and he was screaming. I blocked his knife with mine, then I broke the clinch first and ran the blade down his arm. The Frenchman ran his bayonet right into Guy's chest. Angus' knife was at the Frenchman's throat.

I threw the Indian over my back. He was momentarily stunned, but quickly regained his feet. This time, I threw the knife. It buried itself in his chest. The whole incident had taken mere seconds.

"Quick," Angus prompted. "His saddlebags. We need that second control." I found it, along with a map that looked like a location in a street in town—maybe it was Alexandria—maybe it was the time car—maybe we could find it. That was too many maybes for my comfort.

We retrieved our belongings and sprinted out of the woods. It would be important to tell Washington of the gallant fight Captain Guy put up so that if in later years Washington were to mention the incident in his writings or memoirs, Guy would get the credit and we would not be mentioned. This time, unlike Gettysburg, there was no way PATCH could guess that their operatives did not die in battle. Either way, they had failed and PATCH would not be happy about it. They of all people should have known that the events in history do not always go the way you want them to go.

We rushed for the wagon as Abigail waved and cried out. We clambered aboard. Abigail said to Angus, "You treat your life as if it was nothing, pas de importance. Did you never realize that you may be precious to someone?"

At this point in the conversation, I reckoned it might be better to go sit up front with Daniel. We were still dodging musket balls. We were approaching a location where tree branches laced together overhead, forming a long, leafy tunnel. Daniel said, "When we get to them there branches, watch out for someone dropping into the wagon. Got me a feeling."

I managed to reload one of the muskets. When we passed below the point he indicated, Daniel got more speed out of the horses. One of the Indians dropped out of the tree into the wagon. The other missed, sprawling on the ground. When he tried to climb onto the wagon, Angus' boot caught him in the face. The second Indian struggled with me, attempting to get to Daniel and stop the wagon. He was tougher and stronger than I was, until Abigail whopped him with the butt of a rifle. He fell like a sack of potatoes. We pitched him out of the wagon.

"Merci bien, Abigail," I said, returning her pistol. I had not loaded it, for I thought that on an ammunition wagon there would be no shortage of ball and shot.

She shrugged her shoulders and smiled. "C'est rien."

We ploughed on till we reached Fort Cumberland. At least, what was left of us. What we had not known was that Governor Dinwiddie had wanted Dunbar, the now-commander, to take the soldiers from Fort Cumberland and go back for another attempt to take Fort Duquesne. Thankfully, Colonel Dunbar, as the now-commander, was of the "nobody in his right mind" school of thinking and decided to take the shorter and less dangerous route to Philadelphia.

Daniel got us back to Alexandria. Abigail had a sister in Alexandria. Angus went with Abigail to her sister's home to be introduced and to find out where she lived. I found the minister's home where Meryl and Sebastian had been left behind. When I saw it in the distance, I ran.

Meryl was working in the garden along with Sebastian. Sebastian saw me first and nudged Meryl. Looking up, she squealed with joy and ran into my arms. I broke into tears and I didn't care who saw them. I just held Meryl fiercely and kissed her again and again.

For a long time, we were too busy kissing to engage in conversation. Finally I said, "I never thought I would see you again. I love you." That seemed to call for renewed hugging and kissing.

"I never thought I would see you again either, Drew. We heard rumors about the attack and the mess that Braddock got everyone into," Meryl breathed. "We even received word that you had all been killed."

Mrs. Calvin, the minister's wife, joined us. "Thank God you are safe!" she exclaimed. "Your wife has missed you." She nudged Meryl. "You know the brown room? There is a bath in there and a double bed. I think maybe you need to use both. I have arranged for food to be taken there, as well. When you have rested and reacquainted yourselves, you can come down and we'll talk. Off you go, the pair of you."

Before we took Mrs. Calvin's advice, I thanked Sebastian for being there and watching out for Meryl.

"Man, she done missed you!" Sebastian said. "She was like a bee buzzing around n' couldn't find no flowers to land on. This is the happiest she look since I can't remember when. I feel a big hunk o responsibility just come a'tumblin' off my shoulders. Feels good, man! Like going from slave to free all over again."

Having found out where Abigail was staying, Angus reappeared suddenly and patted Sebastian on the back. "Man! We sure could have used you!"

"Hey, iffin I had been there an' got lost in the forest, wouldn't nobody have ever found me. Law, I could have snuck up on Les Francais an' they'd never would've seen me, 'specially not at night time. Glad to see you back, man, an wid all your right parts all in the right places!"

Angus and Sebastian sat under a tree and the maid came out with cold drinks. Mrs. Calvin approached and I heard Angus say, "He's not my slave. He's my friend and my brother and I owe him my life." I could not help thinking that Abigail would have been proud of him if she could have heard him.

Meryl and I went to the bath and the bed and did exactly what Mrs. Calvin had expected us to. After the physical relief lovemaking brought us both, we lay in each other's arms. "I love you," I told Meryl. "That horror of a battle showed me that God was real and I want to make love to you the right way—as my wife. I don't really know much about God, but my gut tells me that He would want it that way.

"We've already gone past the time we planned for getting back to Bellefield. God alone knows what is happening to the folks there. It was going to be ten minutes on the clock, and probably weeks have passed. Angus got the PATCH people and they tried to kill Washington, but failed. Angus has the controls—or what he thinks are the controls—for the time car and a map of its possible location. We will have to…"

She finished the sentence for me. "We must destroy our time car. Apparently, they are rigged to explode."

I nodded and continued, "What we don't know is if their time car has the fine-tuning that ours had."

Meryl sighed. "It could be weeks back at Bellefield since we left. What a mess."

She snuggled against me. "Drew, darling, after we're married, I want a baby as quickly as possible."

I sort of gulped. "Okay. That sounds good. Maybe a sister for Mi-Ling. I'm sorry for just being a man—and slow of understanding when it comes to women—but why the change of heart? I thought you were more the action type than the domestic type, Meryl."

She sat up. "I've been talking to Reverend Calvin. I guess he helped clarify for me what is important—what's lasting. Jesus, first, Reverend Calvin said, "then my husband and our children. I couldn't tell him we weren't married. That made me feel petty and dishonest. Living a lie under an honest man of God's roof. That's why I want to marry as soon as possible—whenever possible. But for now, darling, perhaps we should go and join the others."

Rev. Calvin had sent word that he wanted to see Angus and me. I had yet to meet him, since he had been so ill when we left. He lay on a couch reading and I knocked at the door of the study. "Come in," he invited in a cheerful voice.

I introduced myself and we shook hands.

"Please, sit down," he said, indicating a chair. "I hope you are comfortable and my wife has been taking good care of you."

"Yes, sir, she has," I assured him.

He nodded. "My Libby is a fine woman and a fine wife. I am one blessed man." Then he changed the subject, "God spared you and your fellow soldier, Angus. God is good. I would have hated to have seen Mrs. Faulkner's heart broken. She has been kindness and mercy to us. And a hard worker, too."

There was something about his eyes that held me. He could look right into my heart and I was powerless to stop him or hide from his gaze.

"Maybe God has spared you many times before," he surmised. I knew he didn't expect a response. He knew the truth and he knew that I knew that he knew the truth. We talked. He reminded me very much of Sir Charles Gray in Foochow, China.

"Andrew," Rev. Calvin said. "God is trying to call you to love and trust Him. He wants you to know that all the wrong of the past can be forgiven. Drew, what you did for Mi-Ling and the life you took her away from is what Jesus is doing for you in the spiritual sense. Jesus says in Revelation, John 21:5…" As Dr. Calvin was about to speak, I heard another voice; a voice that flooded my heart with peace—a voice of pure love and gentleness, but of great authority. "Drew, behold, I make all things new."

Dr Calvin saw the tears in my eyes and struggled up to pat my shoulder. "Andrew, don't fight Him."

If I could have put that voice aside as tiredness, or any other of a hundred-and-one excuses, I might have. But I knew I had never heard anything like that voice before. Had I heard the voice of God?

While I remained riveted to my chair in contemplation, Dr. Calvin urged me to action in his gentle voice. "We must go and take sustenance. We must support our soldiers and militia."

After the meal Mrs. Calvin produced some tea, announcing, "There is nothing like a cup of English tea all the way from China."

I savored the taste. It was Oolong and I remembered Mrs. Jamieson and the way she pronounced the word lengthening the "O" to Oooolong. I wondered how she was and then remembered that she would not be born for another seventy years or so.

"Ooolong," I said.

"It is indeed Oolong. Do you know something about tea, Andrew?"

"Mmmm…a little," I admitted.

Angus asked, "Can we go out to your garden, Mrs. Calvin? We need to talk."

"Of course. We shall not disturb you until you are ready."

Before we headed out to the garden, Angus slipped the map out of his pocket. "Does this map mean anything to you?" he asked the Calvins.

Libby did not recognize it, but Dr. Calvin did. "This is to the north side of town, near St. Gertrude's Church, which has sadly been abandoned and is quickly falling into disrepair. To the right of the church, there are a couple of caves, but not much else. If you must go there, try to have some torches with you and watch your feet. You may run into serpents of various kinds. Normally, they won't bother you, but sometimes one or two of them have a bad day and forget."

At the mention of snakes I had a feeling of déjà vu that followed me all the way out to the garden. I decided that when I retired—if I lived long enough to retire—I would go to a place where there were no snakes. New Zealand came to mind, but it would not be mapped by James Cook till 1769. I hoped Meryl would like it.

Angus said, "We need to go to the caves and try to locate their time car, or at least get the Kairon out of it. If that doesn't work, we have to use theirs and destroy the one in the forest. It's rigged to explode within a certain distance of the control box. We won't know how much time has passed in Scotland until we get back."

Sebastian said, "Law, is someone there in for a surprise!"

After our hurried conference in the garden, I told Dr. Calvin of our desire to go to the caves, using the excuse of some interesting bats we had heard frequented the cave.

Dr. Calvin looked at me and said, "Go during the day. The bats will be in the caves and serpents will be less active. Please, be careful. I can't help but think that you have another purpose for going there, but I shan't meddle." He paused. "Drew, God is taking care of you. Meryl is a lovely girl and you must take care of her. I can't help feeling that there is something special in the future for both of you. No, for all of you. Something that in your wildest dreams, you could not imagine."

It was hard for me to take his words seriously. I had dreamed some pretty wild and fantastic dreams—but none of them matched the reality of time travel with its dangers and travails.

Angus excused himself and went to see Abigail. He was gone all night.

Meryl and I slept well, awaking refreshed both in our bodies and in our love for one another.

After breakfast, Sebastian, Angus, Meryl and I headed for the caves and the old church that was located close to the caves. The town was still full of soldiers and wounded and refugees.

Sebastian carried the luggage, explaining, "It will look bad if I ain't doing the toting. That's what folks expect. Are you sure there ain't no slavery in your time?"

I sighed. "I would love to be able to say that there isn't any slavery in our time. Only, sadly, there is. It's just different from the form you know. It's evil and hidden and it still stinks."

Sebastian looked at me, "Ain't people learned nothin' yet? 'Do unto others as you would have them do unto you.' Like Jesus said. Law, listen to me! Miz Calvin, now, she's been tutoring me on my speech and I done used 'ain't' about three times in a row. She says ain't ain't a word. So how as I can judge others if I a—haven't even got that right?"

We came to the caves and it seemed quiet. Sebastian said, "I'm going in first. Nobody will see me in the dark even with a light."

Angus followed him. Meryl stayed outside with me. I kind of watched my feet in case the branch I thought I trod on decided to move.

Angus and Sebastian came back to the entrance of one of the caves after a few minutes and waved us forward. We tried to be as casual and romantic as possible—a man and woman disappearing into a cave.

We went far enough inside to need the torches. Thankfully, the cave was cold. We stood carefully against the wall in a kind of alcove. We didn't know where the time car would appear. We didn't even know if it would be this cave or the next one.

Meryl and Angus had a quick confab and Angus said, "Okay, here goes nothing." He threw the switch on the PATCH control box—without results. We tried the second switch—still nothing.

"Aw, great!" Meryl said. "Why can't the bad guys get some decent technology?"

I chirped in like the specter at the feast. "Looks like we are stuck here in 1755. It's going to look good on my grave: born 1988 died 17—whatever."

Sebastian looked at us and shook his head. "Law, I do love it when y'all be so cheerful!"

"I'm open to suggestions," Angus told him, somewhat tartly.

"Now, looky here, y'all. We had a pump on the plantation that had two handles coming from it. If'n you used one handle then you got nothing.' If you done used the other handle, the result was still nothing.'"

Meryl looked up to the sky, at least as far as you can see if someone is looking upwards in exasperation in a dark cave.

"But..." Sebastian continued nonplused, "if you operates the handles at the same time, it works real good."

Meryl looked at Angus and Angus looked at Meryl. He handed her one of the time controls. "After three," he directed. "One, two, three..."

There was a short silence followed by the sound of thunder. A time car emerged from a portal at the back of the cave and the sleepy bats decided that maybe an early exit from the cave was wise. They blasted past us in a thick cloud that made us duck and cling to the walls.

There was another silence and then Sebastian's voice drifted through the darkness. "Hey, that's okay. Y'all are welcome."

We started to laugh. It felt good. I was starting to think that we had forgotten how to laugh.

Nobody came out of the car, thankfully, as we approached it with care. The door opened. A cursory inspection proved that the car looked just like ours inside. Thus, according to Angus, the Kairon should be in the same place. A search found the Kairon unit.

What presented itself was a dilemma. If we took the Kairon unit out this machine, then it was stuck. It would just sit in the cave where anyone could find it. Not only did the Kairon provide the power to change time or move through time, but it was also the means of propulsion. After debating the issue, we agreed that we could not take out the Kairon from the time car in the cave and attempt to fit it into the other one in the forest. We noticed that the targeting scanner in this time car had a place for not just year, but the month and day as well. We needed to get this machine to our HQ and to Adrian, to see what he could use from it to stop PATCH. It was like being in a sort-of time traveling cold war.

If we returned to the cave with our personal effects, it might be that when we summoned the time car again, there might be some 'heavies' on board, armed to the teeth. In our favor, Angus said, was the fact that it had been a comparatively short time since PATCH's attempt to kill Washington failed. Angus thought it was possible that they didn't know yet. However, the longer we left moving, the more likely it would be that PATCH would collect intelligence and formulate a plan either to get their boys back, or find out what went wrong and who was responsible.

We exited the car and stood to the side. We made the assumption if it took two switches to get it here, it would take both switches to shift it back.

Meryl posed a question that had been bugging me. If someone at the PATCH end had programmed the time car to arrive here, they would expect it to collect their two agents. If we sent it off un-programmed, it would need to have an automatic homing program—a kind of failsafe destination that could only be changed by someone programming it from the inside.

The car vanished as quickly as it had come. We guessed we had to move fast. As it turned out, fast was not to be on the agenda.

We walked out of the cave into dusk and hoped we could remember how to get back to the Calvin's vicarage. We were not thinking about much else when we turned back to look at the cave again. Startled, we suddenly realized that the cave had started to glow inside. The glowing grew more intense. There was a pulsating noise and Angus cried out in alarm, "Flat on the ground! Now! Put your fingers in ears! Now! Face the cave! Now!"

We dropped, put our heads down, and there was an almighty explosion. We felt the shock wave pass over us and we must have passed out. We came too with sore heads. When we looked where there had been caves, there was only a seriously big pile of rocks. Half of the old abandoned church had also been destroyed. I later discovered that the blame for this was put down to French Agents.

We looked at one another in despair, except for Sebastian. He leaped up, raised his hands skyward and exclaimed, "Thank you Jesus!"

"Sebastian," Meryl said crossly. "What have you got to thank Jesus for? We're stuck!"

"Miz Meryl, I'm thankin' Jesus that we wasn't still in that cave!"

Okay, he was right. We were lost, but at least we were alive and lost.

Angus said, "That was a sonic charge. They must have known it would bring down the cave. Their sonic technology is more advanced than ours—way more advanced. We need to watch for this again. I guess we went through some kind of laser warning that set the charge off after so many minutes."

The walk back was silent, almost. "Well, guys," I said. "I guess the party is over."

Angus agreed. "I guess we'll split up the gear and go our separate ways. I'm going with Abigail—if she'll have me."

All of us had a pretty good idea that she would.

Sebastian looked at Meryl, then at me. "I guess the two of you will set up home somewhere or go for a log cabin in the frontier. I can work for you if you want me, but I'm in trouble. I ain't got—sorry—I don't have no proof that I ain't——that I'm not a slave."

Looking directly at me, he added, "I'm guessin' you done don't know a whole heap about buildin' a cabin in the wilderness?" Then he shook himself. "What am I sayin'? I don't believe that God had you done do what you done did for Mi-Ling just to leave her daddy stranded in time. No, sir! I jest don't believe that. Y'all wait and see. God will get us out of this. You wait now and see if Sebastian ain't——isn't right."

CHAPTER 9

By the time we got back to the minister's house, we had realized and agreed that we must try to get rid of our broken time car. We hoped that blowing it up would do the trick—except for Sebastian who was still counting on a miracle from God to make it work.

I had been told that the time car was constructed so that you could fire a cannonball at it and it would bounce off. If that were true, it must be destroyed from inside by setting off charges rigged on the inside.

The trouble was that none of us could remember where we came from. We made the assumption that Kitchi and his fellow warriors would know, that is if the Powhatan still supported Les Anglais. Kitchi and his friends had promised to hide our "cabin" for us. The thing that bothered me was that Kitchi had seemed to take a shine to Meryl. As the husband who stood in his way, something unfortunate could happen to me in the forest. Perhaps I was being cynical. Still, I must discard my insecurities if we were to accomplish our mission. So I suggested the idea to the others. Meryl acquiesced with too much alacrity for my comfort, adding that Kitchi had been kind and comforting to her when she and Sebastian had been informed that everyone on our mission had been killed. The thought of Kitchi having "comforted" Meryl further worried me.

We found that Kitchi and his friends, who had been hunting, were willing to take us back. It had become more dangerous in the woods, he warned, so we must be careful. Kitchi asked Angus pointedly why he was willing to put the woman in danger of being kidnapped. Meryl was a Karate black belt. Anyone who tried to carry her off against her will would find himself with his hands occupied.

Angus, whose astuteness never ceased to amaze me, said to Kitchi, "I need her wisdom to help remove some of the things from the silver house in the forest."

Kitchi nodded. "Mmm, that is so. We have such women, too."

So, it would prove an early start the next day. Indians never seem to need sleep. As for us, none of us slept well—meaning Sebastian, Meryl and me. We couldn't speak for Angus. He had spent the night with Abigail and her sister. As far as Angus was concerned, this burgeoning relationship was getting serious. Abigail was nice girl. If we had to stay here in 1755, it gave Angus the promise of a family.

Meryl and I lay in each other's arms, just to be close.

Meryl's soft voice silenced the moonlight. "I can hear you thinking, darling."

"Thinking what?" I countered.

"Wondering if I'm going to go off with Kitchi if we are stuck here." I couldn't speak and fought the slow burn of tears as I thought with renewed horror of that possibility. She continued, "The answer is, no. I'm not."

Relieved, I got up for a sip of cider. She mused, "But he does have a sexy body."

I threw a bolster at her and she giggled.

We both lay awake trying to figure what we were going to do in 1755. Meryl thought it would play havoc with her pension. The real difficulty, I realized, would be trying to get land and build a home, even with Sebastian's help. Meryl thought she might be hired to teach. She certainly had the knowledge, and maybe after splitting wood with her hand, to attain Black Belt status, she might not have discipline problems. Yet in twenty years, there would be the American War of Independence and we would have to take a side—difficult when you knew in advance which side won and when you hailed from the losing side. Furthermore, what would happen if one of us fell ill? Or if Meryl had the baby she wanted right away? So many women died in childbirth...Meryl dead? I had come so close to losing her so many times. I didn't think I could survive the heartbreak of losing her in reality. The Indians knew about herbs and natural remedies and they could set bones, which might have been some comfort. But, quite rightly, the Indians began to turn against white settlers as white settlers herded them off their land in a ruthless, unforgivable land grab.

What got me was Mi-Ling. She needed her daddy. I guess if the truth were told, her daddy needed her even more. I missed her dreadfully. The memory of her smile and laughter haunted me. And what was happening to Lucy? Had Bryant turned up? Was Anton still there? I wondered if Myles and Caroline had married and left by now. If so, that would leave Lucy with Anton. If Anton grew bored, he might return to Russia and Lucy would be left on her own. I could see her going back to China to teach. She had been happy there. I wondered if she even thought about me and I knew the answer to that even before I had asked myself the question. But meanwhile, what were they all saying about us? Where did they think we were? What had they thought Meryl and I had done? Again, I knew the answer to that question even before I asked myself.

I finally drifted off to sleep, and the next thing I knew, there was a knock at the door and the Calvin's maid, Rhoda, brought in hot water. We dressed. Meryl said she would love to wash her hair, but there was no shampoo and not enough water. Maybe there was lye soap? We were going to have to get used to this idea of doing without and living outside our comfort zone. It was the first time I had thought about a power shower, and when I thought about it—I discovered that I missed it dreadfully. I think they were called "the good old days." You are never thankful about how far things have progressed until you have to regress. No shower was no fun. However, thankfully, everyone smelled the same.

There were oatcakes, apples and spring water for breakfast. I was glad of this, for the majority of the liquid you drank was in varying degrees alcoholic. Sometimes you just longed for something to quench your thirst. The Calvins had good water in their well. The water seemed to be running up between two stone cracks. We were already thirsty and could tell that it was going to be a hot, humid day. We all drank heartily. Angus met us, promptly on time, as usual.

When we got to the edge of town, Kitchi was waiting for us, along with two of his friends. He looked at me in a different way from before.

"Your deeds in the battle with Les Francais are known," he said. "The Shawnee you killed with the axe in the battle after you re-crossed the Monongahela River was in your language, Red Knife. He had killed many Powhatan. Now he is dead, and many will have peace in their heart at his death. Your name in your language would be, He Who Swings The Axe. You will find few will wish to fight with you. It is an honor to assist such a noble warrior."

I knew he was not kidding. Meryl's face mirrored surprise. "You killed a famous warrior with an axe?" she asked.

"Well, he was scalping someone who was still alive." I shuddered. "I will never forget that horrific sound—and his scream—oh, my God—his scream."

Meryl took my arm and whispered, "Poor Baby. If we ever get out of this, I will buy you a coffee at SavaJava and a chocolate brownie, and then we can go some place and make mad, passionate love."

Kitchi had overheard the promise. "Who is SavaJava? Is that one of your gods?"

"No," Meryl explained. "It's a place, like a tavern, where you go and drink a drink called coffee."

Kitchi scratched his head. "I have taken this drink. I do not think it will become famous. People come to drink this at this place with the strange name? Why does their woman not make it in their lodge?"

"Because," Meryl said, "it is mainly the women who do the drinking."

"What do your warriors do?" he asked.

"They pay gold to buy coffee."

"So they and their woman go to this place and pay gold for coffee that the woman could make in her husbands lodge?"

"Yes," Meryl agreed cheerfully.

"The ways of the white man are indeed strange," Kitchi murmured.

I had to admit that his way of thinking was brilliant.

We continued walking. Angus was speaking to the other two Indians with Sebastian as a very good rear guard.

"I have one question," Kitchi said. "Your cabin we are taking you to, how did it get into the forest? There were no horses and no prints from feet or boots, but the cabin is there. It was too great for you to carry. Did some god put you there?"

"Kitchi," Meryl said. "I don't know how to explain, except to tell you the truth—no matter how hard it may be to understand."

"Kitchi will believe what Sun In Her Hair says."

Meryl smiled at him and I felt a small knot tie itself in my stomach.

"Kitchi, you know how the sun rises and then sets? It is light and then dark and when the moon comes out, it is the end of a day. We rest when it is dark and then when the sun comes out again, a new day starts. Then another day and another. That is called time.

"Time goes on." Kitchi replied. "It moves and the seasons change."

"Yes," I said, entering the conversation. "But what Meryl is trying to tell you is that we make journeys not just in time—but through time."

He looked at us. "This I must think upon."

"Don't feel bad," Sebastian rejoined. "I don't understand a thing about what they done told me."

We walked on in silence. Kitchi was thinking. He finally said, "This is the year according to the white man's calendar 1755. Are you from the year 1755?"

"No," Meryl said. "Our travel ship is from another time."

"What time?" he asked

"In white man's years, about 2013"

"Why can you not leave? In your time have things got worse than the threat of war?" he asked.

Meryl answered. "Like you need wood to keep a fire burning, so we need fuel to cause our travel ship to move. We've run out of fuel. It's a yellow-colored rock. You can see it glow even in the dark.

Kitchi thought and said, "We have a place where the rocks are yellow and glow when there is no sun. It is not far from here. People are afraid for they think it is evil spirits that do this."

Dared we hope that it just might be Kairon? Dared we hope even more that it might be usable Kairon?

"Angus," Meryl shouted.

Angus jogged back to where we were and Kitchi repeated what he had already told us. He also said that we had time to get there, get to our cabin, and then get back to the Calvin's house before dark.

Sebastian clapped his hands and hollered. "Praise the Lord! I done told y'all that God would provide!"

I wished that I could share his confidence.

The place to which Kitchi took us was strange. There were no birds —just silence. It was creepy. We went forward and Angus took out the Kairon detector. It went off the scale.

Angus warned us, "We don't know what exposure to this stuff can do, but someone has to go get a chunk of it. We have the sizes of the container in which it is situated in the time machine. We need to grab it and get to the time car, pronto."

There were two saplings nearby and we cut them down. Angus looked at Meryl. "Can you take your petticoat off?"

"Pardon?"

"Your petticoat—below your skirt."

"What do you want it for?"

In response, Angus took the two saplings. Meryl removed her petticoat while we looked the other way. Angus took the undergarment from Meryl and slid the two saplings along either side of it and made a stretcher. He went into the trees and came out with two large chunks of yellow rock and placed them in the stretcher. Then he washed his hands carefully in a running stream.

Angus and Sebastian picked up one end of the "patient," and Meryl and I grabbed the other two poles. Kitchi lead us to the time car. It was well camouflaged—Kitchi and his friends had done a good job.

Meryl and Angus went inside the time car. We stood outside with Kitchi and the others. There were thumps and bangs from inside and the sound of a drill. Angus was amazing! Where had the guy found a drill— he must know these machines as thoroughly as he knew self-defense!

Kitchi mused, "I thought that time was quieter than this. It is truth that you do not notice getting older, but it is time advancing. When you move in time do you become older?"

"No," I said, pointing to the time car. "That moves through time. We stay the same."

Angus came back out to us. I think it fits and works. Meryl pressed a switch three times and the car kicked back into life. Kitchi's eyes opened wide—the eyes of his friends even wider. "Sun In Her Hair has fingers of magic," Kitchi said reverently.

Normally, I would have suggested a dry run, but Angus negated that. He pointed out that we needed to get back and get our luggage and our possessions.

"You mean we ain't—isn't stuck here?" Sebastian asked in wonderment. "An' I ken go wid y'all and get me one of them salary things you was talkin' 'bout?" We assured him that was the case and he whooped for joy. "That's shore enough good news! Thank you, Jesus!"

Kitchi promised, "We will take you back to the edge of the town. If you wish, we will bring you tomorrow and say goodbye."

He turned to Meryl, "You will go with them, Sun In Her Hair? Will you come back and see us again?"

"Yes," Meryl promised. "We will."

As we walked back, the focus of our thoughts began to change. Meryl and I began to think of what awaited us in 1867. Sebastian had never seemed to have any doubts and he was eager to go back to the future with Angus and begin training. Of course, there was the small, possibly technical point that we had to get back to those places. I discovered that being some two-hundred-fifty-plus years and 3000 miles away from my destination was cause for alarm.

That evening we sat with Dr. and Mrs. Calvin. "Tomorrow," I told them, "We shall be away. Thank you for your kindness to us."

Libby smiled and looked at Meryl. "You have been a joy to our house and a blessing," she praised. "And when it comes time for you to bear your child, we know God will bless you."

My mouth fell open. Speechless was not the word. "You hadn't told me," I finally managed.

She smiled demurely. "I was going to tell you. I wanted it to be a surprise."

"Surprise is hardly the word for what I'm feeling right now, Meryl!" I was going to be a father of my own child as well as Mi-Ling! So why was that knot tying itself back in my stomach again?

****

The following day, we said good bye and set out. Kitchi and his friends met us. By this time, we were able to recognize part of the path. Surprising Sebastian, the Indians helped us carry our things. Angus had said goodbye to Abigail. We could tell from his face that it had been anything but a happy parting. "You will come back here?" I asked.

"Yes," he replied in a soft un-Angus-like voice. "In the short time I've known Abigail, she's changed my life. But, first, we must finish what we set out to do."

Kitchi said to Meryl, "My heart is filled with a great sadness Sun In Her Hair. To lose the company of such warriors and to lose…and to lose…" He did not finish the sentence, but walked quickly to the front of the column. Meryl never took her eyes off him.

The knot in my stomach tightened. I remembered when I was a boy in Edinburgh and I had come to a street corner. I could not go around the corner. I felt danger. It turned out there was a rabid dog. Had I blundered around the corner, I would almost have certainly run into it.

"Meryl," I said with tears in both my voice and my eyes. "I won't be having a coffee and brownie with you at SavaJava, will I?"

She looked at me then looked down. "Of course, you will. Of course, you will. Yes, you will. Why wouldn't you?"

God in heaven, why couldn't I believe her? Why did I feel so sick?

As we approached the area where the time car was, Kitchi warned, "Shawnee. They have found your machine. I must go for help. There are too many for us to fight, even for great warriors like you. You must wait here."

We had divided up the gear at the start of the journey, leaving behind what was not necessary. We had, of course, kept our weapons—a good thing because there must have been twenty Shawnee.

"Please, do not move, Sun In Her Hair. There is great danger." He pointed to the other two braves. "They will go back and get help. I will stay here with you."

Angus said to Kitchi, "We thank you for your honor and your friendship. But we have weapons that will deal with them. You must leave now. Quickly! After we go, you will be on your own and you are greatly outnumbered, for all of your courage and bravery."

Kitchi turned to Meryl. Having only read biased accounts of the savagery of the Native Americans, and having erroneously thought them to be imperturbable, I was astounded at the reflection of pain and suffering—agony even—mirrored on his face. "I will come here each day, Sun In Her Hair and see if you have returned. In my heart I know truth."

I, too, knew truth—or thought I did—and it was killing me inside.

Kitchi and his friends melted into the forest. Meryl watched until they vanished. Angus took the Uzi from his backpack. I had the Heckler and Koch. Sebastian was given a pistol and Meryl had another. But would she be able to quit focusing on Kitchi and turn her attention to the hostile Indians?

Angus directed, "Clear them from the door first. Our aim is to get inside, not kill them. I programmed the machine yesterday. All we have to do is get inside and throw the switch. We move at the count of five. Do not fire until they start—and let's hope they're bad shots."

Sebastian looked through the underbrush at the Indians. "Just one thing," he asked. "When we get back into that machine and throw the switch—hopefully before we gets scalped—how can I be sure we will get to where we are supposed to get to, and when we are supposed to get to instead of winding up somewheres else?"

"You can't be sure," Angus said honestly.

"Okay," Sebastian replied. "Just thought I might ought to ask."

We waited for Angus' count, "One, two, three, four, five. GO, GO, GO!"

We yelled and screamed like banshees. The Shawnee started to come toward us. It took a burst from the Uzi, when four fell, and a burst from the Heckler and Koch, when another four fell. We made it to the door with shots bouncing off the casing, slammed the door shut, hit the activation switch, and hit the floor, and we knew we had moved.

CHAPTER 10

Scotland 1867

We came to a halt. Sebastian said, "Can I go back and get my stomach?"

Meryl and I got ready to leave. I still had one of the controls.

Angus said, "Okay, then, laddie. I'm off to get Sebastian clued up to 21st century living."

I overheard part of a conversation between Sebastian and Meryl. "You will get money, Sebastian. When you do, one of the first things you need to do is to go out and eat somewhere. And let other folks serve you."

"What about my color? In case you ain't—isn't noticed, I got black skin. I can't jest go a'waltzing into a place amonst white folks and sit down to eat. It jest ain't—isn't done."

"In 21st century, no problem. Honest, no problem," Meryl promised. "And if and when we get to meet again, I'll take you out myself. My treat. It will be an honor and privilege."

Sebastian shook his head, unable to believe in a world where the color of his skin didn't divide him and exclude him from full participation in life.

When we opened the door, I was relieved to see the basement of Bellefield.

How much time has passed here since we left? I asked Meryl.

She did a quick calculation, "About four weeks, I would think."

Angus said, "Well, good luck guys. I'm here if you need me. By the way, you look a sight for sore eyes."

We stood back. Sebastian called out, "Well, reckon we had better go before I meet myself comin' back."

The time car shot off. We were on our own and I wished we were back in Gettysburg. I figured that dodging snakes and Yankee Cavalry at Gettysburg would sure be a lot easier than what was coming.

We headed upstairs and went to our rooms, one at a time. It was decidedly colder and our clothes were Virginia July attire, not January Scottish attire.

Meryl got upstairs without being seen. I was not so fortunate. I didn't really care, because I still hadn't figured out what to do and how to handle things and postponing the moment wouldn't ameliorate it. When I left, I had been engaged to Lucy and it had been a mere three days before the wedding. Now—oh, heavens, what a mess!

To say I had heavy steps was an understatement. Then there was a scream, followed by a cry of joy. "Papa! Papa! Oh, Papa!" Mi-Ling appeared from nowhere, jumped into my arms, buried her head on my chest, and broke into sobs. Tears stung my eyes. I felt like crying with her. I clung to her in mingled love and relief. I had been so fearful that I would never see her again. She didn't care that I must have smelled like last week's dirty washing. She loved me.

"Mi-Ling!" I heard Lucy approaching. "Mi-Ling, what's wrong?" Then Lucy saw me. She looked at me with an expression of what amounted to disbelief. There was no welcome or love evident in her expression.

"Drew," she said slowly, "is it really you?" She stared and wet her lips. "Where have you been?"

So, still holding my clinging daughter, I told her the truth. "In Gettysburg in 1863, and fighting with General Braddock in 1755. The first was by intent. The second by accident."

"Don't stand there lying to me, Drew," she said coldly. "Haven't you already done enough damage and hurt enough people? And where is Svetlana? Anton is in prison in Aberdeen. They think he murdered her."

Can we talk somewhere warm? I've just come from high summer in Virginia and it's cold here."

Her voice matched the coldness of the room as she asked again, "And Svetlana is…"

"Svetlana is here." Meryl's voice floated downstairs. She followed it.

"Only my name is not Svetlana. I'm Meryl. I work for the organization that got Drew to China to meet with you. I was Drew's girlfriend before he came to work for Vanguard."

"You knew each other previously?"

"Yes," Meryl admitted readily. "But we split up. I wasn't with him in China except once in a sword fight to save his life. Except that even though we didn't plan it, we fell in love. Drew gave me up for you, but I couldn't let him go."

"I don't believe it," Lucy said in icy tones. "I don't believe any of this! I don't believe either of you! You are making up a ridiculous story to cover a sordid little affair."

"I can prove it to you," I told Lucy gently. "Remember, I told you in China that I was a time traveler, but I don't think you believed me."

"As I still don't believe it now, Drew. Why aren't you man enough to tell me the truth? I'm woman enough to take it. Why do you think you must lie to me? That shows a further lack of respect along with what you've already subjected me to—like leaving me at the alter three days before our wedding!"

"I can prove it to you, Lucy. I can take you to meet your mother."

"My mother is presumably dead. She disappeared."

"Lucy," I reminded her, "the letter, the half-coin on the chain, the picture."

"Forgery. Someone who looked like her."

"You've ripped me to ribbons without giving me the chance to prove what I say is true."

Mi-Ling slipped out of my arms and sat down on a step. After a moment, she got up from the step. It was only then I noticed her black-shadowed eyes and slow step. She went into one of the rooms and shut the door.

"See!" Lucy cried. "You've upset Mi-Ling with your anger. Oh, Drew—how could you be so cruel? And not just to me—to your own daughter!"

"Is this a private argument, or can anyone join in?" I started as Luke Carter walked out of the dining room and joined us. "I didn't know that indigestion was on the menu for breakfast," he explained. "You must admit, time travel does sound far fetched."

"Luke," I directed. "Look at me and think back." I turned to face him fully.

He sneered, "I see someone who needs a bath and a shave."

"Luke, Gettysburg. In the barn near the Brafferton Inn. The three Yankee cavalrymen we turned over to you. You were a lieutenant. You wore a blue spotted bandana. You rode a gray Appaloosa"

I continued, "Remember, we also met at Sir Charles Gray's ball in Foochow, China, and I shot the assassin who tried to kill him. When you saw me, you said, 'Have we not met someplace before?' I said, 'no,' but I knew you had remembered me."

Then the look of recognition flashed into his eyes. "At Gettysburg, there were two of you. You were part of the British delegation. What was different about the third guy that was with you?" he asked.

"He was black."

"Luke," Lucy demanded. "Is he telling the truth?"

Luke sighed and ran a hand through his short-cropped hair. "Yes, Lucy. Strangely enough, he is."

"Has Bryant showed up?" I asked.

"He threatened to show up at the wedding," Lucy said slowly. "In case you had forgotten, Drew. And for some reason, there was no wedding and there will be no wedding. Could the reason behind no wedding have been that the groom was conveniently missing?"

"I'm going to have a baby," Meryl announced unexpectedly.

Lucy looked at me in horror. "Drew how could you? This on top of everything else!"

Meryl shook her head at Lucy. "You are putting two and two together and getting five. My child's father is a Native American named Kitchi. He lives in 1755, and is waiting for me to return to him."

Lucy looked caught on the hop. I was instantly and completely devastated. I heard what I thought to have been the truth from Meryl. It was a bit like illness you could cope with until the doctor handed you the official diagnosis. I would have thrown up—except I couldn't in front of Luke.

"Lucy," I begged, in an attempt to hide my own shock and recover from it. "Let me take you to see your mother. I need to point out that you will be taking a risk by time travel. You may have a bad heart. Your mother barely survived the journey. Still, if you're willing to risk it, I want you to see your mother. And I want to prove to you that I've been telling you the truth. It's not for me, Lucy. It's for Mi-Ling. We have to make some decisions about her future."

"How long will this so called journey take? Days? Weeks? Months?"

"Minutes," I replied. "Just minutes."

She had flipped her valve, and now realized she might have been, at least, partly wrong.

"Look," I reasoned. "If Bryant is around, he wants revenge on me. He hasn't seen me and there's been no wedding. He knows something's wrong, but doesn't know what it is. I assume police took Anton away and the sight of them may have put Bryant off."

I paused and asked Luke, "Luke, will you and Meryl go to Aberdeen to West Prison and get Anton out? Take Mi-Ling with you. Then Lucy and I can head for Victoria—she's Lucy's mother. We need to do this."

We kind of all looked at one another and decided to move quickly.

Mi-Ling did not look well and when Mrs. Fraser heard that we proposed to take her to Aberdeen, she contested hotly. "Mr. Faulkner, you are not dragging that wee pet out into the cold all the way to Aberdeen. She's not well enough and I won't allow it!" She stood like a colossus, and that was the end of the argument.

I went to Mi-Ling's room to visit her. Mrs. Fraser was right. The child looked ill. "Darling, Amma and I have to go on another journey."

"Papa, can not Mi-Ling come with you? I will try to be good." She held my hands tightly.

I could not stop the tears swarming into my eyes. "Darling, daughter, this is one time you can not come. Mrs. Fraser is right. You are precious. We don't want you getting ill. But, sweetheart, look at your clock. What time is it?"

"It is three o'clock," she responded promptly.

"Watch your clock. When the time changes to seven o'clock, I will be back here with you. I promise. Mrs. Fraser will come and sit with you in the meantime so you won't be alone."

"Is Uncle Luke going to be here?"

I looked at my daughter and thought in somewhat of a shock, Uncle Luke! Was there something Lucy had neglected to tell me in her angry tirade about my actions? To Mi-Ling, I explained—calmly, I hoped—"Luke's gone to get Anton out of prison and bring him back. Where is your Carol-lady?"

"Carol-lady be married now. She go to be with her husband. She be very happy. She promise to come back and see Mi-Ling." She thought for a moment and asked, "Papa, why do the people you love go away? It was good when we were on the boat. We were all together. Papa, Mi-Ling is tired now and wants to go to sleep. Mi-Ling loves you. She will wake up and see Papa when the clock gets to seven."

She hugged me, closed her eyes and curled up on her bed. It terrified me. What was wrong with Mi-Ling that caused her to need a nap during the day at her age? I was frightened that something was drastically wrong. I felt like a reptile. Life had thus far dealt her more pain, anguish, terror and hurt than any human of any age should have to experience. And it hurt her all over again that all the people she loved were going away. What about me? What about Lucy?

I took a bath, shaved and met Lucy, ready for the journey. "Where do we go for this journey?" she asked.

"You are one skeptical person. First, we go down to the basement," I said.

We went down and I thought I could get into a whole heap of trouble if things went wrong. I wanted things to be right for Mi-Ling. She needed love and stability. She deserved love and stability. Every child did.

I instructed Lucy to stand by the wall. I stood beside her and pressed the switch. At first, nothing happened. Then the time portal opened and the car stopped beside us. The look on Lucy's face was indescribable.

"Well, come on and get on board," I prompted her. "I promised Mi-Ling I would be back by seven o'clock."

"Yes, Drew," she acquiesced, slipping inside where Meryl should have been. "You are right. We must get back to Mi-Ling. I'm worried about her. I've taken her to several doctors and they can't find anything wrong with her. But you have only to look at her to realize that something is wrong. And I haven't had a chance to discus it with you because you've been gone."

I got inside next to Lucy, set the time and date for when I had left, and pressed the switch.

Oh, Lord Jesus, I messed things up bad. Could You un-mess them? Please?

We shot off and Lucy let out a frightened gasp. It seemed minutes. We came to a halt.

The door opened onto the lab, from which I had left.

"Are you well?" I asked anxiously.

"Yes," she said looking around. "I seem to be."

I still had my card and the same two guards were still there. They nodded and I ran my card through the door. Then I told Lucy, "Look into that light." She did and the door to upstairs opened. I took Lucy to the upstairs of her own house.

I met Adrian. "Drew! What the blazes are you doing here? It is you?" He put his hands on my shoulder and peered into my face.

"Where's Victoria?" I asked.

Then Adrian looked past me and saw Lucy. His mouth fell open. "God, it's Lucy!" He turned on his heel and bolted upstairs shouting, "Victoria! Victoria!"

Lucy and I followed and I saw Victoria come rushing down the stairs. "Adrian, what's wrong?"

Lucy and Victoria screamed simultaneously. "Mummy! Mummy!" Lucy rushed past me and mother and daughter fell into each other's arms. The two of them sat on the top stair and cried and cried.

Adrian tapped me on the shoulder. "Let's leave. Come on, fill me in. Angus McTurk filled in some of the details in his reports and, boy, oh, boy, does he ever speak highly of you!

And I have only got to look at you to see the change. It's good to see you, Drew, and to see Lucy so happy."

"Can we change the subject?" I asked.

"Why, what's gone wrong?"

We got to a comfortable room and two of those deep leather chairs in which you sit and get lost. There was a fire, a plate of snacks euphemistically called "nibbles" by Adrian, and good coffee. We could also hear crying and exclamations from the stairs outside. Still, who could blame them after two years of thinking they would never see each other again?

"Uncle, with God's help, I did I did what you asked. Got the ship, tea and Lucy here, or—perhaps it should be there. Plus, we have stopped PATCH twice. Angus did the bulk of the stopping."

Adrian rose to his feet, "Before you continue, old son, there is someone I would like you to meet. I'll go get him." Adrian left the room and came back with a man in army uniform. He came over to me and extended his hand.

"John Carlisle. How do you do?" The voice and presence exuded an approachable confidence.

"Colonel Carlisle?" I ventured to suggest.

"Well, yes. But I am glad to finally meet you, Andrew. Your reputation precedes you."

"Reputation? It was Angus and Meryl and Sebastian who did a lot of the combat."

"Good. That's fine. Can't stand conceit. Conceit seems to be the standard bottle of sauce with PATCH."

I liked Colonel Carlisle. I assumed he was the Vanguard boss.

"The PM has given this top priority. Even has the leader of the opposition. They may fight like cat and dog in the House of Commons, but they very much agree on the danger to the world as we know it if PATCH gets its way."

I objected. "Surely you would be better with specially trained agents apart from Angus and Meryl?"

He smiled and replied, "No, for this we need someone human who has not had the humanity trained out of them. Besides, you are doing very well from what I hear. What was it like to be three inches away from a fifteen-foot white shark?"

I shrugged my shoulders. "What do you want me to say? In all truth, I was terrified."

"Good. So would any of the super-trained operatives have been."

"How can you stop Professor Reynolds?" I asked. "He seems to be one of the leading lights in PATCH."

Adrian perked up. "When did you hear his name?"

"The PATCH operative in Gettysburg used his name when he was trying to get the time portal to open."

Carlisle looked at Adrian. "You were right," he said. "Bang on." Then he explained to me, "We didn't know for sure, Andrew, but that is important. Confirmation is better than suspicion."

"My suspicion is," I said, "and you have probably come to the same conclusion. That PATCH is going to step up its attacks having been thwarted twice. If it can't change history, then its reason for being ceases. Professor Reynolds has to be being bankrolled by someone."

There was a silence. Then Colonel Carlisle asked, "How you getting on with young Meryl? Pretty girl."

"Yes. She is. I owe her a great deal. She's one of the calmest people in a crisis. But how far can she go on? Because, as you probably know, she's pregnant."

The Colonel looked startled, then grinned. "No, I don't think so, Andrew. It's one of the things that young female operatives volunteer to give up. Without going into gynecological detail, they undergo a procedure that stops them from getting pregnant. It can be reversed, but if ever any of them got stuck somewhere, it saves them from having a child to take care of."

For a moment I was stunned. So Meryl had deliberately lied. Was it out of unselfishness to protect my relationship with Lucy, or was it a more sinister reason: to put me off her so she could leave me with a light conscience and go back to Kitchi?

In an attempt to hide my confusion, I told Colonel Carlisle about Mi-Ling and how she had saved my life by stopping Lancaster. "Now," I finished, "I want to adopt her."

He was okay about that. Then he added, "Right. You are officially in Vanguard now. You are a full military captain in the Royal Scottish Regiment, but as it was only formed recently, you had better stick to the Gordon Highlanders. Also, you're on the payroll. You won't be doing this, however, up until the time that you need a zimmer, so what money you get is a salary—a pension as well. Do well and promotion will follow."

I sighed, feeling empty and smashed inside. "Meryl and I made a good team."

"That's why you should continue to work together." He stared at me. "Captain, we protect that which we love."

"What if it came to Meryl or duty?" I asked.

"That only you can answer if, or when, the time comes."

The subject of Johnny Branson came up, the agent who had gone freelance aboard Bryant's ship. Carlisle shook his head ruefully. "Johnny had large gambling debts. We tried to warn him that it could give the bad guys a way to hook him. He didn't listen."

"I guess you have people inside PATCH?"

"Yes," Carlisle admitted, "but not at the levels we would like."

There was a gap in the conversation.

"You want to get back don't you?" Adrian asked.

I looked at him. "Lucy needs to go back, too. If I turn up without her, Mi-Ling will be heartbroken. Plus, I will get arrested for murder if Lucy just vanishes."

Adrian took out his pipe and emptied it carelessly on the floor. I wondered if Victoria ever got upset with her husband. "I'll talk to her—and to Victoria."

"One thing more," I asked both Adrian and Carlisle. "It is possible to…I'm not sure what I'm trying to ask. If someone is seriously injured, or shot, is it possible to travel back in time—even ten minutes—and save them, or warn them? If Bryant shoots one of us, is it possible to reverse that?"

Adrian fiddled with his pipe, stuffing new tobacco in the bowl. He seemed to enjoy playing with it more than smoking it. Which, in view of the cancer factor, was good. "Yes. Technically. Providing the person was still alive where they were at the point in time to which you went back. If they are shot at 3 p.m., say, and die at 3:05, you can't go back to 2:55 and stop it. If they are still alive when you go back, then that means they would be still alive when you warn them, even if they are wounded. If they die in the time you are in, then they stay dead."

"Oh by the way," Carlisle said, "Sebastian was a good find. He'll make a fine agent."

"It would be good to work with him again," I acknowledged.

Carlisle nodded in agreement. "Well, we'd better let you get back. Good to have finally met you, Drew. Don't worry, Adrian, I will see myself out." Then to me again, "Good show. Well done." With that, Carlisle left.

I said to Adrian. "It was a bit nervy when I thought we were going to be stuck in 1755. But for now, I must get back. I promised Mi-Ling."

Adrian looked at me. "She really means a lot to you."

"I cut cards for her to get her out of a Chinese child brothel. She saved my life, and I can make a difference to her life. Give her what every child deserves—love, hope, a good education, and a future."

"And what about Lucy?" he asked

"I have to tell her that I love Meryl. Besides, there might be someone for her in 1867."

Adrian studied me, knocking his pipe against his palm and spilling loose tobacco on the floor. "Are you sure, old son, that you want to carry on?"

"How can you settle to a desk job after doing this?" I asked. "I've seen places and people that only a handful of others ever have or will. I'll never forget the sight of Pickett's Charge in Gettysburg. The other thing is more personal. I owed a lot to Sir Charles Gray. I want to find why Bryant had him murdered. Bryant has got to be stopped. If he and PATCH ever meet up, then we could be in real trouble."

Adrian nodded in agreement, if not total understanding, flinging his pipe aside, and further dislodging loose tobacco. "Now, about Lucy. We have a dentist on the premises and we're going to give Lucy a check over and a quick medical."

I knew how important this was. In Lucy's time, most women lost their teeth in their early twenties due to lack of dental care.

Adrian added, "She feels okay about it. Even with travel time, you should get back by the time you promised your little girl with some thirty minutes to spare.

I decided to have a power shower while waiting. How long had it been since I had indulged in the luxury of one of these? Then, I went for a drive. Amazingly, I could still drive. I went to Huntly and bought a jar of coffee for Meryl. My watch assured me I still had time, so I decided to go to the library and look back at some old newspapers stored on microfiche. It had been something like January 14, when Lucy and I had left to visit Uncle Adrian and Victoria. I made a perusal of the old papers, then found the one the one dated January 15th.

"*The Bridge at Port Elphinstone, over the Don,*" I read, "*was washed away in a flood. It was found that very probably the structural integrity of the aforementioned bridge had been undermined by the effects of inclement weather and possibly by human activity. Although the authorities cannot be certain, they are investigating possible criminal action and intent. At this time, there has been no danger to human life or any known casualties. Mr. R.J. Burnett, County Engineer, has indicated that all possible steps to secure the area and repair any damage are underway. It is hoped the inclement weather will cease in the near future.*"

Sometimes things do not always register. In the films, you see the hero realizing something—sensing danger then coming up with an extraordinarily clever and wonderful plan. The report about the bridge didn't 'click' with me, mainly because there was no mention of casualties or fatalities. Then I remembered that in 1867, search facilities would be extremely limited. Folks would have had no reason to suspect any casualties. Urgently, it hit home that the bridge at Port Elpinstone would be along the same road that Luke, Meryl—and hopefully Anton

—would be taking to get back to Bellefield. What worried me was the reporter's use of the phrase, inclement weather and possible human activity. Was it just 1867-style vandalism, or was there something more sinister? Was I just being paranoid, or did I have good reason to worry? Oh, Lord what do I do? I had never been a big fan of the phrase if only...

I drove quickly back to Bellefield and caught up with Lucy and Victoria. Lucy's teeth sparkled where they had been polished and she spoke with a numb mouth where a couple of fillings had been done. She kept rubbing her tongue round her lips, I guess to see if they were still there. Normal dental proceedings were both new and unexpected to her.

"Lucy," I told her, making no effort to hide my alarm. "We've got to go back now. I've just read in the local paper from the day after we left, that the bridge over the Don, on which Anton, Luke and Meryl will pass, had been tampered with. The paper was not specific, but I have a horrible feeling that the tampering was done by Bryant and a few cronies and the weather did the rest. I've got to get to the bridge and stop Luke, Anton and Meryl. Bryant won't just go away. He has to be stopped!"

Lucy pulled the edge of her skirt from under her shoe. "Drew, they have told me I can stay here in this time with Mum if I want to."

"What about Mi-Ling? She will miss you."

Tears welled up in Lucy's eyes and I realized I had said the wrong thing—but I wasn't sure what I had said that was wrong. "Drew," Lucy said quietly, with pain etched in her voice, "I thought if you got an opportunity, you might just say that you wanted me back for me, because you wanted me there. Not just for Mi-Ling's sake. Drew, after all we have been through! Remember that night we danced at the ball in the Embassy at Foochow? We had eyes only for one another."

She took my hands in hers and her eyes lit up, the tears intensifying the green sparkle. "Drew, darling we were so nearly married. Surely, there must be something still there, some embers we can reignite. Give me some hope."

I was cut to the quick and tried a practical approach. "Lucy, we need to get back to save the others and we need to get back for Mi-Ling. Then we can sort this out. I promised Mi-Ling."

She let go of my hands. "What about the promise you made to me?" she asked in a small voice. Suddenly, she seemed very small and young and vulnerable. Somehow, swimming with sharks and getting attacked by Indians seemed a sight easier than this.

"Lucy, Major Carlisle—the man in charge here—said that we can go back in time to prevent something horrible from happening to someone. He also said that if they die in the time span where we are, we can't go back before that time to try and prevent their death. If Anton, Meryl and Luke are killed on February 15, 1867, we can't go back to the 14th to warn them. Just now we can. Just now we can stop them. Don't we at least owe it to them to try? The lives of three people are dependent on what we do now."

She nodded, determinedly wiping away the tears, and took my arm. I grabbed the case she had brought with her. Victoria chatted away to Lucy and there was a distinct relief in Victoria's voice, created by the knowledge that at the push of a button, Lucy could return to modern times.

Lucy and I fell silent as we headed back to the time car. I had been worried in case she decided to stay. Was she coming along to be with me —which in my heart I hoped was not the case—or was there another reason? I thought about the first time I had seen her picture. I remembered the enigmatic smile and of the nights that I had lain awake just thinking about her. I remembered how head-over-heels I had been. How tongue-tied when I first met her and Carolyn after plodding back to land out of the water in the harbor where I had rescued the young boy who had fallen into the deep water. Lucy had been shy, but animated then. In China, it was almost like she had her reason for living. Then, she had blossomed like a rose. But now, I had taken her from that and put her into a time and life where she need not be concerned about anything. She had all she needed. She was like a rosebush that had been taken out of the center of a garden where she had blessed what she touched. Taken and put into a pot and set on a window ledge, where she was expected to look beautiful; where people could come and admire —but when they had all gone home, she was still on the ledge, watching the moon come out and seeing the early morning birds getting on with life and listening through the glass to the wind blowing on the trees. Yet the rose longed for the kiss of the sun, the touch of the wind and the refreshing touch of the rain on her petals; to be out in the center bed of the garden holding court in her beauty, with all the things big and small that made life to her worth living. Being admired for how she looked was not enough. Lucy needed to be needed and needed to be wherever that need existed.

When I had finally realized this, for the first time in a long time, I felt peace in my spirit. God had used this trip back to modern times to let me know what was right for Lucy. But before I could release Lucy into the life that was right for her, we had to get back to prevent the possible death of three people.

The time car came to a halt and I assumed we were back in 1867. Lucy came slowly out of the time car, shaking her head. "All the things I've just seen and the places to which I've just been were real, weren't they? I really did see Mummy and she is well? I'm sorry for not believing you. We must hurry and try and save the others." She sighed.

In saying that, it was like she was drawing on inner resources and strength. She would do her very best, no matter what happened. In Act III of William Shakespeare's play Henry V, he and his weary men were besieging the city of Harfleur, in North France. They had made a breach in the city walls, but were pushed back. Henry rallied his men with a speech: *Once more unto the breech dear friends once more…Or close the wall up with our English dead! In peace nothing so becomes a man as modest stillness and humility: But when the blast of war sounds in our ears, then imitate the action of the tiger; Stiffen the sinews, summon up the blood, Disguise fair nature with hard- favour'd rage…"*

Lucy had had enough of running. She was going back to the breech; was going back to fight; and the effect was awesome. Never before, even in the portrait hanging on the wall of Bellefield some one-hundred-and-fifty-years later, had she looked so intoxicatingly lovely.

CHAPTER 13

Lucy went to find Mi-Ling. Mrs. Fraser said that the others had only left a couple of hours ago. I changed into uniform and went out to find the ghillie, Jock Shepherd. Thankfully, I could cover the scarlet of my uniform and I did not feel like I was sticking out like a sore thumb.

When I found Jock, it was almost as if he had been expecting me. "Jock," I said. "We must go after the two Russians and Mr. Carter. First, can you get me to the magistrate's house as quickly as possible?"

"Aye Mr.—er, Captain Faulkner. Let me get ma guns and we can be off."

Jock drove faster than Ben-Hur and I had a job keeping my balance. We pulled up outside the magistrate's house and I knocked on the door. The magistrate, Duguld, was a cheery soul, like a Scot's version of Mr. Pickwick out of Charles Dickens, 'A Christmas Carol.' I explained to him the danger and what might have been done to the bridge at Port Elphinstone.

"Sabotage ye say, captain?" he asked, with the stare of a surprised owl.

"Aye, that is my information. Can you get people down there? One other thing, how long would it take to get someone out of prison who was being released after being found not guilty? The Russian—Anton Devranov. The case was in the papers."

He thought for a moment and said "Aye, he killed his traveling companion, the Russian lady."

"Svetlana Simeonova?" I asked helpfully.

"Aye, Captain. I will take your word for it."

"Well, Miss Simeonova is on her way to the prison to get him out."

"My goodness! Why did the lassie no come forward at the time o the trial?"

I explained, "She was out of the country. Ye ken these hot blooded Russians? The course of true love never runs smooth without a duel or a murder. They're the reason why the saboteurs are trying to damage the bridge. The chief is an American called Caleb Bryant, a Nantucket sea captain. He's also wanted for questioning about the assassination of Sir Charles Gray, the British Ambassador. It took place about fourteen months ago."

Duguld scratched his head. "Mmm…I'll see if I can rouse the telegraphist and get him to wire the West Prison and they can hold the three of them. We can get our newly formed Volunteer Rifle Company to the bridge. I only hope we are in time."

"Be careful, Mr. Duguld. These are desperate men."

"Aye, but some of our laddies are just itching for a fight. Oh Captain, John Grant's stable is near the jail. Mention my name and he'll change your horses."

I went outside. Jock had lit the carbide lamps at the side of the coach.

"It's going to be a night ride. Jock, these are desperate men. Will you help me? We need to get to West Prison."

He shivered. "Aye, Captain. Glad to help out. The name o' that place maks me shiver. Once we are finished at the jail, we can head for the bridge. Twa-legged game will make a change from four."

I laughed. "I guess the difference is the four-legged ones don't shoot back."

So off we went. It took hours and we could not afford to tire the horses. I was so glad it was a bright moonlit night, but it was cold. Thankfully, Victorian winter clothes, including uniforms, had been designed to combat cold.

Talk of grim: the sight of the prison was enough to terrify me. I expected to see a sign above the door, Abandon hope, all ye who enter here.

Luke, Anton and Meryl were in the assistant governor's office. Anton looked rough. This place was no health resort. I gave Meryl a big hug. She was dressed in a long skirt and riding cloak, with a matching hat. "Miss Simeonova, it's good to see you again."

The Assistant governor, who did not look happy about the whole thing, handed a paper to Anton. "Well, Mr. Devranov, here is your release. Of course, there is no record and as an innocent man you are entirely free. Miss Simeonova is alive and well, and you are free to go with your friends. I hope no hard feelings. The law is the law and has to take its course."

Anton looked at the assistant warden. "In Russia, when they put you in prison, there are two things with which the Czarist government is unconcerned—your innocence and your feelings. You will pardon me if I do not put at the top of my list of things to do, to thank you for your hospitality." Then he turned to me. "Let's get out of here."

Luke looked bemused by the whole thing. "I thought Andersonville was bad, but boy! This place sure is rattle on the rattler's tail."

We had crossed Port Elphinstone Bridge on the way to the prison, but by now Bryant and his gang might be working their mischief. I decided that everyone, especially Anton, needed food. A gun battle could wait.

There was an open restaurant, and I was on the bell. I needed to rally the troops, including Jock. A full stomach worked wonders for morale. I needed to try to explain everything, especially to Anton about Meryl and me having known each other before. He listened attentively, then sighed. "And I thought Russian life was complicated." I had expected—and perhaps deserved—anger and accusation from my friend. But either he was too drained after his stint in prison, or else the philosophical side of his nature had triumphed. Either way, I admired him and was more thankful than I could say to have his continued friendship.

Aberdeen is a port, and even in 1867, we had hit on a restaurant that advertised: A New Alcoholic Beverage from the East. To keep the cold out and the heat in, with Russian Vodka you always win. There was a long label on the bottle and Anton studied it.

"What does it mean in English?" we asked

He started to laugh, "Bear Sweat"

After eating, we headed back for the carriages. Our total weaponry included two shotguns, a rifle and three revolvers. Not much to face a gang of desperados. Nobody wanted to turn back. None of us wanted to leave Lucy or Mi-Ling alone for any longer. Jock was an old soldier and we all hoped the Volunteer Rifle Company would already be there. How were we to get across the river if they weren't?

I asked Luke, "If you were going to blow up a bridge, would you post a sentry?"

He thought for a moment. "Reckon if it was up to me, I'd get the charges lit and hightail it outta there, and wait for the bang."

"Suppose," I said, "you wanted the bridge to collapse when anything passed over it?"

He considered. "Blow the struts on the bridge and hope the weight does the rest."

"How long would it take to set the dynamite?"

"Depends the size of the bridge, but probably about seven minutes. Then, you have to be able to see the bridge and light the fuse and stop what you want to stop from crossing over. During the war, we had to blow bridges, but we tried to be sure there were no civilians on them. We didn't make war against women and children. How about your time?"

"Things have changed. It's no longer called war—but Terror—and the higher the innocent body count, the happier they seem to be."

He looked thoughtful. "I guess my time is not so bad after all. I guess you guys get used to the time you live in."

"Yes, we have become immune to tears and orphans, and we consider ourselves a generation that does not need God. Or the god we view, has become so callous that he brings with him the odor of death instead of love and life."

Luke nodded grimly, then said, "Before we get to the bridge, let me off. I doubt whether Bryant has professional soldiers with him. Probably a gang of ruffians wanting easy money. I might be able to neutralize the sentry so he can't warn them of our coming. If the Rifle Company is there and the fire fight has started, then we will have to assess the situation once we get there."

We rattled on and after a while Jock stopped the carriage and announced, "The bridge is about half-a-mile away, sir."

Luke got out from the other carriage and faded into the shadows, in spite of the moonlight. We waited to see if he would return and he did after about twenty-five minutes. "He will have a headache, and I left their sentry bound and gagged."

Anton joined us, making patterns in the damp leaves at his feet and asked, "Is countryside like this on both sides of bridge?"

"Aye, sir," Jock replied.

"Wind is blowing to the north. Yes?"

"Aye, sir" Jock answered. I had the impression that Jock was on Anton's wavelength.

"Old Russian saying. A bear cannot eat what it cannot see."

My mind was not sharp.

At that point a voice came from behind us.

"You are surrounded stand to your feet with your hands up."

We did, in case the voice had decided on the policy of shoot first and ask questions later.

"Caught in the act. Which one of you is Bryant? You're all under arrest. A woman as part of the group—unscrupulous in the uttermost."

I displayed my red uniform underneath my coat.

"Captain, my apologies." He came to attention and saluted. "Lieutenant James Argent, 1st Volunteer Rifle Company."

"At ease, Lieutenant. To answer your question, Bryant is on the other side of the bridge with his gang and Miss Scott is the match in fighting skill of any man here."

Lieutenant Argent was obviously not used to hearing about such Amazons and possibly didn't believe me.

Anton joined us. "In this moonlight, if you go across the bridge, people are going to be killed. You will be like the sitting pigeons."

The lieutenant pointed out, "I think it's ducks, sir."

"Of course to duck is a good idea," Anton agreed. "Especially when someone is shooting at you."

The others of the Rifle Company were feeling the cold. "Any ideas, Captain, of how we may accomplish this task?" Argent asked.

Anton answered for me. "In old country, that is Russia, we hunt wolves. They can be dangerous and they can hide in forests and caves. You go into the cave and they find pieces of you later. If you light a fire and pile leaves on it and make smoke, the wind blows it and the wolves come out pretty quick. Of course they are upset, and not in the happiest of spirits, and if your rifle does not fire when it should, you are presented with problem which requires immediate attention.

"So I would suggest that you get your boys to light fires. The wind will carry the smoke across and cause Bryant and his men to move or do something. Two of the Rifle Company can wait at this point and stop any traffic trying to get across. Be careful when you light the fire. Take your time. Remember, we are after smoke not flame even though it's jist starvation."

They nodded assent, even giving Anton's idea the respect of a whispered, "aye, aye."

So far, there was no movement on the other side of the river. They had lost their sentry, but he, to all intents and purposes, could have fallen asleep. Maybe crawled in some place trying to get warm. I had not asked Luke but I thought Bryant's man would be out of the picture. So we had to light and wait—maximum smoke, minimum flame. Half these guys had been born in the woods and knew their way round tinder and flint.

Smoke began to drift across and after about ten minutes, we heard the sound of coughing. Then from across the river came a voice. "Am awa oot o'here. A fecht is aye thing. Gettin' kippered is something else."

Two or three voices spoke, all the louder for trying to be quiet. "We blow the bridge and go," came an American accent. I knew Bryant's voice. There was a silence, then a fizz as a fuse began to burn. It lit up and headed for under the bridge. I tried to think what to do—but my thinking was too slow.

Jock Shepherd headed across for the fuse. "Ye'ill nae blaw the auld briggie," I heard him say. Two shots rang out. Jock's body fell across the fuse. We fired in the direction of the shots. One had been a flintlock, and we heard a cry of pain and a thump. Luke ran out and ripped out the fuse and gave Jock a firemen's lift back to our side.

I lost my temper. "Bryant, you gutless coward! If I see you, I will kill you! You're a murdering animal!"

"Anytime, boy." Then there was silence. My gut feeling was they had fled. I took my revolver and ran to the other side. It was a risk. Two of the rifle company followed me over. There was a body on the other side. I rummaged through his pockets and got identity. He was signed with the Allegheny—Bryant's ship. He was still alive.

"You gotta get me to a doctor," he pleaded.

"Where is the Allegheny?" I asked. "There will be no doctor until you tell us.

He swore at me and was still.

Dawn was pushing in and I suddenly felt very tired. Luke suggested that we try to move the explosives. It turned out they had wired the struts and we did get all the explosives, or so we hoped.

Jock had been taken to the local doctor, but had died shortly afterwards. It would be my sad and heavy task to tell his wife and sons. I was determined that Jock would get the credit for having stopped the explosion. If there were any heroes, and perhaps remuneration from a grateful town, it belonged to Jock. He had died a hero's death saving others. Guys like Jock were rare. I felt sick and sad inside.

One day Bryant would pay. Surely God would not let that nefarious soul continue his path of plunder and destruction. We were a sad bunch as we headed back to Bellefield.

Mi-Ling seemed a little better. She ran up and threw her arms round my neck. Then she saw Anton. "Uncle Anton, it is good to see you again! My eyes are no longer sad."

Anton picked her up and spun her round. "How is my little cabbage?" Mi-Ling laughed, a sound I had not heard in a long time.

We filled Lucy in on what happened before I prepared to see Jock's widow. Meg would have already heard about her husband's death, but it was my duty to tell her how it happened and the part of a hero that her husband had played. A pall came over Lucy's face. "Will we be ever rid of that cursed man? He is like a disease that won't go away. Do you want me to come with you to see Meg?"

"No. I was with Jock when he got shot. He acted with huge courage. Meg needs to know all this. I guess the eldest of Jock's sons could be the next ghillie?"

"Of course," Lucy agreed. "We must do all we can to help."

Anton was staring out of the window. Meryl was talking to him quietly, with her hand on his arm. Briefly, he leaned his head against the window frame. Then he shook himself slightly, nodded at Meryl, and amazingly to me, gave her a hug before coming over to us.

"It is good to be back here," Anton said to Lucy and me. "I will not be putting the West Prison in Aberdeen on my places to visit for Russian friends. I am just glad you turned up when you did. That place was cold."

"Drew, Meryl, can I talk to you?" Lucy asked. "Maybe after tea. Food first, then conversation. I think Drew needs to eat before he goes to see Meg."

Meryl and I looked at one another apprehensively, then nodded our agreement to Lucy. After a quiet tea, Lucy siphoned Meryl and me into another room. "Sit down," she said. "I have a bee in my bonnet and its not even springtime."

"Well, I can…" I started to say.

Lucy ignored my interruption, and as she continued, I realized that I had hold of the wrong end of the stick.

"Things are going to get hectic for Bryant. With poor Jock's murder and the attempt to blow the bridge. These added to his being an accessory to Sir Charles Gray's death. Bryant is a wanted man. Luke is going to pass on Bryant's details to the American authorities, so that if the Allegheny shows up in an American port and someone has been notified, his ship won't get out."

"Good," Meryl said. It looks as if the noose is tightening."

"Quite so," Lucy agreed. "But do you think Bryant could have any idea about time travel?"

"Time travel from whom?" I asked.

"What about Johnny Branson, that agent who changed sides?" Lucy suggested.

Meryl and I looked at one another.

Lucy continued, "Being told something is one thing. Actually believing what you are being told is another. Time travel may have sounded as far fetched to him as it did to me. I know it's true. He doesn't know it's true, but he may try to put together all the things he was told. The possibility of being able to start again in another time where nobody knows you would appeal to Bryant. Maybe in 1800."

"Or 2000?" I quizzed.

Meryl said, "We don't know what Johnny Branson told them. Did he give away all his cards?"

Lucy frowned. "We thought Bryant was only after revenge. Maybe now he wants a way out. That worries me. I'll never feel safe until he's caught."

I nodded. "We don't even have a photograph of him. We can't give any picture to the staff here so they can keep an eye out for him. Could he know about the house and the basement being where the time car comes in?"

Meryl sighed. "It's impossible to know what he knows. We need something to get his attention. To force his hand. I can think of one thing that will do it."

"What?" Lucy and I said almost simultaneously.

"Announce your wedding. That will force his hand."

"We had a task returning all the presents the first time," Lucy said. "Maybe a quiet wedding."

"No," Meryl objected. "It has to be well known, broadcast. It depends if Bryant's ego is bigger than his fear of getting caught."

"Ego," Lucy asked, "what's that?"

"His big-headedness. The 'no woman messes me around' attitude," Meryl explained. "Now, I'm going to leave the two of you to talk over the idea. I wouldn't leave it too long. I think Anton wants to go home. I can't blame him. It's a decision only you two can make."

Meryl's idea floored me. Lucy looked at me expectantly, waiting. What do I say? I thought. Then to Lucy, "We have to stop Bryant."

"Drew..." Lucy said.

"Nobody is going to get any peace until he is stopped ..."

"Drew ..." Lucy said again.

"He'll probably make his move soon when the announcement goes out."

"Drew!" Lucy said loud enough to get my attention. "Do you love me?" She pushed the question at me.

I gulped. "No, Lucy, I don't. Well, that is...I don't know."

"You knew on the ship, nothing would have separated us." She looked at me and accused, "It's Meryl! You still love Meryl, even though she loves someone else. She's even carrying another man's child. Drew, I can offer you more. I've never been with any man. I can offer you a home and children—your children."

"Lucy, can't we try it out? I forget the words. Marriage of convenience—that's it! Just until Bryant makes his move. Then, once he is stopped, we can part if you want."

"I don't want a marriage of convenience, Drew. I want a husband and children. I want someone to love me, to lie beside me at night. Someone to talk to me and hold my hand and tell me they love me."

"If we marry and go through marriage, we can be like brother and sister. Like friends. Just until Bryant makes his move. It would make Mi-Ling happy. Then we can decide."

"Drew, do I have to spell it out? I love you! Don't make me beg." Her voice fell to a whisper.

My grandmother had once told me, "that which we love can so easily turn to hate." If Lucy started to hate me, it would make Bryant's job two hundred percent easier. Divide and conquer and you are home and dry. "Look," I told Lucy. "Just let me sleep on it. I just want to be sure. Tomorrow, I promise. I'll give you an answer tomorrow."

I needed to go out for a walk to clear my head and seek surcease for my wretched heart, and I needed to tell Jock's family what had happened. I found Meg Shepherd surrounded by her sons, and by neighbors who left when I got to the cottage. She had a gentle voice with a musical lilt. I tried to tell her how sorry I was, but words proved illusive and ineffective.

"It's funny Captain Faulkner," Meg mused. "Jock regretted leaving the army. He was scared of growing old." She dried her eyes with her handkerchief. She reminded me of a wounded swan missing its mate. "Jock was scared of being useless. Now people will remember him for a courageous act and he could have wanted no more than that." The swan's head bent down.

"When Jock saw that the fuse off the explosives was heading towards the bridge," I told Meg, "he acted. There was no thinking twice. 'Y'ill nae blaw the auld briggie,' he yelled. He got killed, but his body fell across the fuse and put it out. One of the two guns that fired was killed by our return fire but the leader got away." Meg and I looked into the fire as if it held answers we lacked. "You stay here rent free," I added. "It's the least we can do. The cottage is yours for as long as you need it."

She took my hands in hers. "Thank you, Captain. Thank you."

"Meg it should have been me that went across first, my body lying across the bridge."

She smiled and shook her head. "You have your whole life ahead. I'm sure Jock would have been glad to know that you and Miss Lucy and the wee lassie Mi-Ling will be happy together. God bless you and I wish you a long and happy life."

Somehow her words made my decision much more difficult. Before I left the cottage, I found that Andy Shepherd would take over his father's job. I tried to describe Bryant and asked him to inform me if he saw him.

Then the bombshell hit. Tam Shepherd, the youngest son, came running out. "Captain! Captain! Can I have a minute of your time?"

"Surely. Tam, isn't it?"

"Aye, sir."

"What can I do for you Tam?"

Suddenly, he became very mature. "Sir, the man who murdered my father. Do you know what he looks like? Can we not put up his likeness everywhere so that people will recognize him?"

"No, Tam. I wish we could. But we don't have a picture of him."

He looked around, as if he did not want anyone to hear him, and dropped his voice. "Sir, when I am not working, I love to draw. My brothers make fun of me. Dad didn't. Maybe I could draw a picture of Bryant from what you say. We can rub out something if it's not right. By the time we are done, it might be enough for folks to spot him. We can start as soon as you like."

"We have soft lead pencils up at the house and erasers. Can you come this evening about seven?"

"Aye, sir." And he ran off.

When I got back to the house, I told Lucy and Anton about Tam's offer and asked them to rake their memories.

"Tam will do the face one part at a time. We say yes or no or how it can be improved. If we can get Tam's drawing lithographed, then Bryant's face could soon be all over the place."

We felt as if perhaps now we were close to being able to strike back. Of course, it depended how good an artist Tam Shepherd was.

It turned out that Tam was as good an artist as his father had been a ghillie. With our help, two hours after Tam arrived, Bryant's face began to appear. Tam nearly choked when I gave him £30 and insisted on him drawing a second copy. I explained, "We can get one of these to the police, they will be happy to get it."

Mi- Ling, who had been watching Tam at work, asked if he would draw her picture.

"No Mi-Ling," I objected quickly. "Mr. Shepherd is busy. He has got a lot to do."

Tam smiled at Mi-Ling. "For this wee lassie, I will become unbusy. Now you must promise to smile. I canna draw frowny faces."

Mi-Ling giggled. "Mi-Ling promise to smile for Mr. Tam."

"Now, Miss Faulkner, ye muaun bide still. Still as a moosie when the cat's aboot."

Miss Faulkner. What Tam said hit me like a sledge hammer. I looked over at Lucy. I knew she had picked up the same message of what folk were thinking. I watched Tam as his hand flew over the paper .There was something in his eyes—as if he were drawing Mi-Ling's heart on paper. He caught the smile, the look, the wide eyes and the trust. He could look at her and bring out the best. All traces of Mi-Ling's seemingly chronic illness vanished under his touch. Tam was a gifted man and he did not even realize how gifted.

Mi-Ling looked at the drawing and smiled in joy. Then, slowly, her tiredness returned and it was as if her flame had gone out.

"Leave the drawing wi' me," Tam promised Mi-Ling, "an I will do a second one for you."

I thanked him and Tam said if he came again he would tell Mi-Ling stories about the animals in the woods. He wished Mi-Ling goodnight, as did we, and Mrs. Fraser took her up to bed.

Dinner was a subdued affair. Anton said it was time for him to be getting back home. Meryl accidentally knocked over a Mycenae vase. "Miss Scott," Lucy raged, "did you have to be so clumsy? That was a very expensive vase. And a very thoughtless gesture from a guest who has been so well treated!"

"I'm sorry, Lucy. I didn't do it intentionally."

"I wonder what you do do intentionally. Like stealing other people's fiancés."

"Pardon?"

"Don't play innocent. I know what your plan is. It's a pity you are carrying another man's child. You sit there night after night, pretending to be what you never can be, while you hatch wicked schemes. You should be ashamed of yourself! Flaunting yourself and throwing yourself at Drew. A lady would have more respect for herself."

My mouth fell open.

Meryl made an attempt to control her anger. "Speaking of schemes, Lucy, just who put forward the idea of you and Drew getting married again?"

Enraged, Lucy drew in her breath and spat, "A cover! A lie! A wicked, deceitful lie! You hoped that it would make Drew turn back to you again in spite of being with another man's child. And, anyway, you hoped we wouldn't have to go through with the marriage! You don't want Drew to marry me—you want him for yourself. And you've been..."

"Lucy, stop it!" I ordered.

"No, Drew. It's time I had my say, so I am going to have it! I'm sick of all the slyness and pretense! I don't deserve to be treated like this! I haven't done anything wrong!"

Her words stung. She was right about one thing—she hadn't done anything wrong.

Luke got up from the table. "Well, Miss Oxford, you won't be troubled with my presence much longer. It's more than time I was getting back to my unit. To tell the truth, after tonight I will be glad to get out of here. Real glad. I hate histrionics."

Anton looked up from his plate and shook his head. "I know what happens when thieves fall out, but when the watchdogs fall out, then it is easier for the wolf to get amongst the lambs. You've just done Bryant's job for him, Lucy. You've accomplished in five minutes what he couldn't do in months. Congratulations. You should be in politics."

Anton looked at Luke. "Captain Carter, I will share a coach with you tomorrow. I, too, need to wire a passage home."

"Look what you've done now, Lucy," I sputtered. "Got everyone upset and mad. They're all leaving. That means I leave, too. We're not married yet. I can't stay here alone with you until we are. The folks around here wouldn't stand for such obscenity. It's the wrong century. So I guess you will be facing Bryant alone when he shows up again."

"I'll wire Carolyn. She'll come stay with me and help me."

Luke commented, "It may have escaped your attention, but Carolyn is married now. She may value her husband's company over yours. Bryant and his gang come along and Mi-Ling's defense is you, Carolyn and Mrs. Fraser? When he sees the coaches leave, Bryant will be rubbing his hands in glee. Well done, Lucy."

Meryl said, "Please. The rest of you stay until you catch Bryant. I'll leave. I'm the problem. I'll pack and be out of here first."

Meryl left the dinning room and we all followed suit, leaving unfinished food on our plates.

CHAPTER 12

Dear God what a mess! I had come to the end of my tether. I could go back to my old job. I had run on shallow, empty living all my life and another few years would not make any difference. Anton would go back to Russia. Luke would go home to Texas. I had thought he was attracted to Lucy, but he seemed to have suddenly recovered from that attraction. As for Lucy, she could join her mother in modern times. No miracles, no happy endings—but, hey! What was new about that? That was life. Reality. And sometimes, real life stunk like rotten onions.

But what about Mi-Ling? I asked myself. Then I remembered that Meryl had lied to Lucy about the baby because she loved me. She was willing to give up everything and stand aside to watch the person she loved marry another because she thought it was best for him.

"Oh, God, please help me," I begged out loud.

The answer flowed in, startling me. "How about the shark, the snakes, the pirates, not getting shot, surviving knife attacks—how am I doing? Or is there something else you would like? Faith, Drew, is not just believing God can, but that He will. I can help you through this, but not if you run away. I have entrusted you with Mi-Ling. You must trust Me, even if things seem to get worse before they get better."

"I am finding it hard, Lord, to think of an event that got worse before it got better."

"How about Jesus dying on the cross before He arose to live forever? Drew, trust me."

I fell asleep on the top of the bed and woke minus my shoes. Lucy must have come in and removed them while I was sleeping to make me more comfortable. Could that possibly mean that she didn't altogether hate me? And why should I be eager to assume that—as if it mattered? Today had to be faced and I could not run anymore. God promised to help and I knew I was going to need it.

I washed and went downstairs. Lucy was there by the table. "Drew I said some things last night I shouldn't have said. I gave vent to anger and I hurt you and everyone else. I'm sorry."

"Meryl dropped that vase by accident. And she's not pregnant."

"What? Why would she say...how do you know?"

"Colonel Carlisle told me that all female operatives get an effective but reversible surgical procedure done to stop them from getting pregnant. To protect them in case of rape or other dangers."

"Why did she say she was?" Lucy asked

"You're a woman. Why do you think? Meryl doesn't know that I know she's not pregnant. In Virginia, we were away for weeks. Meryl had been told that we had all been massacred. That meant she was effectively stuck there. Kitchi, the Native American, had helped us. He was the one who found the Kairon to get us back home. Like 1867, in 1750, a woman needed a man's protection. I don't know if anything took place between them. She may have been saying that to push me towards you, thinking that it would be the best thing for all of us."

At that point Anton came down. Lucy went over to him and said sweetly, "Anton, I want to apologize for my outburst last night. You have been such a big help—and an entertaining guest and companion, as well. Please forgive me."

He smiled broadly. "Old Russian saying: Whether a rose blooms in a palace or a prison, she is still a rose. Maybe this palace has become a prison for you. Just now it is a very cold prison. I wonder if someone has left a door open someplace."

Lucy kissed his cheek and thanked him. "You're right about the cold, Anton. Yet, the fire is still burning. It shouldn't be so cold."

Luke, who had gone for a walk before breakfast, came through the front door and hung his coat in the hall. Lucy hurried over to him, and I couldn't hear their words. There was nodding and Luke pointed upstairs towards the direction of Meryl's room. Then he kissed her cheek, and she looked relieved.

Meryl came down and it was this moment that Lucy had been

waiting for. The autumn color of Lucy's hair moved in rich waves as she nodded or shook her head. Meryl's blonde hair nodded and she looked over at me.

Luke looked around and asked, "Is Mi-Ling feeling worse? I know she's seemed fatigued and a bit ill at times, but she's usually here to greet all of us with a cheery good morning. Has she been down for breakfast already?"

Conversation stopped. Everybody looked around. Heads shook from side to side. "I'll check on her," Lucy said.

We had returned to our breakfast when there was a loud scream from upstairs from the direction of Mi-Ling's room. Forks clattered on plates as chairs were rudely shoved away from the table. All of us ran to Mi-Ling's room .The window was wide open and fingers of cold invaded the house. Mi-Ling's bed was ruffled and a blanket was missing. Most frighteningly, Mi-Ling was missing.

Lucy cried hysterically, a note clutched in her hand. "I found this on Mi-Ling's bed," she sobbed, holding it out to me.

Never had I felt so cold and bereft as I did then when I spotted Bryant's name at the end of the tirade: I have the Chinese girl. I am a fair man I will do a straight swap. My Lucy for the girl. I know about time travel and it can be my way of getting out of here for me. You have caused me a lot of trouble. You all thought you were going to live happily ever after but that goes for me too. When Lucy marries me, then I will release the girl. Oh, I wish I could see your faces. If you don't agree, the Chinese girl will be sold to a very busy child bordello I know of, and you will never see her again. I will be in touch later. No tricks, or the girl dies. I have nothing to lose now.

I passed the note to Luke who read it and noted, "I could be wrong, but this looks like a woman's handwriting."

Anton broke into Russian then said, "I lost my daughter. Not again. I'm going to do all I can to make sure you don't lose yours. I'll kill him if I see him."

"Lucy, Drew, I am so sorry," Meryl said, tears in blue eyes testifying to the truthfulness of her words. "I'll go tell Colonel Carlisle and the

155

others, but I will come back quickly. I don't want Anton ending up in prison again."

"A sentiment for which I am most grateful," Anton acknowledged.

Luke took charge. "Okay, everybody. Back downstairs and we have a council of war. Drew, you might want to close that window so we don't all freeze while we plan."

As terrible as Mi-Ling's kidnapping was, it served to pull us back together into a solid unit. Then I remembered God's words, "Trust Me even if things seem appear to get worse before they get better."

"First," Luke directed, "we need to get that picture of Mi-Ling that Tam drew and get it to the sheriff. They can copy it and have her picture all over the place. Offer a reward. That will sharpen people's vision."

He turned to me and asked, "Would Tam take the pictures he drew of Mi-Ling and Bryant along to the magistrate?"

"I'm sure he would," I said. "He would do anything to help catch the man who murdered his father."

Luke nodded and continued giving orders. "Lucy, you must go about armed at all times. Meryl, you get back to your HQ. Tell them what has happened and if your time is as advanced as you've said, then won't they have a file or details on Bryant that might help? Check on it, please. Drew, you guard Lucy. Remember, she's the target. Mi-Ling is only the decoy. Anton, you and I can go around and search the ground from Mi-Ling's window. We have both tracked before, and I've even found children who were kidnapped by Indians and returned them to their parents. Believe it or not, some of them didn't want to go back to their families. They wanted to stay with the Indian tribe that had adopted them."

Luke paused, "The girl, Connie—Mi Ling's play friend—has a dog. His nose might be put to good use. He would know Mi-Ling's scent. It would be worth a try. It's ten o'clock. Let's reconvene at five this afternoon. Any questions?"

No one had questions. "Good. Don't worry. We'll find her. Okay, let's go."

I contacted Andy Shepherd, through Mrs. Fraser, and gave him the details of what had happened. Mrs. Fraser said she would get Tam to take the pictures along, and would check on Meg, as well. I was afraid to leave Lucy alone.

Lucy and I went into the living room together. Now what do I say? I wondered. "Are you going to go through with this marriage?" I asked. "To Bryant?"

"We have to get Mi-Ling back," she said evenly. "That comes first. I think if I found Bryant, I would kill him."

"You don't often talk like that."

She crossed to the window and looked out, but her eyes looked hurt and dead—not up to the task of really seeing anything at the moment.

"No Lucy," I warned. Stay away from the window. He might be out there. We're dealing with someone unbalanced who would kill his own mother and then look for someone else to blame. He's never wrong, everyone else is."

"Drew, I think it's this place. We've been unhappy here since we arrived. If I believed in luck, I would say it was a bad luck place." She put her hands behind her back and began to pace the floor, her skirt making a gentle swish as she walked back and forth.

"I think I have an idea." I said.

Lucy stopped pacing and turned to face me. "What idea can you have?" Then she thought for a moment and added, "I'm sorry. I didn't mean that the way it sounded. What's your idea?"

"The other thing that must be close on Bryant's mind is revenge. He's been seriously upset, whatever his plan was. Killing me, if the chance is offered, might suddenly climb to the top of his agenda. I love Mi-Ling. I want to adopt her. But equally, I can't ask you just to pass yourself over to Bryant. I still remember Sir Charles Gray's ball and the girl I danced with. You deserve the best Lucy. If I challenge Bryant to a dual and give him the chance to shoot me, we might get Mi-Ling back. It might be enough. He might not kill me—just wound. In a duel, the challenger has the right to have the pistols reloaded until honor is satisfied."

Alan T. McKean

She gasped and stood staring at me, wide-eyed. "Drew, I can't let you do that! You're brave and courageous to even think of that, and I thank you, but..."

"You can't not let me do it. I'm not handing you over to Bryant without a fight."

"What will Meryl say? I know she loves you."

"Lucy, I'm tired. I never meant to, but I've wound up hurting a lot of people. I can't take the past back and build it up the way I should have built it to begin with, but now, Bryant has to be stopped. That I can do."

Lucy began pacing again. "Have you told Luke about this?"

I took a deep breath. "It's not his concern. He's a good guy, but this is something only I can do."

"Luke will never agree to this."

"Then we don't tell him. It's that simple."

"How are you going to contact Bryant?" she asked.

"He said he would contact us. So we leave him a message."

"Where can you leave it?"

"Pinned to the front door after everyone else has gone to bed. Bryant is watching this place, or having it watched. He will know that any message will be for him. All we can do is pray that he will respond in the way we want him to. There are dueling pistols in the gun room. I assume they still work. Anton will know all the rules."

When I looked into her tender green eyes, I saw my wavering reflection through her tears. Lucy whispered, "No one has ever cared enough about me to do something like this for me before."

"Yes, they have, Lucy," I reminded her. "It was you who told me of what Jesus had done for you and for all of us. He defeated the one in a dual that could be killed by no physical weapon. Compared to that—this is easy."

I thought for a moment, then added, "I can leave a message written in such a way that Bryant's manly pride can't ignore it. Once he has accepted, then we can tell the others. We can't back out once the challenge is offered. Otherwise, Mi-Ling will be in real danger.

"Perhaps you're right about this house, Lucy. Maybe you could be happy with Luke. He certainly would be happy with you. I do want you to be happy, Lucy. Our life since we came here reminds me of one of the most tragic Italian operas ever written. It's about a girl who is forced to marry the wrong man instead of the person she loves. It's by the Italian composer Donizetti, written about thirty-two years ago. She, in a fit of madness, kills the man she doesn't love but was forced to marry. When it is announced outside the castle that Lucia has died of a broken heart, the man who loves her kills himself, rather than attempting to live without her. His hope is that they will be reunited in Heaven. The opera is called Lucia di Lammermoor. Lucia is your name in Italian."

Lucy sighed and nodded. "I know the book on which it was based. The Bride of Lammermoor by Sir Walter Scott."

We waited and talked and read until the five o'clock deadline that Luke had set, when everyone started coming back as per Luke's suggestion. The drawings of Bryant and Mi-Ling were in the right hands and would be distributed as soon as possible. The printers were working all night to get the picture of Mi-Ling up by morning. We had offered a reward of £300, which was a great deal of money in 1867.

Anton and Luke had failed in tracking Mi-Ling and Bryant. "We lost the signs shortly after the house," Luke said grimly, "and then not even the dog could get anywhere."

I decided not to share my plan with the others, even though with Luke and Anton's failure to make progress, it seemed my plan would have to come to the fore. If I killed Bryant, we would never find Mi-Ling. I had to aim to wound him. He, on the other hand, with great delight, would aim to kill me.

Dinner was ready and there was still no sign of Meryl. Nobody had seen her. Maybe she was following up some clue. She had promised to come back. Perhaps Colonel Carlisle had detained her or had refused to let her come back because of the danger. I didn't know.

The steak and kidney pie was good. We were just beginning to appreciate it when Meryl appeared at the dining room door. "What's a girl got to do to get some food around here?" she asked jokingly.

"It's not been a good day," I said, "so by all means join us and enjoy the food—but forgive the somber mood."

"Oh. Sorry." She paused and then asked Luke, "How did you guys get on in tracking Mi-Ling?"

He took a deep breath and admitted, "Not good. We got nowhere. I thought there would be more signs—more indicators to follow. She and Bryant seem to have just vanished."

The resulting silence could be cut with a knife or any other sharp instrument that came to hand.

"I know someone who could find Mi-Ling," Meryl said quietly.

"Who?" Three voices simultaneously.

"Kitchi."

"Who is Kitchi?" Luke asked.

"A Red Indian from 1755."

Lucy nearly choked on her food. "But he's in 1750. What good does that do us now?"

"Err…well, I took the precaution of bringing him with me, which is why I'm late for Luke's deadline."

Lucy's face brightened. "Well, don't keep the poor man out in the cold! Bring him in."

Meryl stuck her head round the corner of the dining room door. "Kitchi, Eagle Heart, please come in."

We never heard a sound as he entered the room. We all had the grace to stand up. He wore a coat of furs and thick shoes on his feet. He carried a pack, his rifle and a knife. I felt a sharp jab of pain under my ribs. He was an even more attractive man than I remembered, big, bold, strong. Even Lucy seemed awed.

Kitchi surveyed the room. "Your lodge is big. There must be many families here."

"No, only one," I said, feeling a bit guilty and decadent from the sheer opulence of Bellefield.

Kitchi greeted Luke and Anton as they were introduced, then looked at me. "Maybe you are troubled that I am here?"

"No, Kitchi. Believe me: it does my heart good, for I understand the wisdom of She With Sun in Her Hair's action in bringing you here. And I thank you for being willing to come."

"Eat something" Lucy invited.

He shook his head. "There will be time to eat later. Even though the sun is not in the sky, I will take a torch and see what can be discovered. When you are looking for the tracks of a rabbit, they are more easily seen before a herd of buffalo passes over them."

Anton smiled. "I like this man. He has his own old Russian sayings."

Kitchi went outside and disappeared into the night.

Meryl said to Lucy. "If anyone can find them quickly, it's Kitchi.

The rest of us were back to waiting. There was a professional on the job. Kitchi came in thirty minutes later carrying a hair ribbon. "Does this belong to the little one?" he asked Lucy.

She looked at it, brushed tears from her eyes and replied softly, "Yes. That's Mi-Ling's."

He took it back. "Thank you. That's good to know." He melted back out into the night.

I had to get the challenge letter written, but I couldn't leave it on the front door. Not only because Kitchi would read it, but also because not even Bryant—as quiet as he thought he was—could fool a Native American. If Bryant came to look at the message or to put up a reply, he would be caught, or at least seen.

Regardless of where I found to post the note, I must write it. I couldn't expect Bryant to respond to a note that hadn't been written. So I wrote, "Well done, Bryant, hiding behind an eleven-year-old girl. A real manly thing to do in an attempt to win the woman you say you love. I'm the one who has caused you the trouble ever since the governor's ball in Foochow. You remember Sir Charles Gray, the man you had murdered? You had to get your whippet, Lancaster, to do it because you weren't man enough to do it yourself. Why don't you fight me? I challenge you to a duel with pistols. You can bring your own second. You kill me—Lucy is yours. If you are man enough. Stop hiding in the shadows and come out and face me. 'Unfinished business, boy,' you have told me three times now. Okay, I challenge you. Let's finish it."

"Let me have your answer."

I took it along to show Lucy. "Phew," she said. "Where are you going to put it so Bryant will see it?"

"On the oak tree along the drive just as you come in view of the house." I replied.

I guessed I would be safe taking it down there. Bryant had Mi-Ling. He wanted Lucy. I hoped that once he saw the invitation, he would want revenge more than he thought he wanted Lucy.

Before I went out, I went to the gun room and found the pair of dueling pistols. They were of good quality, made by Joseph Manton of London. I picked one up and discovered that it was heavy. I had made the challenge. Bryant, if he took it, would get the choice of pistol. In a duel, it was best to stand side-on with your head down, giving your opponent as small a target as possible. After that, I hated to think what would happen. In Leo Tolstoy's book, War and Peace, the inexperienced Pierre fought a duel with his wife's lover, Dolokov, and wounded him, even though Pierre stood facing Dolokov's gun, making the widest possible target.

This, however, would not be from the pages of fiction. It was real life and the balls which lay in the case were real.

I had not heard Anton come in, and didn't know he was there until he spoke from behind me. "Are you thinking of fighting a duel?"

"Yes. Err, no. Well, kind of."

"You sound like a nervous bridegroom when the priest asks if he will marry the woman standing next to him."

"I wasn't going to say anything till my challenge had been accepted."

"You are going to challenge Bryant to a duel over the woman you love. You must have Russian ancestors. Old Russian saying. 'A man looks different when you are staring down his pistol barrel.' Even Bryant." He shook his head.

"Even Bryant?" I echoed "I can't just hand Lucy over to him. And if I can wound him, the pain might cause him to tell us where Mi-Ling is, in exchange for medical help."

"Does Luke know? Or Svetlana—sorry, Meryl. It's a pity—she

does make an alluring Svetlana."

I shook my head, "No, to both. I'm just going down to pin my challenge to an oak tree where I hope Bryant will see it without Kitchi seeing him. I invited Bryant to bring his own second."

Anton chuckled. "If it is the kind of company Mr. Bryant keeps, you had better hide the silver and lock this gun room. You need to tell the others."

I took a hammer and nails from the house and went to the tree, hoping Bryant would see the notice before it rained. Scotland was famous for its copious rain.

The others were playing cards when I returned and there was no sign of Kitchi. I guessed he was still tracking. We had asked Mrs. Fraser to feed Kitchi what he wanted, when he wanted it. How Bryant would find to reply with Kitchi around was up to him. I imagined that he was inventive enough to find a way.

Suddenly, Luke blurted out, "You challenged Bryant to a duel?" So Lucy had told him. "Are you crazy?"

"No, just trying to force the issue. My plan is to wound him and make him disclose Mi-Ling's location in exchange for medical help."

"Drew," Meryl said. "Don't put your life at risk. Please. Maybe Kitchi will find Mi-Ling."

"That would be wonderful. Then I wouldn't have to stop at wounding Bryant. I could just kill him and rid the world of at least one evil."

"Have you ever fired a dueling pistol before?" Anton asked.

"No," I said. "But it can't be that difficult."

"I have heard others say that," Anton expounded, "and they all have one common factor." "I probably will regret asking, but what is that my friend?"

"They are all in the cemetery. Dueling is not as easy as it looks."

Meryl said, "Drew, there has to be another way to save Mi-Ling and Lucy."

"Yes," Lucy agreed. "Drew, I'm being selfish to let you even contemplate this. It's me that Bryant wants. He can have me. Anything to save Mi-Ling and stop this duel!"

"Look," I said. "I've put out the challenge. Let's see what the response is. Meantime, Anton, would you act as my second? And I sure could use any tips you have."

"Old Russian saying—eemigrate. And look how successful we were at that. Very!"

The conversation ebbed and flowed. The duel between Aaron Burr and Alexander Hamilton was mentioned and the duel in literature in War and Peace. Everyone except Lucy knew of duels.

One by one, they drifted off to bed. I sat by the fire and the house echoed to the crackle of the fire. The expression, the long watches of the night, came to mind. There was some coffee left that had been put out for supper, and I finished it. All of it. Then I took out my wallet. Inside was Meryl's picture, the one she had given me before I left for China. I sighed. I remembered her laugh and her smile and her warmth and passion. I remembered how when she was with me I felt life had a purpose. She would drink her cappuccino and the foam off it would give her a blonde moustache and I would smile and say, Mmm…it really suits you. Then she would wonder what I meant and wipe it off and giggle. I remembered how we used to hold hands and drink each other in with eyes that noticed nothing else. I hadn't realized just how deeply my love for her went. Suddenly, even with a lot of money and a big house and all the trappings, I would look forward to sleep, because in my dreams, I could get back to Meryl. I could kiss her, and hold her hand, and tell her how beautiful she was. The thought of being without Meryl made life empty. I closed my eyes and said out loud, "Meryl, darling, I love you. Time won't stop me from loving you. Who knows? Perhaps one day."

The answering voice was so soft and lovely that for a moment I thought I had fallen asleep and was dreaming. "Everyday when you were away, I would go out under the stars and hug myself and pretend it was you. Even when they told me you all had been killed, I prayed that somehow it was false and you and Angus had survived."

Meryl stood behind me. She wore a long tartan dress and her blonde hair had a tartan band woven into it. She looked the epitome of the word "beautiful."

We talked. "I know you were not bearing Kitchi's child. Colonel Carlisle told me about the pregnancy prevention that Vanguard operatives get. But why did you tell me that in front of Lucy?"

She walked over and sat by the fire. Every turn of her head caused her hair to shimmer. "I wanted to make it easy for you and Lucy if that was what you wanted."

"Do you love him?" I asked, not really wanting to hear her answer. "I'm guessing the answer is yes, or he wouldn't be here. It doesn't matter if you do love Kitchi. I still love you and I want you to be happy. You are to me the filter through which I look at life, a filter that makes everything beautiful."

She patted the seat beside her. "Come and sit beside me my darling, my only darling. Firstly, Kitchi is married. When you were gone and I thought all was lost—still my heart could not give you up. I knew if anyone had survived, it would be you, especially with Angus close at hand. Kitchi's eldest son took an infection and was dying. I had antibiotics—part of the kit we get—and they worked. The boy was healed. Kitchi said that he was in my debt and if I needed him, he would come. Yes, he is a very handsome man, but he is also happily married and his wife was kind to me and to Sebastian. He is here to help with no wampum expected."

She took out a handkerchief and caught the tears that were unexpectedly rolling down my cheeks. "I thought I had lost you for good," I whispered.

Big hero, me—I began to sob. Meryl took my head and laid it on her lap and I felt the desire for life and living flow back into me. "Hush, my darling. Don't cry. I'm here for you." She stroked my hair and kissed me.

The Lord had warned me: Drew, things may seem to get worse before they start to get better. Even with a dual facing me, nothing could better than trusting that God was in control, and that I had not lost the woman I loved with every fiber of my being.

CHAPTER 13

Meryl and I decided to say nothing of the rediscovery of our love. Now I had a reason to live. Early in the morning, I went to the oak tree. The note was gone. There was no reply, as yet. It made me realize there was a lot to be said for the internet and the speed of modern communication.

Anton was at breakfast. When he saw me said, "You need shooting practice, if you are to survive. Rule One: Always eat a good breakfast. Never fight a duel on an empty stomach."

After breakfast, we went into the basement and piled up sacks and padding.

Anton instructed me. "You start off back to back. You both walk ten paces, and then turn and fire. The pistols are primed and cocked, ready for firing."

He hammered a post into the ground and pinned a piece of an old packing case. "That's Bryant. I know, it's better looking than him, but bear with me. Balance the pistol in your hand. Now, aim. Hold it steady! You're waving about like grain in the wind."

So we aimed and held, aimed and held. Then he loaded the pistol.

"Ten paces." He counted them out. "Turn, aim, fire."

When I pulled the trigger and the pistol fired, I missed. I had not expected such a kick.

Anton shook his head. "Look. Watch like the hawk." He loaded the pistol and went through the procedure. His hand was steady and the bullet smashed into the center of the plank. "It may be that Bryant has not shot that many pistols," he mused. "He gets other people to pull his triggers."

We practiced until lunchtime and Anton loaded the second pistol and we had a real duel minus the bullet. On each occasion, Anton fired first and I was a second behind him. To survive, I had to get my shot off first.

I was a bit down and Meryl picked up on it. She could convey love and encouragement with her eyes. I remembered the feel of my head in her lap, her fingers caressing my head. The chance to experience that again was my reason to survive the duel with Bryant. It is easy to love someone when the sun shines. But when everything seems to go wrong, it takes the love of a person who will still be there, even in the dark. Meryl was my shining light, especially at times when I felt God was far away. Yet, I was just beginning to learn that when God seems far away—that's often when He's the closest.

Anton was a good teacher. Bryant's reply to my challenge came, not in some dramatic form, but through one of the estate children giving Mrs. Fraser a note for me in exchange for a cookie. Bryant accepted. He would bring a second and there would be no tricks. He would be glad to see the end of me. I guess I did always bring the best out in people. If the worst did come to the worst, then Meryl would be with me. I hoped that if I did die, it would be in her arms. Well, okay, maybe I did watch too much opera—but as Anton had said, "a man looks different when you are staring down his pistol barrel."

The duel was set for morning. Bryant said in his note he wanted to celebrate killing me, and that he had a wedding to plan, for he wanted to be sure that Lucy would enjoy her marriage bed. He also had plans for the "Chinese girl." I knew if I dwelt on all Bryant had written, I would crack. Luke and Kitchi were still diligently searching for Mi-Ling and Luke had said enthusiastically that he was learning as lot from Kitchi about tracking. At least his sabbatical would have paid dividends.

I'm not sure how to write now in my diary. It's the morning of the duel. How do I feel? Scared.

Bryant brought his second, Major Otis Brand, whom Luke recognized as a confederate officer who had changed sides. "It seemed expedient so to do," Brand explained. I suppose Benedict Arnold had thought the same thing. The look on Luke's face showed the fact that there would have been a queue for the pistols had things been different.

The pistols were loaded to both parties' satisfaction.

Whether I get to write anymore in this journal remains to be seen. I prayed, "Oh God don't let it end here. Let me have years with Meryl, in Jesus name."

It's strange but the words that are in my mind are Jesus' words, "The thief comes only to steal kill and destroy, but I have come that they might have life and have it abundantly."

Well time to go. Time to let go and let God.

****

Drew had been so careful to keep this journal of all that had happened to all of us that I wanted to continue it after my darling got shot.

Drew walked out into the morning sunshine. Bryant and Brand, looking very pompous, were at the other end. That grinning oaf was the one who had nearly killed me in China. After Drew got me back to the time machine, they got me to hospital just in time. The surgeons and doctors did a brilliant job. I guess I hung between living and dying for days. It's stupid the things you think of. I wished I could get my hair washed. I must have looked a sight. Then, bit by bit, they let me up. The wound hurt, but hurt of the body heals. Colonel Carlisle came to see me. "Meryl," he had said, "I'm so glad you are starting to recover. I'm going to give you the choice. We can transfer you to lighter duties or patch you up, if you will pardon the expression, and send you back. It will take a bit for you to get up to an adequate level of fitness, but Angus and Anna—you'll remember her. Our Swedish dancing teacher and gymnastics instructor at headquarters—the one who taught Drew to dance before he left for China—they can help you."

"Sir," I had asked, "Is there any word of Drew?"

Colonel Carlisle had smiled. "To our knowledge, he's fine. You like him don't you?"

"Is it that obvious?" I had asked.

"Noooo, Meryl," he had joked. "You hide it very well."

I hoped that my acting ability had improved. I hoped that I was hiding my fear now. When the man you love could die, it plays havoc with the female emotions. I ran to Drew and kissed him in front of the others. "I love you. I will always love you, my darling."

Even in the face of danger, he smiled. I could see the sparkle of glad tears in his eyes. "And I still owe you a trip to SavaJava and a brownie... so pray for me, Darling." We kissed again. He touched my cheek and walked unwaveringly toward waiting Death.

Anton intonated the rules. The only one I heard was the one that struck fear into my heart: "On the tenth pace, turn and fire at your leisure."

Drew started walking the ten paces. I stood where he could see me. I looked as lovingly at him as I could. My insides were screaming, No! No! No! Don't let it happen! I could hear my heart thumping in my ears.

I have no clear memory of what happened. They turned and fired. Drew fell back. He had been shot. I felt sick to my stomach and cried out to him.

Bryant was untouched. Drew levered himself on one arm, obviously in pain. Blood ran down one arm.

Then Brand went over to Bryant and Bryant shook his head. Brand turned and his next words chilled me to the core. "As the one who was challenged, Captain Bryant says that honor is not satisfied, and that the pistols are to be reloaded and a second round take place."

Not caring what Lucy or anyone else thought, I ran over to Drew. His lovely face was ashen. He seemed to think humor was a panacea. "It only hurts when I laugh," he said. "Brand is right. I did the challenging. He is entitled to a second shot." Then the big puppy dog eyes filled with tears. "I don't want to die," he said, "because I want time with you. I don't want to lose you."

The pistols were reloaded. Drew took his, but he hardly had the strength to lift it.

"Come on, boy," Bryant mocked. "Remember, we were going to finish it .Your woman is going to look real cute in black." And he started to laugh.

All I can say it was at this point that God stepped in. Kitchi and Luke came running over and Kitchi whispered something to Lucy. She emitted a glad cry, and looking up into the sky shouted, "Thank You God!" Then she diverted her attention to Bryant, "Mi-Ling has been found," she spat. "You have no hold over us now."

Kitchi smiled and assured Drew, "The little one is well."

Even from where I was, I could see the glad relief on Drew's pained face and the color draining from Bryant's face. Bryant said in a voice that was anything but confident, "I'm entitled to my second shot."

"He is," Drew rasped, stumbling slightly and clenching his wounded arm in pain.

"Don't you dare die on me!" I ordered, flinging my arms round his neck.

What happened next struck all of us with awe and disbelief. Lucy calmly walked over to where Drew and I stood together and picked up the pistol. "Is this thing loaded?" she asked in a quiet, menacing voice.

"Yes," I told her. "Anton would do it properly."

Fearlessly, Lucy faced Bryant. "Come on, Bryant. Come and get your second shot."

His eyes opened wide. For all his hubris, the man was speechless.

Brand interrupted. "All this is highly incorrect my ..."

Luke's voice cut across. "Shut up, Brand, you traitor, or so help me I will drop you where you stand." He produced a six-shot pistol.

Lucy walked slowly toward Bryant. "Come on, Bryant, you cowardly pig! Come and get your second shot."

Lucy was like a two-footed tigress. I could not help admiring her, even as I held onto Drew, keeping him upright.

"I won't shoot you." Bryant stammered. "I can't shoot you."

"Well, mister, you had better try, because I'm going to shoot you. You've ruined my life. I would never, never, NEVER marry a gutless murderer like you. Now, I believe it's ten steps. I will fire on the tenth and blow a hole in you head. You killed Sir Charles Gray in China..."

"It was Lancaster who did that, Lucy. Honest."

"You couldn't be honest about where your rear end is, you gutless wonder." I think all of us gasped at the unexpected and un-ladylike language. It was un-Lucy. She continued, "Lancaster pulled the trigger, but you loaded the gun, didn't you?" She pulled back the hammer.

"Yes," he admitted, in an attempt to calm her.

"You kidnapped Mi-Ling. That's her name. Mi-Ling. Say it."

When he remained mute, she screamed, "SAY IT" and took her eyes off Bryant for just a second. His pistol was up and he pulled the trigger. There was a click. The pistol had misfired or not fired, or whatever had happened.

"Now it's my turn," Lucy intoned quietly, raising the pistol. Bryant dropped his gun and fell to his knees. "Don't shoot me, Lucy, darling," he begged. "I will give you anything you want. Please don't shoot. Please. Please." And disgustingly, the evil man began sobbing.

Lucy was unmoved. "On the count of three," her voice cracked like a whip. "One..."

"Dear God, she is going to do it," Drew whispered.

"Two..."

"Lucy! For the love of God! No! No!" Bryant cried, wetting himself.

"You have no love for God," Lucy said tersely, interrupting her count. And God's name has no place in your vile, filthy mouth." She leveled the pistol again, her finger firmly on the trigger.

Just before the count of three a voice cut in, "No, Miss Oxford! If you pull that trigger it will be murder. Drop the gun. That's right. Just put it down."

Lucy began to lower the gun. Passion gave way to practicality. She looked at Bryant with loathing. "You're not worth wasting a bullet on." And before the police could corral the tigress, Lucy smacked Bryant in the face with her hand, spit on him, then spun on her heel and walked away.

The cops had turned up in a nick of time. Fortunately, they had brought along medical help. The doctor came over and began tending to Drew. "Can we get him inside?" he asked.

Luke hurried to Drew. "Come on, buddy, let's get you fixed up."

Once inside, the doctor included all of us in his conversation as he examined Drew's wound. "We need to get the bullet out and the patch of material that will have gone in with the bullet. I have been following Louis Pasteur's work and agree with his conclusions. We need to stop any infection in the wound. I don't think there are any broken bones, but a wee drop of laudanum will help the pain and make him rest a bit."

The doctor singled me out and asked, "Will you help me?"

"I'll do what I can," I replied, kissing Drew and waiting for the laudanum take effect. Drew drifted off to sleep saying, "I can't die. I still owe you coffee and a brownie."

With Drew asleep, the doctor got the bullet out fairly quickly. Still, Drew moved around a lot and moaned. Every movement, every moan made me hurt for him.

"There is a patch of cloth off his shirt," the doctor said, "taken in by the bullet. I must get it out. We need to reduce the bleeding."

"There is an ice house," I informed the doctor. "Would that help if we put ice on the wound? Would it reduce the bleeding?"

He nodded. It's worth a try."

Poor Drew began to get cold with the ice, and then suddenly, the doc pulled out a patch of cloth that matched the bloody hole in Drew's shirt.

"Thank God," he said. "Now, he needs rest to recover. The next forty-eight hours will decide whether he survives or not."

I was torn between my desire to stay with Drew and my duty to get Kitchi back to his family. Kitchi had worked diligently to get Mi-Ling back. I had been to see Mi-Ling, but I don't think Lucy was happy at having me there, and I stayed only a short time. In fairness, I suppose Lucy wanted Mi-Ling to be kept calm and guarded in a stable environment after her harrowing experience. Plus, even to me—a non-parent if there ever was one—the child seemed ill. If I timed it right, I could get Kitchi safely back and Drew would hardly know I was gone.

Kitchi sat outside the comfortable house, his fur cloak around him. "How is the little one?" he asked.

"You probably got to her in good time," I said. "She is sick. We don't know how sick and the doctors can't seem to figure out what's wrong with her. Thank you for saving her."

"She Who Has Sun in Her Hair speaks kindly. My heart is filled with joy that you are pleased."

When Kitchi called me She Who Has Sun in Her Hair, my heart felt a thrill. It was like being seventeen again. I must get him home to his wife and family. There had been enough tears and broken hearts.

"It's time for you to go home, my brother. You can go back with honor and we will miss you. I must then come back here and tend to Drew."

"Drew is a brave and courageous warrior and may you and he have many sons." He smiled. Why do I wish I could have your sons? I wondered, looking into Kitchi's dark eyes. Then I felt guilty for having such capricious thoughts.

I checked on Drew and found him sleeping. Lucy seemed to be taking good care of him in my absence. I went to see Mi-Ling again to explain to her that I was leaving with Kitchi. She was pale and fatigued. I wished we could get her to a modern day doctor. The word leukemia came unbidden to my mind. Come on Meryl, I told myself, you are not a doctor. Leave it to the experts. Right. Kitchi first.

Lucy came to thank Kitchi. "We are all in your debt," she told him, hugging him and clinging to his hand. "We can never repay you for your courage and your kindness."

Kitchi smiled. "To do what is right does not demand thanks. That the little one lives is thanks enough. I hope you find happiness and the path you seek."

Luke, too, thanked Kitchi. "You have taught me a lot, brother," he said. "Now I can teach it to others. Thank you."

They shook hands. "It is a wise man who learns and an even wiser man who wants others to learn from what he knows," Kitchi said. "Knowledge is like a flowing spring that many can drink from."

Kitchi and I made our way to the basement. He said, "It will be good to be home. I miss my family. But that there has been a happy result of my trip, it will make them glad."

We waited for the time car to come and it made a bit of a noise. Kitchi put his fingers in his ears. "Pardon me, but with this I cannot hear the birds sing."

We got inside. I put down my bag that I always carried on any trip. I was dressed for 1750, minus the corsets. Well, even duty has a limit and corsets were it. However, I had slipped a pistol into my skirt pocket in case it was needed.

The trip was not long, but all through Kitchi sang to himself. His voice was soft and gentle. I closed my eyes and imagined him singing to me, and all tension and worry evaporated. His voice cosseted me like the sun on a warm summer's day.

Then we arrived and opened the door to sunshine. Kitchi looked out, and at once became the alert warrior. He looked first into the sky, and thankfully it was a good day. We headed for the camp and memories flooded back to me—memories as soft and gentle as Kitchi's voice.

When we got to the camp, I saw Kitchi's eyes open wide in what could only be alarm. Two people saw him and ran up to him, with obvious distress on their faces. They began to speak quickly. I thought I had better remain silent. We headed for his tepee. I didn't go inside. I waited outside. It was for Kitchi to greet his family on his own. Then I heard the sound of wailing from inside. Oh no, not tragedy, I thought. Kitchi doesn't deserve tragedy. When I looked around more carefully, I realized that some of the lodges had been burned. Had they been attacked? I wondered.

Kitchi came out of the lodge after what seemed hours. His face was like flint. "My wife is dead. Wyanet died defending our children." He stood as if himself trying to understand the significance of what he had just said to me. I saw the pain in his eyes and I felt my heart shatter into a hundred fragments. I wanted to reach out and take him in my arms and hold him.

"Oh, Kitchi, my heart grieves for you! I am so, so sorry." Then I used the cliché, "is there anything I can do?" After having said it, I realized I stupid it sounded and how empty.

He looked at me with eyes that ran right down to his heart. "That

She Who Has Sun in Her Hair is here, takes the poison from the arrow. But you must return to your own warrior. He needs you and I have much to do here."

"I will come back," I promised impulsively.

"Kitchi looks forward to that day. Like before, I will watch for you each day that the sun wakes up to start the walk up into the sky."

I found my own way back to the time car, even though Kitchi wanted to make sure I was safe. His family needed him. As I walked off, it seemed that Kitchi was on his own. I realized that my heart was not my own. I wished I could shut off my emotions. And what about my poor Drew? My poor Drew? Was he?

"God if you are there," I whispered, "I could sure use some help."

I realized I must get a grip. If you let your emotions rule you, then where do you end up? In the wrong arms.

I stopped at HQ and gave a report to Colonel Carlisle.

"Are you sure Andrew is recovering?" he asked.

I thought a moment before answering. "The doctor says the next forty-eight hours will be critical, sir, but so far so good. The doc says he can't be moved."

"I can ask the medics for antibiotics in case of infection and send them along with you. It's good that Mi-Ling is safe."

"She is not well, sir. I'm not sure she could be time traveled. Her abduction by Bryant made her worse. By the way, they never got the woman who helped Bryant. I could think of one or two things that might help jog his memory for names, but in 1867, I am supposed to be a lady."

"What about Kitchi?" Carlisle asked. "That was his name, wasn't it? How is he? Was he of any help to you?"

"Without him, sir, we would never have found Mi-Ling. His poor wife was killed in a raid by another tribe." Kitchi's earnest face studied mine as I spoke to the colonel. The vision was so real that I started to reach out and touch his cheek. I shook my head to vanish Kitchi. "It had just happened before I took him back."

"So you feel you want to go back and check up on him? See if he needs anything?"

"Sort of," I said evasively. The colonel's eyes were sharp: he was not doing this job for no reason, and when I sighed—he had me.

He nodded. "I see. You like him a lot, don't you? Perhaps you even fancy that you love him? If we didn't have feelings, then we would become like those who work for PATCH—mindless obedience machines. Our heart is the one thing we shouldn't be trained to control, Meryl. You have a right to follow your heart. And we appreciate the fact that you've done well from the first day you joined us."

"I can't hurt Drew," I burst out.

"But do you love him? Or only think you do because of all the two of you went through together?"

I sighed. "I'm very much afraid it's what happens when the been through is through and all that is left is each other. We made a good team. But is there enough between us to make things last even when we start to grow old? That's what I am not sure about."

"What about Kitchi in 1755?"

"It's like having lived your life on Christmas cracker rhymes and suddenly discovering Milton or Keats."

He smiled. "That pretty well says it all, doesn't it, Meryl? You really love Kitchi. One thing that makes you such a good agent is that you are willing to learn, even though some lessons are more painful than others."

"Sometimes, sir, I wonder if school holidays ever come?" I sighed. "Colonel Carlisle, can I go into Aberdeen for coffee at SavaJava? A four-shot Americano and some chocolate cake."

He smiled paternally. "Go on then. The break will do you good, and maybe you need some thinking time. Get some money from petty cash and take my car." He pressed his car keys into my hand.

"Enjoy yourself, but leave your 1867 kit here and get some modern togs before you go."

I got into modern clothes and it felt odd. I had slipped on a denim skirt and jacket, a blue blouse and flat shoes for driving. I got to Aberdeen and parked the boss' car, careful to lock it, and headed out into Union Street. Suddenly, I felt eighteen again.

"What can I get you?" asked the Barrista at the coffee shop. "Let me guess—cappuccino."

"No," I quipped, "don't give up your day job. Four-shot Americano (four shots of espresso, topped with boiling water)." I also bought a jar of instant coffee to take back to Drew.

"You a visitor?" he asked

"Yes."

"Come a long way?"

"You might say that," I replied, paying the tab.

"You a student?" I asked him.

"Yes. Is it that obvious? I'm doing a major in American history. Looking at the Civil War and Gettysburg just now."

"Ooo," I said. "And what conclusions have you reached?"

He was taken aback at my question and pontificated, "Do you know much about the American Civil War? The Union won, you know. They were the ones in Blue Uniforms and the losers were the Confederates. They wore Gray Uniforms."

"Butternut" I corrected.

"Say what?"

"The Confederates ran out of gray material, so they had to use a homespun cloth. It was light brown in color and called Butternut."

"Yes, of course." He looked thoughtful. "Lee was a maniac ordering Pickets Charge."

"General Lee was a godly gentleman and a brilliant general."

"You sound as though you've met him in person."

"I have. Actually, I was there when the charge took place. Thanks for the coffee. If I were you, I would look carefully at your text book list."

He stared at me open-mouthed and I laughed. "Told you I had come a long way." Flashing my most winning smile at him, I said, "byeeee," and went out of the shop whistling Dixie. Everyone is allowed to kick their heels up now and again, even time travelers!

Before heading back to Bellefield, I made one more stop and brought a pack of panties. Some "modern" conveniences are worth their weight in gold.

Once back at Vanguard Headquarters, I handed in my keys and put my 1867 dress back on, but decided to hang onto my denim and shoes. Angus McTurk came whistling down the corridor and smiled when he recognized me. One thing for sure, Abigail must be good for him. I filled him in with the news. Sternly, he treated me to a father-like lecture. "If you do go to Kitchi, Drew will be devastated. He loves you."

I sighed. "Love is a two-way thing. It can't be one-sided."

"Lassie, are you really sure? I remember that night before Drew went to China. I know I was hard on you both, but I could see this happening."

"Thanks for caring. And for not saying, 'told you so.' How is Abigail?"

Angus looked down at the ground and then up. "I didn't believe that anyone could love a character like me. When I'm with her, things are so different. I see more, do more, and am more alive than ever before— and my French is coming on in leaps and bounds! I love her so much, yet instead of feeling trapped, her love is so liberating."

I nodded my understanding. "And how is Sebastian?"

"Well, he's clever, innovative. Good in certain combat situations and can think on his feet. Dr. Francis is working with him on improving his written and spoken grammar."

We chatted for a few more minutes and Angus was relieved to hear that Bryant had been caught. "Once he's in prison, I really hope he stays put and doesn't escape."

"Is it my imagination," I asked, "or has PATCH been suspiciously quiet?"

"Now that you mention it, Meryl, yes. The Colonel is expecting to hear from them anytime—all those people who want to 'free' the world in places where the world doesn't want to be freed are like cancers. You never know where they're going to pop up. I wish we could catch Reynolds. Our hope is that he's too paranoid to share his information about time travel."

One last stop. I went to see Adrian and tell him in person about

Drew.

"Oh, but I'm vexed to hear about his wound! I hope it doesn't fester. Are you sure there isn't much hope for him and Lucy? Och, we had great hopes. I remember when he came here he was smitten by Lucy's picture. He sat and gazed at it for hours. You and he didn't get on at that time."

"Yes, he thought I was Lucretzia Borgia."

He smiled broadly. "Aye, but things have improved between you immensely. Any hopes about you and he, sort of settling? Drew needs to settle."

I sighed and shook my head. "Probably not with me. I don't seem to be the settling type—at least not in the time and circumstances he's chosen. Drew is determined to be a father to the Chinese girl, Mi-Ling, which is only right. You know, the wee lassie he rescued from that foul place in China. Unfortunately, she seems to be quite ill just now. So at the moment, Drew is recovering from his wound, trying to figure out a cure for his daughter, and is scheduled to get a Dear John letter from me. As much as I hate to tell you all this, I must be honest. Life for Drew, at the moment, is not at its rosiest."

"Heavens, Meryl! That is a thick pile of dung to have to walk through. Give the boy a break. If PATCH moves, we may need him—and you—and for the two of you to work together. If PATCH has its way, nothing will be safe and no time will be safe. We might need to call on you quickly. Remember, you are one of the highest trained operatives we have."

"Nowhere safe? Not even an Indian lodge in 1755? Thanks for putting my Girls Own Comic-type mind into proportion."

Adrian hugged me. "Love to Victoria," I said as I left. But I felt like a liar and a traitor. I felt selfish and stupid. All I had been thinking about was having comfortable panties to wear, while Drew was in great distress of mind and body and PATCH was determined to ruin the world.

Anyway, I picked up antibiotics for Drew from the medics and headed back to the time car with my bag. I had taken time to wash my hair and it was still a bit damp. Somehow Gettysburg had seemed simpler than this. Your enemy there was the one who was shooting at you. Not unrequited love and not some faceless enemy planting a bomb on a subway or poisoning your water supply. I supposed the expression, All it takes for evil to succeed is for good men to do nothing, applied to women, too. I threw the switch and headed back for Bellefield, 1867. When I got back, I went straight to Drew to see how was after stashing my bag in my room. He seemed a little better.

"Hello, darling," he said. "Suddenly, things have got a whole lot better." He held out his hand to me. After a moment's hesitation, I took his hand as he asked, "How did things go with Kitchi? We owe him a great deal. He did a fantastic job in finding Mi-Ling."

I looked at him and hated myself. His eyes were so trusting. "When we got back to Kitchi's village," I told Drew, "we found that Wyanet, his wife, had been killed in a raid by another tribe. I had to leave him to come back here. I felt so bad. So guilty. I still do. Kitchi had come when we needed him. Yet, in his hour of need—he had no one. Not even one of us."

"Won't the tribe help? His extended family?" Drew asked.

I shrugged. "I guess so. But after what he did for Mi-Ling, I wish we could do more. I stopped off at HQ and filled everybody in on what had happened. They are all concerned about you. The medics have given me some antibiotics to protect you from infection." I handed him the jar of coffee. "Since you can't go get it right now, I brought it to you. I'll finish off all the details in your journal you've been keeping. I'll do that until you are better and feel like taking the pen again."

"I'm up to it now," he assured me.

The doctor was just coming in, so I wrote down the last few words and passed the journal back to Drew.

****

I thought it was time to start writing again. What Meryl had failed to realize was that ten days had passed since she left. Whether she had

over-compensated for the return journey, or what had happened—I just
didn't know.

I felt hopeless and gutted, because after Meryl returned, it was like
dealing with the ice maiden. I thought we had a future planned. Was it
because she didn't want to become a mother to Mi-Ling? I couldn't
believe that. Kitchi had children and that didn't seem to put her off him.
I had to accept and respect her feelings. Isn't that what I had preached to
Lucy? And now, I was getting paid back in kind. For when I read the
words that Meryl had written while she was keeping my diary for me,
truth hit. She was in love with Kitchi. Not me.

So what to do? See if Lucy would take me back? Mi-Ling would be
over the moon. And my poor baby. What was wrong with her? She got
tired so easily—fatigued really. She had lost weight. Was Meryl right?
Could it be leukemia? How could we find out?

I was sick of being in bed and the pain in my shoulder had eased off.
There was no cure for the pain in my heart, but staying in bed longer
wouldn't help that. I made my way downstairs and met Lucy in the
living room, She was at a desk writing. She looked up and smiled when
she saw me. "It's good to see you up and about."

"Thanks for your care when I was crook."

"You're welcome, Drew."

Mi-Ling came in and seemed overjoyed to see me there. "Papa, it is
good to see you well!" My daughter hugged me and the warmth of her
smile filled the room. "Would Papa like a story from Mi-Lings book?"

"Of course, sweetheart."

Her English had come on in leaps and bounds. I don't remember
the content of the story, but I do remember the expression on her lovely
face as she read about the lost duckling that eventually found its mama
again.

Mrs. Fraser came to take Mi-Ling to supper, and I wondered if it
was my imagination, or if Mrs. Fraser often took charge of Mi-Ling
because Lucy seemed so busy.

After she had eaten, I took Mi-Ling for a short walk. We counted
birds and stood and listened to the sweet sounds of life and growth,

carried on the cool fingers of wind. "Papa," Mi-Ling asked, after a long silence. "Will you and Amma get married and live ever after happy?"

I couldn't lie to my daughter. "We don't know, yet, sweetheart."

"Will you go with the Meryl lady instead?" she asked with the candor of innocence.

I put my hands on her shoulders and looked into her face. "Meryl loves Kitchi, the Indian who rescued you from the ones who kidnapped you."

She nodded in understanding. "Kitchi is very gentle and wise. He knows all about the animals and birds and trees and he can make noise like some of the birds. I hope they will be happy people and Kitchi will show Meryl how to sing."

When we got back from our walk, Mi-Ling went to play with Connie. Connie seemed to have the ability to get Mi-Ling to reach deep inside and find new strength and energy. I thought, we expect children to learn from us. Yet, it is often what they can teach us.

Luke was outside target practicing with Anton. Lucy caught me as I came in the door. "Drew, take a seat. I have something to tell you. I've been waiting for you to get stronger and regain your health. Luke has asked me to come to Texas with him to teach. We will get married if we get on with each other. I know this will come as a slight shock to you, but you have Meryl. I have to think of the future. I've decided to give you life rent of the house. Yours for you as long as you live. When Meryl moves in here with you, I want to be away."

"Have you told Luke yes?" I asked. It wasn't a "slight" shock. It was a major shock. I felt as if my insides had frozen solid and it was difficult to move my jaw enough to form words.

"Yes. For a trial period. The Texas climate is different from China, or here. Much drier."

"Ain't that the truth! You'd better believe it. You'll find a lot of differences—just about everything, I would imagine." I hoped I sounded cynical. "Now, while you've been plighting your troth and making plans for San Antonio, Meryl has decided to return to Kitchi in 1750."

Lucy stared at me. "She is not coming here?"

"She is not coming here. Kitchi's wife was killed in a raid and that leaves him free. Meryl believes her heart belongs to him."

"That means you'll be here on your own," Lucy noted.

"No. Mi-Ling will be here with me."

Lucy drew a circle in the carpet with the toe of her shoe. "Well, Luke and I have been thinking. We could take the burden of Mi-Ling with us."

Burden! What language! "No, Lucy. You and Luke are not getting Mi-Ling. She stays here with me and if you try to take her, I will fight you every inch of the way. Do you understand?"

"We're only doing what's best for her."

I turned on her. "We? I would bank on it that Luke doesn't know that you intend to take Mi-Ling. Who are you to decide what's best for Mi-Ling?"

Luke and Anton had apparently finished shooting, because at this point, Luke entered the room. Meryl was following Luke, but upon hearing our heated words, she must have decided that discretion was the better part of valor. She disappeared down the hall.

Luke came to Lucy and put his arm around her. "Drew, I don't want to fight you, but you can't talk to my intended like that."

"Oh, shut up, and stop playing the big hero. You want Lucy? You take her. And may it bring you much joy."

I left the room and Meryl caught me outside, slipping a slender hand on my good arm. I am afraid the milk of human kindness had run out of me by that time. I shook her hand off my arm. "Drew," she said. "You've had time to read about Kitchi and me in the diary now. I wanted to tell you. Only, you've been so sick and…I'm a coward, Drew. Yes, I can swordfight with the best of them. But when it comes to love, I'm a coward. I didn't want to hurt you and I didn't know how to tell you. So, I left it for you to read. I'm sorry. I'm so sorry."

She reached for me again and I pushed her hand away. "Yeah. Sorry. What a wonderful lot that word fixes. I feel all better now just from hearing that wonderful little empty word."

"Oh, Drew!" she said, tears wetting the blueness of her eyes. "I wish

I knew a better way of saying it. I am sorry. Can't we at least part as friends?"

"Are you still here? I thought you would have been away by now into your lover boy's arms. Don't bang the time car door on the way out."

It was just at this point when the friendly, familiar figure of Sebastian emerged from the basement. "Lordy!" he said. "And there was me thinking the Civil War was over. I didn't know y'all had moved it to Scotland. What's all the ruckus about?"

So much for dealing with angst in private. Anton had come down the hall in the middle of my conversation with Meryl. He turned and went back out the door, deciding it was warmer in the winter temperature outside than in the frosty exchange inside.

I was about to flee upstairs to be alone when Sebastian added, "I bring a message from Colonel Carlisle. 'Tell Drew to take it easy and not to get stressed."

Like another dog returning to the fight, Lucy had chosen this moment to come down the hall. With hands on hips, she told Sebastian, "This does not concern you, whoever you are."

"My name is Sebastian. I work for the same group as Drew does. You might say we are kind of brothers, and as brothers, we look after each other's welfare."

Then he focused his attention on Meryl. "Meryl, honey, I want some words with you girl." The two of them headed to a small room. All I caught of the conversation was, "What's got into you, girl? Have you thought it out..."

This is none of my business, I realized. I went outside and found Anton sitting on an ornate metal bench, looking very pensive. When he saw me, he said, "I think I shall call my book Reminiscences of a Roaming Russian. Memories of my travel in Scotland. I would have to explain where Scotland is and whose people fight outside and fight at home. Just like old country.

"My uncle Kiryl—or it may have been Pyotr—had a flock of cows. You put them in the same field and they would kick at each other and sometimes bite. Then one night my uncle, in the middle of winter, had an urge to go and see his cows in the field. There was light by the moon, but he took a—torch, you call them—and his gun. He found his flock close to each other. No biting, no kicking, no pushing. If they had got any closer they would have been drinking each other's milk. My uncle —he could not believe it. Then he saw the wolves going around them, backwards and forwards."

"There are no wolves here Anton."

He nodded. "The wolves, now they are in prison. But you have an event coming up soon. I think it is a listening…"

"Hearing," I corrected. "It's called a hearing."

Anton raised his hands. "Hearing and Listening serves the same purpose. In Bryant's case, I hope the verdict has been decided beforehand."

"This is Britain," I said with dignity. "We don't do that here."

"What happens if the wolf escapes before he goes before the judge to hear the outcome of what has not been decided before hand?"

"But he couldn't. He would be guarded."

He shook his head. "In Russia, czars are guarded, but some of them have been killed by somebody throwing bomb at them, or shooting them. Then there are many questions asked, like how did this come to pass, and will it be big funeral? The czar is still dead. If Bryant escapes, then the wolf is back among the cows. The only way to be sure that a villain will not trouble you is when he has given up the task of breathing. If Bryant escapes, he will be mad and dangerous. For Lucy showed him up to be a coward and less than a man and without his pride, all he has left to feed his evil heart on now revenge. Think about it my friend."

Anton paused. His eyes glittered with faraway thoughts. "I remember the night you saw Lucy at the dance in Foochow. You were the one who had found the treasure then. Your eyes were the brightest things in the room next to hers. Don't forget, Drew, my friend. It was you who went off with Meryl. I wanted Meryl—I brought her here to be with me. But when I brought Meryl here, I was not engaged to be married. You were. Do you not think that Lucy has some right to anger?"

I knew Anton was right. I had built Lucy's hopes up, then callously ground them under the soles of my feet like dirt. Still, I tried to save face. "It's obvious that we were not suited."

"Obvious to whom? Not to Lucy. You fall in love with your eyes, Drew. As a man, I know I am just as guilty as you. A woman falls in love with her heart, then her eyes fill in the rest and her eyes iron out the flaws in the object of her love so that the flaws disappear. The way women see is different from the way men see."

"You heard her in there," I said.

"What I heard in there was not Lucy, but someone who had been hurt speaking. No doctor can heal that kind of hurt." Anton paused. "I remember Irja, my lamented wife. She grew roses. One time when she was away, I had to water them. I did so, except one that I had not noticed. When she got back, it was nearly dead, but she gave it special love and it recovered.

"Drew, my friend, have you forgotten how Lucy faced down Bryant with that pistol? Was it only because he had threatened Mi-Ling, or was it because a hand span to the left and he could have killed you? And you, in your heart—was it just for Mi-Ling you offered the duel, or was it for Lucy as well? My brother, look into your heart. Fighting the duel was a brave thing, a very brave thing."

"Thanks," I said. "I appreciate what you say. Sometimes, we do things without thinking."

He laughed, "Just the type of thing that will make you a romantic hero in someone's book."

I went back inside the house. There was no sign of Meryl or Luke. Sebastian and Mi-Ling were talking in a corner, and Lucy was arranging flowers, cutting the stems into different lengths.

Okay, I thought. Okay, Lord. We've reached the cellar. Now it's time to start climbing the stairs again. Give me the words to say, and let them be as Anton says, from the heart. I don't know where I am going.

"Lucy," I asked hesitantly. "Can we go for a walk together outside? Please?" I expected her to refuse and send me packing. "Just down to the oak tree and back?"

"All right. I will get my shawl." That surprised me. Her voice was not loving, which I had not expected it to be, but nor was it cold and indifferent.

We got outside and walked. "I ...," we both said at the same time.

"You go," she said quickly.

"Lucy, I wanted to say no matter how lame the words may sound for being unfaithful to you..."

"So you and Meryl were lovers?" she asked, in a hurt, shocked voice.

"Yes," I answered truthfully. "It didn't matter what had happened before, but it was wrong this time because I was engaged to you and promised to you. I was wrong. Way wrong. All I can say is that I'm sorry for the hurt I've caused you. And the broken trust. Trust once broken can never be easily mended."

"Are you only saying that because Meryl's gone?" she asked.

"No. I'm saying it because it's true and I owe you the truth. And perhaps the Lord has finally got through past my pride and down into my conscience. When we were in China, I would rather have died than put you through what I have put you through now."

Lucy plucked a flower and smelled it. "Every year, something new and beautiful comes up," she mused. "This garden reminds me of home. The Scent of Home, wherever that is."

"I really do hope you and Luke will be happy," I told Lucy. "And if you want, if you both want, I'll let Mi-Ling go with you. She needs a mum and a dad. A stable home. Her happiness must come first. I won't stand in the way of what would be best for her."

"What made you change your mind?"

"I prayed. I searched my heart. I think talking to Anton helped, too. I realized why I wanted to keep Mi-Ling."

"Why?" Her voice suddenly sounded tender. Or was that just what I wanted to hear?

"Please don't make fun of me, Lucy, when I tell you—but once Mi-Ling is gone—so is my last link with you. That's what I couldn't stand.

But it can't be about me. It has to be about Mi-Ling and doing what's right for her. You and Luke could—should give her a home. I'm sorry if I've upset you. I'll walk you back to the house, if you have had enough of me. All I ask is that you will forgive me." I turned my back on Lucy and started to walk to the house. I stopped when I realized she was not following.

Amazingly, unbelievably, when I turned back to see what had happened to Lucy, she stood with her arms open toward me. I ran back to her and fell into her arms and stated to sob and cry. I kept repeating that I was sorry. The rest of what was said and passed between us…well, it will remain between us.

"There is something else I need to thank you for," I told Lucy, as we snuggled close to one another.

Lucy looked puzzled. "What can that be?"

"For guarding my jacket in China when the boy fell in the harbor."

"Carolyn and I thought you were dashing and brave and courageous. But to keep you from getting too full of yourself, perhaps I should give you the traditional reply. 'You are welcome, kind sir." She smiled and shook her head and titian hair rippled like a field of ripened corn. Then she laughed and I realized that I had missed Lucy's laughter It was something I had not heard in a long time. Sadly, I hadn't taken the time to notice it was missing. It was like I was seeing Lucy as a real person, the priceless personality that shone out of her lovely features, for the first time. "Oh Lucy I am so…"

She sealed my lips with a gentle finger. "Shhhh, darling. No more 'sorry." Lucy took my arm and we seemed to walk forever, never tiring of our circular route. When we finally headed back toward the house, the warm winter sun at our backs, I could not feel my feet on the ground. I kept looking at Lucy as if I had never seen her before. People in love really do walk on air.

Anton was sitting on a bench reading. When he saw us, his smile stretched from one ear to the other—like a benevolent grandfather. "I don't have to ask what has happened. Your eyes are putting the sunshine into the shade. Old Russian saying: 'When you find real happiness, you don't even need vodka anymore." He hugged us both, and invited, "How about Russia for a honeymoon? Eh, but for now, you two will want to be alone." He wandered off singing some Russian folk song, and although I could not understand what he said, it at least sounded cheerful and optimistic.

We headed toward the house. "What about...?" I asked.

Lucy read my thoughts. "I'll tell Luke, you tell Mi-Ling." So we headed off on our first day in eternity.

I found Mi-Ling and took her outside. She was puzzled, but happy to see me. "Mi-Ling..." Her big eyes looked at me intently.

"Is Papa going to say happy words?" she asked hopefully.

"Yes, happy words, Mi-Ling. Amma and I are getting married and want you to come and live with us. Will you?"

I didn't expect her response. With a joyous squeal, she threw her arms around me and hugged me tightly. "Father God answer Mi-Ling's prayers," she announced. He promised Mi-Ling that all would be well. Oh, today will be in my heart always. Thank you, Father, both Fathers."

Mi-Ling ran to find Connie and share the news with her best friend. At times, she ran and played like any child her age. Yet, increasingly, the quick onset of fatigue and her constant need for naps and rest was alarming. She didn't seem to have grown since leaving China and she was no longer slim—she was skinny.

Luke was angry at Lucy's news and confronted her. "How do you know the minute that you turn your back, Drew won't be in bed with someone else? What will happen if Meryl comes back—if it didn't work out with Kitchi? She could wrap Drew round her little finger—then it is bye-bye, Lucy. Think about it before you commit yourself. Can you trust him? He lied to you before. He will do it again.

"Lucy, think!" he added heatedly. "Drew deserted us in the Hanshee caves. The guy is a coward. Is that the kind of father you want for any children you may have? Will they have yellow skin?"

I could understand and even agree and sympathize with Luke's attempt to keep Lucy. But enough was enough. "Back off, Luke!" I ordered. "How is your fiancée—remember the one in Texas? Mary Ellen

Darrow, I think you said her name was. Remember her?" I asked.

"Why you cowardly!" Luke might have said more, but I didn't hear him. He hit me and I hit the floor. He was about to have a second go when Mi-Ling ran up crying, "Papa! Papa!" Somehow, Mi-Ling ran onto Luke's fist and went sprawling on the floor.

Sebastian had seen what happened and he was bigger than Luke. "You calm down, boy," Sebastian warned, "or you are going to get seriously hurt."

Lucy ran to Mi-Ling, who lay crumpled on the floor next to me. "Anton," she said breathlessly, "you know where the doctor stays. Can you go and ask him to come here?" Anton bolted out of the house.

Luke tried to apologize. "I'm so sorry, Lucy! I never meant to… Oh, God what a mess!"

Lucy looked up at him as she cradled Mi-Ling in her arms. "Take one of the carriages and go to the hotel. You can get a boat from Aberdeen. Just get out—now!"

Luke stared at her in disbelief. "But, Lucy, it was an accident!"

"Luke, just go."

It was a sad ending to what once had been a good team. Luke had been away for a while and he would have to get back to his unit, anyway. It would take three months to get back. His career could be in ruins.

I rolled over and got up off the floor, still rubbing my face where Luke's fist had made contact with it. I joined Lucy and took over holding Mi-Ling, who was moaning slightly.

Sebastian spoke up. "Miss Lucy, when I was a runaway slave, I was chased by a Confederate patrol and I hid in a ditch. One of the officers in that patrol came past and saw me. Law! But what I was scared. Miss Lucy, I mean to tell you that I was a cross 'tween bein' terrified and plum tuckered out. I didn't know it then, but that officer was Lieutenant Carter. I know'd him the moment I saw him. He protected me. He pretended he didn't see me."

Luke nodded. "I hated those patrols. I used to 'not see' as many as I could. These were people in trouble not animals to hunt down."

Sebastian held out his hand. "Thank you."

Luke took his hand. "You're welcome, sir."

In the middle of our hall, a former slave shook hands with a former Confederate officer who had been ordered to hunt him down.

"Now," Sebastian said to Lucy and me. "If you two is finished fightin' with one another, why don't we help Captain Luke out? That time machine of ours can take someone back in time to a place where he is supposed to have been but didn't get to on account he didn't have time to get there. Reckon we can take Captain Luke back to San Antonio so he don't get into trouble when he gets back?"

Astonishment stole over Luke's face.

"What ya' say Captain? I can take you back to San Antonio." But Luke clearly didn't know what to say.

I carried Mi-Ling upstairs. Anton returned with the doctor, who shooed me out of the room and let Lucy stay. When Lucy and the doctor came down, Lucy told us, "She'll be fine. She's weak, but it could partly be the illness and we don't know what it is or how to treat it. Anyway," Lucy sighed. "She's asking to see 'Uncle Luke.' So, go see her, Uncle Luke. But don't stay long."

Luke practically flew upstairs.

Lucy turned to me. "I think the time machine is a good idea, Drew. Luke's done so much for us, and I know he didn't mean to hit Mi-Ling. It was an accident. Although," she added severely, "He shouldn't have hit, or tried to hit you either! Why don't you go with them to San Antonio, darling? It won't be long, and if anything does go wrong, it would be good for Sebastian to have a friend along."

Sebastian smiled. "I sure do appreciate that. Just in case it's nighttime when we get there and folks don't see me in the dark!" We laughed.

Luke came slowly back downstairs. "Mi-Ling told me a story about how a friend of hers had trodden on a puppy's paw and hurt it. She hadn't done it deliberately, of course. The puppy got well. She said she didn't want me to hurt because she knows I didn't intend to hurt her. She says she will get well. Will she, doc?"

The doctor shook his head. "She will be fine from the accidental punch. But as to the other…there's a limit to what medical science can do and we have just about reached that limit. Fit we could do with is a miracle straight oot o' the pages o' Scripture."

Luke nodded. "I'll be praying for that, sir." He went to his room to get his things and Anton helped him.

Sebastian excused himself. He said he was away to put some gas in the tank of the time car.

For the first time in a long time I was alone with Lucy when there was no duel or tragedy or something bad about to happen. She was standing at the window. I came up behind her and put my arms round her waist and buried my face in her lovely mane of red hair. "What's the matter?" she asked.

"Matter?" I said. "I just wanted to tell you that you are so very beautiful—inside and out. I want to live forever in the love in your eyes and be bathed by the warmth of your smile. I wanted to tell you that I love you. I want you to know that." We kissed. The herbal scent of her hair and the sweetness of her lips made me forget where we were or why we were there. It expunged the scent of coconut that I had once believed to be the scent of love. Lucy sighed and rested her head against my chest.

After a moment, she looked up at me with softness and trust in her lovely green eyes and announced, "I wish we were married."

"Lucy, I love you. I want you—I need you—to be my wife. Will you marry me?"

"This time, I know you mean it, Drew, and this time the answer is yes. This time let's make sure Bryant is put away for good."

We stood with our arms round each other and looked into each other's eyes. The portrait at Bellefield sprang to life. We looked and kissed, then looked and kissed some more.

"I hated Bryant for what he did to Mi-Ling." Lucy said," but I also hated him for having shot you."

"Would you have pulled the trigger?" I asked.

"Yes," she said without hesitation, her arms tightening around me. "I was a heartbeat away from it. He had hurt the two people whom I love the most. I just wanted to be close enough to Bryant so I wouldn't miss —so the one shot I had would go through his head."

"Phew," I said, and was astounded at my own inept vocabulary.

Lucy smiled at me. "You better throw a few things in a bag in case you get stuck. Like last time. Don't forget clean socks."

I grinned at her. "Yes, ma'am." That obedient reply earned me a hug and a longer kiss.

I dashed up to see Mi-Ling, but she was asleep, so I wrote a quick note to leave on her pillow.

Lucy told everyone goodbye, but I was the only one who received a hug and a kiss along with the words. On the way to the time car, Luke said, "I'm sorry for having called you a coward. It's not true."

I patted his arm. "It's okay—let's get you home—or as near home as a military base gets.

Sebastian said, "I'm drivin' I got de keys."

CHAPTER 14

We left. I had expected just to kind of let Luke off and then to get back. What I had not realized was that the military base at which Luke had been stationed was that which is now the prime building in San Antonio and probably the most well-known building in America—the iconic Alamo. We had even heard of the Alamo in Scotland and that was 3000 miles away!

A generation of children had grown up dressed like Davy Crockett, or carrying a plastic replica of Jim Bowie's knife, or admiring the courage and ever-diminishing hope for help of Alamo Commander William Barret Travis.

We exited the time car in a warehouse in the complex web of streets that surrounded the Alamo in 1867, some thirty-one years after the event. It was busy and noisy like Foochow, only this time I could understand most of what was being said. Luke had on his uniform and any trooper or non-commissioned officer who passed saluted him.

There it was—the Alamo. I tried to imagine what it had been like thirty-one years ago. The Alamo was not just the church itself, but took in quite an area the one-hundred-twenty-eight guys had died defending. They had retired to the church in the end, but they had just been outnumbered. They had known that there was no rescue. Travis had sent out couriers to ask for help, but only thirty-two men from Goliad had responded.

Had the Alamo defenders expected to win? Perhaps not, but while you can kill people, you cannot kill an idea or truth. While the Alamo was being besieged a Texas constitution was being forged in a meeting at Brazos-on-the Washington. A few months later, the tables were turned, and the Mexican dictator Santa Anna was defeated at San Jacincto.

I knew as I stood there what the Alamo would turn into and the enduring freedom it would represent. Many would come to be inspired by what the Alamo defenders had achieved. Their blood had watered the seeds of Texas freedom. To do what the United States Constitution promised: enjoy the unalienable rights of life, liberty and the pursuit of happiness.

PATCH was the modern day threat. They wanted to change everything to suit their own evil agenda. They were attempting to do it subtly. They wanted to steal and kill freedom. In Scotland, Sir William Wallace had planted the seeds of freedom with his blood when Scotland was being invaded by England. After winning one battle, he was defeated and betrayed by someone on his own side. He was murdered as a traitor in London, by a king to whom Wallace had never sworn allegiance.

"Surely things in the future get better and more peaceable," Luke said as the three of us looked at the Alamo.

"Luke, as the expression goes, 'you ain't seen nothing yet.' It really is true that the price of freedom is constant vigilance."

Sebastian and I had stood in awe before the Alamo. Now, it was time to forget about history and leave it in the past. We needed to return to Bellefield—to Lucy and Mi-Ling. We shook hands with Luke, and I asked him to keep in touch. I didn't know how deep his feelings for Lucy had gone. He might not be inclined to keep in touch. He still seemed a bit rankled over Lucy's acceptance of my proposal. I tried to ameliorate the situation. "Luke, I hope you're still thinking about the Marines. I'm told that there are some great guys there. And give our apologies to Mary Ellen for keeping you so long."

With a rather curt nod, he disappeared inside the fort, some of his stuff lugged inside by a couple of squaddies.

Thankful that—this time—we had stopped where and when we needed to and had not stepped into the middle of a war or battle somewhere, Sebastian and I headed back to the time car.

When we got back, I took Lucy aside. "Let's get married as quickly as we can. I love you. I want you as my wife."

Lucy threw her arms around my neck and pulled me tightly to her.

Her head tilted to one side. "You know," she said with a straight face. "You really are quite handsome when I half-close my eyes and squint at you."

"You cheeky character, Lucy Oxford!" I exclaimed, pretending outrage. I ran my fingers through her hair, and kissed her. "We need a honeymoon, but we can't go away for long. Mi-Ling needs us."

"What is it like?" Lucy asked.

"What's what like?" I asked.

"Being one with someone you love? I know I want to be one with you, Drew, and have your children."

Anton rushed in on us before I could answer. "Sorry to interrupt, but Bryant's hearing date has been set. Maybe you should be there."

"Anton," I said. "We're going to arrange a wedding as quickly as possible. Will you be my best man?"

"But, of course. Do you not remember—that is why I came here in the first place, to attend a wedding. Old Russian saying: 'When you have been climbing a high hill, you are glad to get to the top because you know the view is better and there are no wolves.' Congratulations! May you always have tea in the samovar, bread and salt on the table, and a bottle of vodka in the cupboard for wintertime."

Lucy and I set the date for three weeks. There was nothing to stop us from getting everything organized—this time on a much smaller scale. We wanted each other, not fuss.

Lucy blossomed. There seemed to be a million things to do—or was it a million and one? With the wedding scheduled so soon, no sooner was one thing done until three other things took its place.

Sebastian had stayed for the wedding. He came to us one day and announced, "I was thinking about Mi-Ling. She's Chinese, and God willing, she will grow into a lovely Chinese lady. She should keep up her Chinese language. There ain't—sorry—aren't any Chinese here, unless I bin lookin' in the wrong places. So what's about getting someone in to help her keep her language up? She sings to herself in Chinese, but if'n you don't know the words you're singing, it could be all wrong."

Lucy and I looked at each other and realized that Sebastian was right. Mi-Ling was entitled to keep her roots in China strong and healthy.

"But who can we get who speaks Chinese?" Lucy asked. "I know only a little. Not enough to teach Mi-Ling what she needs to know."

Sebastian drew himself up in pride. "Well, y'all will have noticed how real good my English is comin' along. It ain't often I say ain't—oh shucks if'n I didn't just do it." He enunciated carefully, "But it is not often I say ain't now."

"Yes, we did notice," Lucy said. "Well done."

He beamed. "Well, the doctor who's done taught me—excuse me —what's been—the person who's been teaching me speaks not just English but a whole heap of languages, one of which is Chinese—only she calls it Mandarin. She speaks a whole passel of old languages—dead folk's languages. Why she would want to speak dead folk's language, I don't know. Shucks, ain't—I mean—who's gonna tell you if you is right or wrong? The colonel fixed it up for me, and as long as I'm here, my teacher would be willing to come and have a look see. I could go back to headquarters and fix it up. And I could see if they could do anything for Mi-Ling medical-wise. She might not can travel, but what they can tell if'in you give 'em some blood is amazing."

Other than being prone to exhaustion, Mi-Ling was mentally as bright and interested as ever. The stimulation of speaking the language in which she was brought up would be good. No matter how much Lucy and I loved her, Mi-Ling would grow up into a life of her own. She might even want to return to China someday—at least for a visit.

"Darling," I asked Lucy, "what do you think?"

Lucy thought for a moment and said, "I had learned some Mandarin, but it would be good to get an opportunity to learn more. For Mi-Ling's sake now, instead of teaching. Maybe Mi-Ling and Amma could learn together?"

"Just think," Sebastian said. "In the years ahead, we done can have a class reunion. I will get going and get it all sorted out. Reckon the colonel, he gonna be happy. Now I best give you lovebirds some time alone. It appears that y'all's got a lot of catching up to do. When do you reckon the wedding will be?"

I answered, "Well, we've planned it for three weeks from now. After Bryant's hearing."

"Could Angus come?" Lucy inquired.

"Shore enough!" Sebastian exclaimed. After all he went through to get Drew back from China, he's gonna be as delighted as pigs in a melon patch."

"We should leave Meryl out," I said. "I don't want her here and she has enough on her plate taking over Kitchi's family."

"You can invite her if you want," Lucy offered.

"No, sweetheart. All I want is you. Let the past go. Together, we are heading into a long and happy future."

"Right," Sebastian said. "Okay, folks. I will make tracks and see you again soon."

We told Mi-Ling about the Chinese teacher who was coming and she sounded deeply happy. "It is the way I speak at home. My old home. This is my new happy home."

At the time, neither Lucy nor I realized how costly the decision to include Dr. Francis in our lives would become.

We told her that Amma was going to learn some Mandarin with her. Then suddenly, as if it came from their boots, they began to talk to one another very slowly in Mandarin.

A couple of days later, I wandered out into the garden to find Anton reading through telegrams. He shook his head. "They are from Maria, Anastasia, Vera, and Alexia. All saying how much they miss me and asking when I am coming home. Then they promise me things you don't need to know about. Or, perhaps, I'm getting tired of an empty bed. Still, I will see my promise to you both through. You must both come visit me in Russia—even if it's fifty years from now."

"Anton, you don't want to be in Russia fifty years from now. Remember what I showed you in China? How would you like a look see?"

"Let me think about it."

Lucy and I spent a lot of the time just talking. She grew happier and happier. Even Mi-Ling looked stronger again, as if she was drawing strength from Lucy.

The day of Bryant's hearing arrived. Angus McTurk joined us. He wanted to be sure that Bryant was put away. When we asked him about Abigail, he beamed. "She's some lassie. She can throw a tomahawk so it hits the target every time and she is a crack shot with a pistol and can load a rifle faster than anyone I know!"

Abigail sounded like he perfect match for Angus. When Lucy left to check on Mi-Ling, Angus said, "I am glad to see you happy, laddie. I heard about Lucy and the duel. She's a woman worth fighting for."

Hesitantly, I asked, "How is Meryl?"

Angus studied me for a moment before replying. "She and Kitchi aren't married yet. Someone coming into the tribe is put on a trial basis. So she sleeps in one tent and Kitchi sleeps in another tent and Meryl is chaperoned. They have a high moral standard."

"But there will be wedding for her?" I asked. "If they get on?"

"Oh, aye. But she is finding the domestic side a bit rough. In-law trouble, I believe. But she's a strong woman and will tough it out, I hope."

"You can do me a big favor." I said. "Tell her I'm sorry and I apologize for what I said. She wanted to part as friends, but I wouldn't allow that."

"There was a time when I thought you two were joined at the hip."

"Yes. But we've both made other choices now."

He looked at me. "You're doing the right thing, but there is an old saying." He tapped my chest. "The heart, once having loved, loves on until the end. Be aware that what you two had doesn't go so easily away."

I shrugged my shoulders. "I just want Meryl to know that I'm sorry for what I said."

He smiled, in what seemed to be relief. "Okay. I will pass on the message. But for now, let's get ready to see Bryant committed for trial."

I explained to Mi-Ling that we were going to see "that bad man Bryant put in prison, so everybody would be safe."

"Will you put in prison the bad man's friends?"

"No, darling," I said. They haven't been caught yet. But we will get them."

"They were so very shiny. When they come to see the bad man, they hurt Mi-Ling's eyes."

Startled, I asked, "Did they hurt you or hit you?"

"No," Mi-Ling said. "It would be dark. Then as if a door opens, the room would be filled with bright light. Then two peoples would come through the light and talk to the bad man. They would give him things and then they would go back into the light and it was dark again." Mi-Ling yawned. She tired so quickly these days.

"Wait, sweetheart. Don't say anymore. Remember Angus, from the tea race between China and Scotland?"

Mi-Ling nodded. "Mi-Ling's friend."

"Yes. Mi-Ling's friend and Pappa and Amma's friend. Tell him what you just told me. I ran out into the hall and called Angus. He ran up the stairs. "Drew! What's wrong?"

"Mi -Ling tell Mr. Angus what you told me about the bright men."

She repeated the story and Angus listened carefully.

"Mi-Ling, think," Angus said gently. "Did you hear anything they said?"

Mi-Ling screwed up her face, then recollection swept into her dark eyes. "They said to the bad man that PATCH would make it okay."

"How do you remember PATCH?" Angus asked curiously.

Mi-Ling looked down at the floor. "In the bad house in China, my friend, Jasmine, used to get man coming to her. When they would go to room, after they come out, Jasmine would be crying. The man would say, 'Don't cry, my beauty. Mr. Patch will make all better.' Papa, if you think someone is beautiful, why do you make them cry?

"Later my friend Jasmine died. She was covered in much blood. The owner was very angry with the man and said he had to pay much money. Then they saw me hearing them and got angry at me. Many times they hit Mi-Ling." Her little shoulders began to heave up and down as the memory of the nightmare came back.

I gathered her into my arms and kissed the top of her head. "You are a very brave girl. Thank you for telling us this, Mi-Ling. It's very important. Papa loves you and is very proud of you."

A short time later, Connie arrived and they changed into two little girls at play.

Angus looked at me. "They're going to try and rescue Bryant. But when? And more importantly, why?"

"How are we going to get people to believe us?" I asked angrily. "Especially the authorities. We have to be there."

We went downstairs to find Lucy. "Darling, we believe that PATCH may try to rescue Bryant at court today."

Astonishment burned brightly in the pure green of her eyes. "But, Drew, how do you know that?"

"It's a long story, but it's what Mi-Ling remembers seeing when she was captive before Kitchi found her. Don't ask her about it unless she volunteers the information. It's tied to something unpleasant that happened in China."

"Can't you tell the police?"

"How can you warn them that PATCH arrives through a time portal of bright light without them thinking you are insane?"

"Do you want me to stay here with Mi-Ling, or go with you?"

"If Bryant sees you in court, and if his chums are armed, they may try to kidnap you. Angus and I can go to court."

The journey to Aberdeen seemed impossibly long. What we had expected to be an open and shut case was now complicated. I said to Angus, "I don't know how it could be done, but we really need to go on the offensive against PATCH. Slowly, they seem to be getting the upper hand. Yet, I can't think of a way to stop them. We need to be there when they turn up. There must be a base. They must be operating from somewhere. Could there base be in space? If it is, has NASA seen anything unusual? If they come from another time, then when? We damaged them when we stopped them from switching General Lee."

"They are not ones for hanging around," Angus noted. "They come in and strike and leave."

We drove on in silence. "There must be a way to capture one of them and question him. Seeing what beans he will spill, even in PATCH's megalomaniac fashion. You know, 'what is the great plan that PATCH has?' They would be funny, if they weren't so dangerous."

"Baiting a trap?" Angus said thoughtfully. "Hmmm."

Court was busy, and crowded, and we asked an usher where to go.

"Court Two—upstairs on the right. You'll have to go in the public gallery." The building was impressive and awesome. The sounds of justice echoed round the corridors and along the halls. Families came and went, and when the cases were presented, some were put forward for trial. In other cases, the sheriff looked at the evidence and said in a deadpan voice, "There is no case to answer here. Case dismissed." This was Victorian justice at its somber best. Sometimes the accused admitted guilt and sentence was passed.

The Clerk announced Bryant's name and he was brought up from the cells. Angus and I kept a low profile. Bryant was to be charged over the bridge and Jock's death, along with pending enquiries over Sir Charles Gray's death. If all of these changes stuck, Bryant would not be going back to sea for a long time.

The Sheriff had just committed Bryant for trial. Bryant did not look worried, but kept looking around, as if he expected to see someone. Then in a darker part of the courtroom, a light suddenly appeared—somewhat subdued—but there. Mi-Ling had been right!

Five men came through in combat uniform. They were all armed. One nodded at Bryant and pointed his gun at the officers on either side of Bryant. "We are PATCH, People Allied Together to Change History. This man is with us. We are removing him from this place. Anyone who tries to stop us will be severely dealt with. We change events in history so that one day, WE WILL RULE."

The Sheriff, who had recovered his voice asked, "Who are you? What are you doing in my court?" Then he remarked to the clerk, "Mr. Baxter, all this is most irregular"

Mr. Baxter had the sense to keep his mouth shut.

"You will be brought to book for today's events," the sheriff warned.

"Shut up and sit down," a PATCH operative ordered.

The sheriff was indignant. "Don't tell me to be silent in my own court room!"

The leader of the group shot him, yelling, "Obedience must be learned!"

The sheriff slumped in his chair. Nobody else moved. The intruders, with Bryant, headed toward the light. Angus had a pistol. "We must try to get above the light. I can't risk firing unless there is a clear shot. We can't risk hitting an innocent member of the public."

A PATCH gun went off again, and a police officer fell. "The next attempt to hinder our progress," the PATCH operative ranted, "will result in the death of five others. We will not be stopped."

Angus crept above the light source. Four men and Bryant went through. As the fifth was going through, Angus fired two shots and the last man fell. Two others came running out of the portal and dragged the body back inside and the light closed down. Angus and I sat down in the court along with everybody else. We didn't want to draw attention to ourselves. Angus had fired his pistol and he didn't want to get blamed for the sheriff's shooting.

Pandemonium broke loose and armed police swarmed into the courtroom. Statements were taken, descriptions given. We managed to slip away. Then we began to think of what had taken place. What were we going to tell Lucy?

Angus had been deep in thought. "What I can't see is why they rescued Bryant. I can't believe it was because one of them wanted a sea cruise. At least it makes it more difficult for Bryant's ship to move about. The navy will be wanting him, and if that Sheriff dies, there will be an accessory to murder charge to add to the list."

"It's going to be interesting what the newspapers will make of this," I said.

We got back to the house and Lucy met us at the door.

"Well," she asked cheerfully, "is Bryant safely committed for trial, locked up and hopefully someone lost the key?"

Angus shook his head.

"They didn't let him go, surely!"

"No," I said, not bothering to soften my words. Lucy deserved the truth. "Bryant got sprung and one of the PATCH people shot the sheriff."

"Bryant is loose? Oh, no! Drew, what now?"

I took Lucy in my arms. She was shaking. "I'm going to tell Colonel Carlisle and see what he thinks about your idea of baiting a trap. Then, my little red haired sunrise, we are going to get married as quickly as possible. It will be easier for me to protect you if I'm in the same room as you. Not to mention the other joyful reasons for being in the same room and the same bed."

Lucy managed a laugh. She pressed her head against my chest and sighed. "I am so looking forward to that!" Then she blushed and added quickly, "And to not being parted for the next—maybe sixty years. Loving, hugging, reading and maybe going places. Even when we are old, my eyes will still long for you and we can still hug—providing we're not too creaky! Then we will be bombarded with grandchildren. Mi-Ling and her children and our other children and their children. It will be lovely."

I wanted to share Lucy's belief in that future. We tried to dismiss Bryant from our minds. Angus supplied Lucy with a .32 caliber revolver that she could keep it in her dress pocket, and a second arm for her bedroom, which she slipped under her pillow. He gave her a crash shooting course. Angus was thorough, and Lucy proved a good pupil and an even better shot.

"That girl has got the steadiest hand I have seen in a long time," he remarked.

I congratulated Lucy and she explained, "It's easy. I just imagine Bryant in front of me, and I shoot to kill."

The wedding banns were called in church for three Sundays. "There is a purpose of marriage between Captain Andrew Sinclair Ian Faulkner (I got called Asif at school because my parents could not see the predictability of my school friends getting the best mileage out of making fun of my name. Still, in my class at school, there was John

Andrew Neil Edgar, who at an all-boys school had to put up with his initials being made into Jane. "Jane" worked hard and got a Karate brown belt—after which he became John overnight.) There is a purpose of marriage between Captain Andrew Sinclair Ian Faulkner bachelor of this parish and Lucille Victoria Denise Oxford, Spinster of this parish. Then asked for any objections.

We had a rehearsal in the church. Anton was my best man or, sidesman, as it was called then.

The minister met with us and decided to his satisfaction that we really meant it this time and that I would not be going AWOL again.

Carolyn and Myles arrived for the wedding. Carolyn looked radiant, and Myles looked a happy camper. Carolyn said she had never yet been seasick. Mi-Ling was over the moon to see Caroline again. "Carol Lady comes to see Amma and Papa get married!" she told everyone joyfully.

In spite of her long dress, Caroline dropped to her knees and gave Mi-Ling a big hug. The deterioration in Mi-Ling's health clearly worried Caroline and she shot me a warning look that translated into, "We'll talk about this later." Then to Lucy, "Luce, I'm so, so happy for you! So very happy for both of you."

At dinner, Carolyn said to me, "In China, after you had visited us, Lucy used to say to me, oh, I wonder what it would be like to be married to him? He's so handsome and nice."

Lucy blushed. "Shush, Carolyn, or Drew won't be able to get his head through the door."

"I used to wonder the same thing about you," I admitted to Lucy. "Now, thank God, we are going to find out—together."

Carolyn smiled graciously. "You can tell me in sixty years whether you did the right thing or not."

"Oh," Lucy said. "Around 1927. I wonder what it life will be like then?"

The girls had a lot to catch up on and Mi-Ling wanted to be with them. She loved Carolyn and was thrilled to see her again. They spoke to each other like mother and daughter.

Myles wanted a pipe of baccy, so we wandered outside and I filled him in on Bryant.

Miles said, "They must find his ship. Heaven alone knows what he has on it."

I agreed, then asked, "How is Captain Searcher?"

"Both he and the ship are doing well. The crew has really pulled together. They say they miss you being on board and they have made you an honorary seaman."

I was honored and touched. "Give them my best and thank them... Myles, if you were Bryant, as regards to your ship—what would you do? Where would you go?"

He thought. "Well, the one thing he will need is money. A crew either lives on pay or booty, but they don't work for nothing. Especially the type of crew that Bryant would attract, no matter how skilled they may be."

"So he's going to need money."

"Aye," Myles replied. "And his ship is going to need repaired and maintained."

"If he wanted to change his ship—swap or buy another one, or whatever the nautical term is, where would he go?"

Myles thought and then replied, "Russia. St Petersburg. No questions asked."

"Thanks," I said, and we switched to other conversational topics.

"Carolyn is looking well and happy. It's good to see her so cheery."

His brows came together. "Don't know whether I should tell you this... Carolyn misses Mi-Ling. She would never tell you or Lucy, because she wants Mi-Ling to be happy and believes she would be the happiest with you and Lucy. And of course, like the rest of you, she has noticed Mi-Ling's illness and is greatly worried about her. But I understand that you've taken her to all the doctors around here and they can't find anything wrong with her. So Caroline realizes that you're doing all you can, and probably more than we could aboard a ship."

"Let's go and find the girls now," I suggested. "We've given them enough time alone, and I like to keep an eye on Mi-Ling, even though I don't really know what to do about her or how to help her."

When we found the happily chatting, giggling trio, Lucy announced, "Drew, darling, we must get an outfit for Carolyn and Mi-Ling for the wedding. That means a trip to Aberdeen." Hugging each one in turn—even Carolyn since Myles was there—I nodded my agreement, then kissed Lucy and Mi-Ling. "We men folks will be back downstairs if you need us."

Myles and I suited words to action and found Sebastian pacing the landing, waiting for me. "This sure looks good," he announced, "a shore enough wedding! Bout time you two jumped the broomstick."

By the time we reached the living room, Lucy, Carolyn and Mi-Ling joined us. Mi-Ling looked tired, but determined not to miss a minute of Carolyn's visit. Sebastian shuffled his feet and coughed. "My teacher is here. The one what's helped me with my English and will help Mi-Ling with her Mandarin. Upstairs unpacking. We'll be right back down."

Sebastian went upstairs as Anton came down, asking, "Who's for a game of bridge?"

"Perhaps in a while. We're about to meet Sebastian and Mi-Ling's teacher," I explained.

He snorted. "A doctor of languages! Probably some grouchy old man like a wolf with a wounded paw—or some old lady who has retired from teaching and is eking out her pension to make enough to live on. She probably lives in the past and talks endlessly of the good old days."

Sebastian came in alone. We looked at him questioningly and he explained, "Dr. Francis is very shy. Dr. Francis, please join us."

Anton had his back to the door when a voice said in perfect Russian, (so he told me later) "I will do my best not to disappoint you, and walk at a pace that will allow you to keep up with me."

"You are Chinese!" I exclaimed in lively surprise.

She nodded and smiled. "This has facilitated the speaking of Mandarin to a most wonderful extent."

"And you're a girl!" Anton added.

She nodded. "This, too, my beloved parents noticed and made due allowance for."

"Ohhh!" Mi-Ling said, enthralled. "You are very beautiful. And young. Not like Anton saw with his eyes already before he looked and really saw you."

Dr. Francis laughed. "Thank you, dear one. You, too, are a pretty girl—also inside where it means the most. You will make my job of teaching a joy because you are kind, thoughtful and intelligent. This I know from the words of your heart."

Dr. Francis went over to Lucy and said something in Chinese. All I caught was Colonel Carlisle's name."

Lucy replied and Dr. Francis complimented her. "Your grammar and accent are very good."

"Thank you," Lucy said. "You are very kind. And do you wish to be called Dr. Francis—or do you prefer a different name?"

"I didn't speak out of kindness. I spoke the truth." She looked around at us. Anton, especially, seemed spellbound. "Friends call me Francis. I hope we will all be friends."

Mrs. Frasier announced dinner. It amused me during the meal to find Carolyn and Lucy attempting, in that peculiar female way of elucidating information without making it seem obvious, to learn all they could about our new houseguest. Francis, being female herself, knew the rules and the questions and how to reply to them without disclosing more information than she thought appropriate.

"Is it Miss or Mrs. Francis?" Lucy asked, with the subtlety of a sledgehammer.

"Mrs. Francis."

The look of relief on Lucy's face was almost palpable. The look of disappointment on Anton's face was almost theatrical.

Francis smiled in Anton's direction. "I'm a widow. My husband was in the United States Marine Corps and was killed in Afghanistan three years ago—well about a hundred and fifty years into the future."

Anton's countenance brightened. "Sebastian said you speak dead languages."

"She shore enough do." Dr. Francis' eyebrows lifted and Sebastian corrected, "Yes. She surely does. Veni, vidi, vici."

"Latin," Anton told Sebastian. "I came, I saw, I conquered."

Slowly the ice began to melt. The ladies retired and the men went to take their port, even though I didn't drink anymore. Anton was effusive in his praise of Dr. Francis, so effusive that he spoke in Russian and was unable to translate. He said the pages in his English grammar book that covered the superlative had been eaten by a mouse. Anton added, "Old Russian saying. When you have a face like that, you do not need vodka."

I laughed. "I hate to throw cold water on things, lads, but we're here for Lucy's wedding."

Anton nodded sagely. "Of course, my friend. We are here to celebrate your wedding, but by the coldness of the Neva, the views here have just improved."

"Anton, you are incorrigible."

"I may be what you said," he acknowledged, "but that is what makes me so lovable."

We rejoined the ladies. The conversation was varied, but it registered with me that Dr. Francis not only spoke Greek and Latin, but also Aramaic and Hebrew. "Aramaic was the language of Jesus," she explained.

It was Mi-Ling's bedtime and Dr. Francis offered to read her a bedtime story. Hugs and kisses were exchanged, and Carolyn wrapped her arms around Mi-Ling and held her tightly before releasing her.

When the women had retreated upstairs, Sebastian asked, "Well, what y'all think? Can she stay?"

Anton moaned, "Oh I hope so."

He felt our eyes on him and said defensively, "Well, what are you looking at? I only put into voice what the rest of you were thinking."

CHAPTER 15

Over the next few days, the rest of the wedding details were finalized. Angus happily agreed to give the bride away. We invited the Shepherd family, and Connie and her mum. All we wanted now was a good day, with plenty of spring sunshine. Spring had come early that year, almost as if it wanted to share in Lucy's happiness—and mine too. For I was happy. It was almost as if I had found my purpose and the right person and a future. None of us wasted time thinking or worrying about Bryant. Lucy had bested him once. His pride wouldn't bring him around again. Besides: he had been safely whisked away to some unknown location and time by PATCH. PATCH would demand repayment for his rescue and would press some evil assignment on Bryant, just as surely as if he had sold his soul to the devil. Which, in a way, he had. No, Bryant wouldn't attempt to spoil the wedding. PATCH owned him now. That ruthless organization would not be interested in Bryant's love life and agendas. They had their own.

Mr. Thorburn, the minister, came for a last pep talk.

"You have the rings," he said in a chipper voice. "The banns have been called. You've got the schedule which we sign at the wedding. Carolyn and Anton are the witnesses. One might say it's all over, bar the shooting. Sorry—I mean the shouting. There will be a lot of people coming to watch and share in this most blessed and happy occasion. My goodness, but it makes such a refreshing change from funerals! One gets weary of seeing so many tears."

"Indeed," Mr. Thorburn. "So I can imagine. Thank you for your help."

"Yes," Mr. Thorburn," Lucy said. "I echo my fiancés sentiments."

The day arrived as good days do. You look forward to an event and think of all you've been through. I was going to be with the woman I loved in reality and truth.

I stayed with a neighbor the night before the wedding, holding with the traditional superstition that the groom should not see the bride on the day of the wedding before the wedding. Ian Hunter had been a good friend and had helped us when we first arrived at Bellefield.

Ian and I both wore kilts in true Scottish fashion. Mrs. Hunter looked at me after I got dressed. "Man, Drew! She won't be able to take her eyes off you."

I grinned my thanks and said, "So I hope!"

Mrs. Hunter was a bit of a character and added, "I hope you got a good sleep last night. That commodity might be in short supply tonight."

I had spent a sober stag night with Anton, who drank my vodka. "As you are not allowing the spirit to enter you, then I must bravely stand in your place," he had explained.

We had gone to eat and Myles had joined us. "Last night of freedom," Myles said.

"Yes, my brother," Anton had added. "You have four hours and twenty six minutes to do what you always wanted to do before you got married. If this were Russia, I could offer quite a few suggestions for places to go." He turned philosophical. "Mmmm…someone in your bed every night. Someone to love and welcome you. To be your friend and companion and to share the world and life with. But for all of that, just think of the freedom you are giving up. To be able to go where you want to go and do what you want to do every night of the week and to come back each night to a cold and empty room. Maybe marriage has some good points after all."

His eyes went dreamy, assisted by vodka. "Now that Chinese lady, there is a woman worth getting married for. She could teach me Russian."

"Uh," I had pointed out, "you already speak Russian."

He was far away. "Yes, but she could teach me it all again and find out that I am both a willing pupil and a quick learner."

"One day the right woman will come along for you," I said encouragingly.

"Old Russian saying. 'When you have found gold, who can settle for silver?"

It had not been a long stag night. Myles was anxious to get back to Carolyn and Anton was busy dreaming about Dr. Francis. When they had dropped me back off at the Hunter's house, I had gone straight to bed and spent the rest of the night tossing and turning—counting the hours until I could hold Lucy in my arms as my wife and lover.

Arriving at the wedding in a carriage was not pretentious. It was the way things were done and it helped local trade. Anton said to me like some ancient philosopher, "I remember that night you danced with Lucy and there was nobody else but the two of you on the floor. You were both totally lost in each other and now you have found each other. Did I ever tell you about Irina?" He looked round about and sighed. "Perhaps I will save that story until you come back from honeymoon. If I told you my gem of wisdom about Irina, with you having one or two other things on your thoughts, you might forget and that would be tragedy."

The closer we got to the church, the more people had gathered. They actually cheered, which was a surprise. Anton and I walked up the line of well-wishers. There were pats on the back and, "God bless ye," and, "a 'lang an happy life to ye baith, Captain."

Mr. Thorburn met us and escorted us up to the front of the church and we had our backs to the people. The organ was newly installed and was being pumped with gusto to make the bellows go. So we stood and waited and I knew it was the bride's prerogative to be late.

Anton whispered to me, "It is the task of the sidesman to stop the groom from running away." A mental picture of what tonight would bring flashed into my mind—and suddenly—running was the last thing on my mind.

I noticed Colonel Carlisle in the back of the church. He had a clear view of the front and I appreciated his presence.

Suddenly the music changed and the organist played Handel's Largo from Xerxes, music that has seen the entry of countless brides to their futures. I had to turn around and look. Lucy was mind-blowing. She was everything that was pretty and feminine and gentle. Her dress was white as snow and, unusually, it was not wide. Two panels of lace fell down the length of the skirt either side. Her sleeves were Tudor design and she looked like Juliet out of Romeo and Juliet, for she wore a Juliet-type cap to hold her veil. Round her neck, peeping from beneath her veil, she wore the same ruby necklace that she had worn at the dance in Foochow. Her Titian hair hung in ringlets. She redefined beauty at every step and with every breath. Her bouquet was orange blossom. Where had they found orange blossom in Scotland, I wondered.

Mr. Thorburn looked happy. There was no professionalism and no cold-fish voice. He was celebrating a joyful occasion. For once in my recent life, there were no guns or threats—just quiet joy and deep peace.

Mr. Thorburn began. "Dearly beloved, we are gathered before Almighty God to celebrate the wedding of this man and this woman… Then suddenly, it was, "I, Andrew do take thee, Lucy, to be my lawful wedded wife. To have and to hold from this day forward, for better or worse, for richer for poorer, in sickness and in health, for as long as we both shall live."

"I, Lucy, do take thee, Andrew…" and every word she spoke sounded like a movement from the most beautiful symphony ever written.

"I now pronounce you man and wife… You may kiss the bride."

To the distant sound of clapping and shouting, I lifted her veil and Lucy's lovely emerald eyes shone with love. I kissed her and she breathed, "Oh, Drew! I'm so happy…so, so happy."

We turned and faced the congregation and walked down the aisle and out into the blessing of sunlight and spring breeze. Then—dear God help me—the light opened in front of us and Bryant stepped through and shouted angrily at Lucy. "You rejected me! If I can't have you, nobody will!" He lifted a gun and pointed it at me. Lucy pushed me to the side and Bryant shot Lucy twice in the chest. Then, as I grabbed my fatally injured wife, Bryant laughed demonically. "Have a good honeymoon, boy! I would kill you, too, but it will be more fun watching you suffer for the rest of your life."

His demonic laughter echoed through the shocked crowd. He stepped back into the light. Just before the light went out, Colonel Carlisle's pistol went off and Bryant clutched the top part of his arm and swore.

Clutching my dying Lucy to my chest, I screamed, God curse you, Bryant! May you rot in hell." Then he was gone.

I lowered Lucy gently to the grass and tried to compress her chest to stop the flow of blood. Her beautiful white dress absorbed more red-blood color from every faint beat of her heart. The now crimson-stained orange blossoms lay beside her.

"God, Lucy, don't die! I love you! Please live!"

Her soft voice floated up toward me. "I love you, my Drew. These last few precious weeks have been the happiest of my life, but I'm going home to Jesus now. Live your life, darling. I will always love you. I will love you through eternity." She took my hand and I held her in my arms.

"Lucy, Lucy! NOOOOOOOOOOO, don't leave me! The color drained from her face and she was still. The doctor came over to me and held my shoulders as I shook with sobs. "Laddie, she's gone. I am so sorry."

I think I let out a howl that could have been heard in Texas.

The one person who did not freeze was Meg Shepherd. She came over to where I knelt and put her arms round me and Lucy and said in a soft lilting voice, "There, there. Let it all oot, bairnie. Let it all oot."

CHAPTER 15

It was up to me to tell Mi-Ling. She had been in the church with Dr Francis. Sebastian had stayed at the house just in case Bryant showed up there.

First Mi-Ling shattered. I held her as she sobbed in my arms. Then my brave little girl straightened herself up and looked unblinkingly into my eyes. "It make me think of my friend Jasmine," she said. "I had bad pain inside. Papa, you have big, bad pain."

"Yes, Mi-Ling. Big, bad pain."

Once home, we sat in front of the fire. "Papa, Mi-Ling is cold." I placed a traveling rug around her and held her in my arms. She snuggled against me. "Papa, Mi-Ling loves you. Will you be here when the sunshine comes tomorrow?"

"Yes, I will be here for you Mi-Ling."

There was a silence, then she said, "Papa, that bad pain inside. If we cry, it will help."

So there we were, father and daughter, arms round each other, crying. Mi-Ling put her hand in mine. When both our reservoirs of tears ran dry, we fell asleep.

How long we had been like that, I didn't know. I awoke to Carolyn's voice in my ear.

"Drew, Myles and I will take her to sleep with us. She shouldn't be left alone."

I nodded and Myles, with a gossamer touch, lifted the tired little body and carried her up to their bedroom.

"What about you?" Caroline asked.

"I want to be alone. I'll be okay."

"If you need anything, knock on our door. Promise?"

"I promise, Caroline. Thanks. Goodnight."

Colonel Carlisle had wanted me to come back through to Vanguard HQ. "Get the medic to give you a quick deco," he had suggested.

I had thanked him, but negated that idea. "No, sir. My place is with Mi-Ling."

"I understand, but we are here for you. That's what Vanguard is all about."

Now the fires were lit and the lamps were low. When I closed my eyes, all I could see was Lucy's face and that horrible moment when the breath left her body and the bloom hemorrhaged from her lovely cheeks. Every night I had prepared a stone hot water bottle—her piggy—for her. Tonight, I did the same thing. "Darling," I called out. "I've got your piggy. I'll just go put it in your bed." I went to her room and there were the cases for our honeymoon, one of which was open. On top, lay a beautiful nightgown. I picked it up and carried it in my arms to the bed, took off my shoes and trousers and undid my shirt and put the piggy in the bed. Then, holding the nighty in my arms, I slipped under the sheets and laid my head on Lucy's pillow. I could smell her scent— the wild flowers over which she presided as a rose. I began to cry again. I cried out her name several times, and then fell asleep, thankfully not waking until the enquiring sun worked its way through the curtains. With dawn came the pain and the emptiness.

****

Over and over, I kept replaying it in my mind. Lucy had seen Bryant's gun before I had. She had pushed me out of the road. If I had been quicker, I could have got in front of Bryant and protected Lucy. "I am going home to be with Jesus," she had said and sounded so peaceful.

Mi-Ling woke up early, wanting to see me and reassure herself that I was still there.

Some of the local women came to wash Lucy's body. They asked me how I wanted her dressed and I asked them to put her into the nightgown that I had slept holding last night, the one she had intended for our honeymoon. Mr. Thorburn had agreed to her lying in the church so that people could come and pay their respects.

I couldn't stand the thought of Lucy lying in darkness in a hole in the ground. I asked Myles and Caroline about a sea burial. The Night Arrow was in Aberdeen, and when Captain Searcher received my request for a sea burial, he readily agreed. Not only that, but when the crew heard who it was, representatives told Captain Searcher they didn't want to get paid—it was for Miss Lucy. These men did not make a lot of money, and I was deeply touched by their sacrifice.

There would be a service in the church and then the body would be taken by horse-drawn hearse to Aberdeen Harbor. Then we would proceed to deep water and the earthly shell that was my Lucy would be committed to a watery grave that could not hold her spirit.

Anton and Carolyn helped me get through the next few days. Sebastian and Francis were also a comfort. The night before the service, Anton kept insisting that I should accompany him to Russia to get away afterward. He grew sad and pensive. Lucy's death had brought back memories of his wife's death.

I had taken Mi-Ling to see Lucy in the church. Lucy lay still and cold. Her hair was still as red as it had been in life. I thought of Shakespeare's play, Romeo and Juliet. When Juliet's father thought she was dead, he quoted: Death hangs on her like an untimely frost. I had let out a sigh and said, "Lucy, Oh, Lucy. I love you." I had felt Mi-Ling's little hand slip into mine. Mi-Ling had been tired and cold, but it was amazing in one so young what love could overcome. She loved me and she had loved Lucy. Mi-Ling had been a trooper and I had tried to comfort her. I don't know whether she helped me more, or I helped her. We tried to decide what heaven would be like and what Jesus would be like.

With confidence, Mi-Ling informed me, "Amma will never be old or walk with a stick or lose all her teeth. She will be always beautiful. Jesus will take away all her hurts like He did for Jasmine."

I began to sing an old Negro spiritual to Mi-Ling. Nobody knows the trouble I've seen, nobody knows my sorrow; nobody knows the trouble I've seen, nobody knows but Jesus.

I lived and relived our time in China, going over every word spoken, every event I could remember. The sparkle in Lucy's eyes glowed in my heart.

I wasn't angry at God. He hadn't killed Lucy. It had been an evil man and an evil organization that had extinguished t the light of my life. Yet, it was only out for a few minutes because Mi-Ling kept rekindling it. I was needed. No matter how I felt, Mi-Ling needed her papa. She was like an anchor to stop me from slipping into despondency. She had been hurt enough. I was determined she would not be hurt anymore. She also did something else. I hated Bryant, but then realized that love and hate cannot coexist.

I either focused my hate on Bryant, or focused my love on Mi-Ling. Yes, I wanted Bryant brought to justice, and if he was killed, well, that could not be helped. If he was caught, he would suffer the death penalty for his cold-blooded murder. Yet, on the other hand, Mi-Ling was the future, even though she was ill.

I sat in front of the fire in Bellefield. It was about ten at night. I thought everyone had gone to bed. I was glad Carolyn and Myles were there. They comforted Mi-Ling immensely. Mi-Ling kept saying the, "Carol Lady is Amma's good friend." Love by association.

There was a polite cough and Francis stood at the living room door. "A penny for them," Francis said. I started to hear the phrase that Meryl had used so often tumbling out of this stranger's mouth. "If my presence upsets you, I will retire." Dr. Francis added quickly.

"No," I said. "I think I would welcome company. But what kind of company I will be, I can't say."

"I think I know and understand a little of how you feel. My husband was a doctor. He had treated soldiers and wounded Taliban and in the end, he was shot. John had spent his life only doing good. He had pulled his fellow soldiers out of combat. Where there was a need, he helped. He had helped many local people. In the end, the people who could only hate killed him.

Why do those who preach only hate call it life?" As she spoke, I remembered the rantings of PATCH and their desire to rule, to take away freedom.

"Dr. Francis," I asked, "do you have a first name, or do you want me to continue to call you Dr. Francis?"

"Everyone calls me Francis, and I didn't think it was right to mention my first name. Not even Sebastian knows. Are you sure you want me to tell you? Please don't get upset."

"Nobody will get upset. Least of all me."

"My first name is Lucy," she said quietly.

I was taken aback, but not wounded. "Lucy. I never thought I would mention that name again. It should have been me that died, not my Lucy."

Dr. Lucy stood in front of where I was sitting for a moment. Then she and went on her knees before me and took my shoulders gently in her slender hands. "Captain, listen. You can either remember what you last saw—your wife's death—or you can remember you gave her the happiest weeks of her life. She spoke only of you and Mi-Ling. When she mentioned your name, there was a joy in her eyes. She would sigh deeply when we girls got together and talk dreamily of her hopes for the future. All those hopes were wrapped up in your name and person. Andrew, I've never seen anyone so completely happy.

"Lucy's joy didn't come in a Christmas cracker. It came because of you. She had more fulfillment in her life in weeks than many women get in years. The cause of that was you." She spoke with passion, and when she spoke, her eyes had a way of holding you because what you were hearing came from her heart.

After a moment, she added, "Remember the good, the happy times. She got called home with a heart filled with love and hope. You gave her that. Andrew, that is a priceless gift—please believe me that when hope is gone, there is nothing left."

I had been openly crying in front of Dr. Lucy. She must have thought I was a weakling. She produced a white handkerchief with a lace border and gave it to me. "Dry your eyes," she said gently. "Your Lucy would not like to see you so sad."

I mopped up my tears and handed the handkerchief back to her.

"Keep it," she said, "a reminiscence of China." She stood up and said, "I perhaps should rest now. Tomorrow will be a hard day, most of all for you and Mi-Ling, and sleep is good. Goodnight, Captain." With graceful steps, she headed for the door.

I called after her, "Lucy, thank you for being here, from both of us." Then I sat holding the handkerchief in my hands, idly running it through my fingers remembering that the first gift my Lucy had given me in China had been a white lace handkerchief just like this one.

****

The following morning we headed for the church. The place was mobbed. Mi-Ling wanted one more look at Lucy, as did Carolyn. Not me. I wanted to remember her alive. The butterfly had flown from its cocoon, and now she was free.

I carried my Bowie knife. I didn't know why. The church was packed. Ram-jam full. The front pews had been kept for us. Mi-Ling took my hand. "Mi-Ling is here, Papa."

She and I walked up the aisle where only a few days before I had walked down with Lucy. Lucy's blood still stained the stone work and my eye caught a fragment of orange blossom that the cleaners must of missed. I picked it up and wrapped it carefully in the hanky Dr. Lucy had given me.

Mr. Thorburn, poor guy. What a job he had to do. The question all of us were asking him, he could not answer. Why?

"We can either look at the shell of Lucy Faulkner that is lying in the coffin," he intoned, "still beautiful—a masterpiece of God's creation and make the choice to be miserable with our loss, while we think of what could have been—or we can celebrate the life she had here and rejoice that she has exchanged this perishable shell for everlasting life in heaven where there is no more death, or dying, or illness, or sorrow. We can only shadow guess at how her husband Andrew and her daughter Mi-Ling feel. It's our duty as Christian brothers and sisters to support them and comfort them. We can reach out to them with our offerings of life and hope, or we can make a choice to grieve and mourn. But I knew Lucy. That selfish choice of grief and despair would grieve her. Her trust was in Jesus, Jesus Who did not make promises about a future life here on earth, But Who said, "I am the resurrection and the life.' Lucy had begun her walk into life here. Now she is in God's Kingdom. Our loss is heaven's gain. As the Bible promises, Eye has not seen, nor has ear heard, nor can the heart of man conceive what God has prepared for those who love Him. Lucy is finding that out now, even as I speak. 'If I prepare a place for you,' Jesus said, 'I will come again and take you to be with Me, that where I am there you may be also.' Lucy closed her eyes here seeing the face of the man she loved the most and opened her eyes in heaven to see the face of the God who loved her the most."

We finished the service with the hymn, Just as I am.

Two of Jock Shepherd's sons, along with Anton, Angus, Myles and I, carried the coffin out to load it up on its journey to the Night Arrow.

I had put my scarf around the back of a pew and forgotten it, so had to dash back in to retrieve it. The crowd had mostly worked its way out, and I passed one girl whose face I could not see, but who smelled softly of coconut. I knew only one person who carried that scent on her person, but by the time I realized that, she had lost herself in the crowd.

The Harbor was crowded and busy. Cargo boats, fishing boats, and trading ships vied with each other for space. It was strange being on board the Night Arrow again. It was good to see Captain Searcher. He shook my hand and said how sorry he was about Lucy, then chided himself for the inadequacy of his words. Daniel Cavendish and Joshua Hemphill came to see me.

"Oh, sir, we are so grieved for you, so grieved—and for the little lass as well. She's a trooper, if there ever was one." I thanked them and asked how they were. They mentioned a couple of new faces that had joined the crew. "We even have another American in the crew, as well as the cap'n. Tom Tyler, from Maine. I think that is about as far north as you can go in the United States. You can meet him, if you want?"

I got introduced to Tom, who predictably said how sorry he was. "I was trying to find an American ship," he explained, "on the chance of getting home. We passed one. It was flying the American flag, even though the sails were furl'd. Nobody was paying much attention, but I caught the name. The Allegheny. That's a river back home."

"Where was that?" I asked, trying to remain calm.

"I will have to ask so I get the right name. I'm not from around these parts and get confused."

Tom Tyler left and returned with Daniel who said, "Crawton Village, between Aberdeen and Stonehaven. It's a fishing village and they repair boats. Pretty place."

I found Angus and told him, "Bryant's ship is at a place called Crawton, near Stonehaven, on the coast between here and Stonehaven, and the guy who told me said the sails were furled though it still flew the American colors. He heard the name, Allegheny.

"Right," Angus said. "We can tag the ship so we'll be able to find it. We'll need to involve the Americans. Bryant is an American citizen. But just now, you have enough to think about without thinking about how we can capture him. Maybe if we give him enough rope, he'll hang himself and save us a lot of trouble."

I suppose I had been trying not to think of this time—the time when we could do nothing else but commit Lucy to God's hands. Yet parting still hurts like hell.

There were a good number of people on board. Mi-Ling didn't look at the coffin. To her, Lucy was already up in heaven. What we were putting into the water was not Amma in a box. Amma, like a butterfly, was gone.

Mr. Thorburn went to the side of the ship and completed the service and brought to an end what must have been one of the worst days of his life. "Lucy has gone home. We commit her body to the deep in sure and certain hope of resurrection to eternal life."

Jock Shepherd's two sons tipped the coffin platform up, and Lucy's coffin slid out from under the flag—and she was gone. Little did I know then that I was to see Lucy one more time in unbelievably different circumstances.

Mi-Ling and Dr. Lucy were further back from the ship rail.

Suddenly, the time portal opened up—aboard the ship. Two figures came through first with guns, followed by Bryant. "PATCH has come to administer justice to the little murderess known as Mi-Ling. She shall come with us for punishment, that justice might be served. Long live PATCH!"

The two goons pushed Dr Francis aside, grabbed Mi-Ling, and started to drag her toward the light, still pointing pistols at the company. Mi-Ling screamed.

Angus and Anton were four rows back. I flipped. I screamed language I would be ashamed to record. "Nooooooo!" I pulled out my Bowie knife and stabbed one of them as hard as I could in the chest. The second had just raised his pistol to fire when a tomahawk spun through the air and smashed the man's hand. I made a lunge for Bryant. If I had caught him, I would have killed him with my bare hands. He was a coward. He disappeared into the light and vanished.

I ran to Mi-Ling. She threw her arms around me and began to sob. I held her close and sought to soothe her. "There, there, sweetheart. Papa is here."

Carolyn rushed over and hugged Mi-Ling. Gradually, with the love and assurance, Mi-Ling's tears began to subside, but her physical condition seemed to worsen and we had to hold her up to keep her from collapsing on deck. She began coughing and complained of weakness in her muscles.

Angus examined the dead PATCH operative. The wounded PATCH operative, with part of his hand hanging off and blood steaming down and dripping on the deck, was holding his injured arm with the good arm and groaning. Just above him, embedded in the mast, was the unlikely and unexpected weapon—a tomahawk.

I took the tomahawk out of the mast and considered it thoughtfully. "You are weak!" the injured man taunted. "You don't have the courage to complete the task. Go on—finish me."

Angus came over and said to him, "Oh, no, mi bucko, you are going for questioning. We think there is a lot you can tell us and we have some very persuasive friends. Oh, yes. Very persuasive."

"I will tell you nothing," the man ranted. "We are the master race."

A voice behind me asked quietly, "Can I get my tomahawk back, please? It's the only one I brought back with me."

Meryl looked at me with uncertainty in her eyes. I hugged her for long enough for her to say, "Drew, I am so sorry. I really did want you and Lucy to be happy. You must believe me."

"I believe you," I told Meryl. "And I'm sorry for what I said when we parted. Please forgive me."

She crinkled her nose in reply. I squeezed her hand and let go.

Angus said to me, "Let me get a few of the boys to take these two down to the hold and let's see if our time car will arrive on the ship. I don't want to risk PATCH turning up to take away the scum before we get some answers."

We were taken back to shore at Aberdeen Harbor by rowing boat. I knew Angus would have a lot to tell and show Colonel Carlisle. In my heart, I felt more at rest. Reflecting, I realized that peace had begun stealing into my heart right after I had handed Meryl's tomahawk back to her.

****

Two days later, I was asked to a meeting with Colonel Carlisle and the team assigned to combat PATCH. I knew all the people in the room, except a man wearing a United States Marine Corps uniform. I was told that the force would be split between dealing with PATCH as the organization and trying to trap Professor Reynolds. The Marines would deal with Bryant.

The Colonel said to me, "Let me introduce you to Captain Craig Carter, USMC."

We shook hands and he said with a broad smile, "Delighted to meet you, Captain Faulkner. I believe you knew my grandfather. He spoke a lot about you right up till he died. He was afraid that when he got back to San Antonio, they would shoot him for overstaying his leave. So he joined the Marines."

"Your grandfather was Luke Carter!" I exclaimed in lively surprise. "And he did join the Marines!"

"Yes, sir, he did. Rose to the rank of General."

"The rogue did it! Did he marry Mary Ellen?"

"Yes, sir. They had five children: Lucy, Meryl, Anton, Andrew and Sebastian."

I laughed and exclaimed out loud, "Nicely done, you old rogue! Nicely done!"

Angus interrupted my conversation with Craig. "The PATCH operative no longer wants to be part of the master race," Angus announced, "and he is singing like a bird. We have a lot of answers already and expect more soon."

Colonel Carlisle said to me, "Thanks to your quick response and team work, we are getting enough information to catch Bryant and to start to take PATCH apart stitch by stitch. Well done, Major."

"Major! You mean I've been promoted to major? A real major this time and not a proxy major like in the American Civil War?"

He nodded. "Oh, yes, one other thing you might like to know," he added. "Meryl has been reinstated as a Vanguard operative."

Lightning Source UK Ltd.
Milton Keynes UK
UKOW02f2253050616

275688UK00001B/27/P

9 781612 962023